I0761247

LOVE GOES VIRAL

LOVE GOES VIRAL

Camille Stochitch
Alexander Berman
AND
Estelle Laure

SIMON & SCHUSTER BFYR
NEW YORK AMSTERDAM/ANTWERP LONDON
TORONTO SYDNEY/MELBOURNE NEW DELHI

An imprint of Simon & Schuster Children's Publishing Division
1230 Avenue of the Americas, New York, New York 10020

Jacket design by Laura Eckes

Interior design by Hilary Zarycky
The text for this book was set in Garamond.
Manufactured in the United States of America
First Edition
2 4 6 8 10 9 7 5 3 1
CIP data for this book is available from the Library of Congress.
ISBN 9781665950626
ISBN 9781665950640 (ebook)

To Alex, Anton, and Misha, who taught me what true love is—C. S.

To my father, who would've been very proud—A. B.

For my father, Michel, who gifted me writing, music,
big dreams . . . and (apparently) dance—E. L.

CHAPTER ONE

Love

Before I even really knew who I was, I wanted the world to know my name. I don't remember learning how to sing or dance. It's just something that I had to do to get where I was going, like crawling or walking.

That's why I'm stretching for the second time this morning, studying my form in the mirror, as Mom's voice rattles in my head—*Every trophy's built on busted ankles and bloody toes, baby. Nobody claps for the bruises.*

She would know.

My hamstrings protest for a second before they give over and let me lay my torso flat on the ground in a full split. You don't get anywhere by wishing. You dance through the hurt. And one day, soon, I'm going to dance through it right out of here. Los Angeles, by way of Nashville. That's the plan. Making it is preparation plus luck, and I have to do everything possible to be ready when the opportunity finally comes my way. Which—judging by the fact that Mom had to pull yet another extra graveyard shift last night—needs to be soon.

I just have to finish high school first.

"Love! I'm back, hon. It's almost seven thirty. We're cutting it close!" Mom taps on my door as she calls out.

"I was waiting for you!" I pull myself out of my bendy state. "Just putting on my shoes!"

"Well, okay, but . . . oh, damn it." Her phone rings, muffled. "Hello?" She drifts down the short hall, sounding upset, which means I have a pretty solid idea who she's talking to.

I force myself not to think about him and open the closet, humming the bars to the Lil' D song I'm going to be covering for the next upload to my channel. Lil' D, or Damien Hunter to the fans as obsessed with him as I am, is one of my favorite artists, so I've been working extra hard on it. You never know which video is going to hit, but if this is the one, maybe he'll actually see it. My voice is more fire-in-the-veins than technically perfect, but even I can hear the emotion in it, can hear how it's different from what's already out there. Only Damien Hunter matches my energy, which is why I'm planning something extra special to pay tribute to his music.

My closet is organized according to color, then subdivided into shirts, dresses, pants, and skirts, and it's the one small bit of space I can claim as my own. I don't have much, but I've spent hours and hours in Austin vintage stores, picking out the things that feel exactly me, and it always gives me happy shivers to see it all right where it should be. Except, when I retrieve my dance bag, looking for my lucky sneakers—

A pinprick of rage settles in my throat.

"That little knee-high pilferer," I mutter.

My brother Forest loves to steal my shoes. I spent the entire summer working at the Cinnabon at Barton Creek Square in Austin, dealing with kids so much better off than me, to buy them. Perfect, beautiful, unscathed Air Force 1 sneakers in metallic gold. They're like my ruby slippers, except for getting me out of here instead of going home.

I should have known better. Literally nothing is sacred in this house. One of the many (many) reasons I'm planning my escape.

I sling my bag over my shoulder, slide on my baseball cap, and rush down the hall, past the disaster zone my brothers call a bedroom, into the living room to confront the littlest menace.

I see Mom first though, still in her cute black scrubs, her hair a halo of frayed curls—as she unloads and puts away the groceries she must have picked up on her way home from the hospital. She must not hear me come up behind her, because she continues talking.

"I can't reschedule, Will," she says. "It's your weekend and I need some rest!" She throws a zucchini into the crisper so viciously, it splits. "Oh, dang it," she mutters. Then, "I do have a life. Well . . . that's none of your business, now, is it? As I recall, you didn't want it to be, and whether I curl my hair all weekend or go on twenty dates has nothing to do with you. So you can just f—"

She turns and catches sight of me and stops herself, grimacing instead.

Sorry, she mouths, and tilts her head toward the door, meaning she wants me to get the boys and skedaddle into the car to wait for her. She doesn't like it when I hear her fight with the man who has major commitment issues and an empty wallet to go with them . . . aka my father.

She and my dad hate each other, is what I'm trying to say. She pretends they don't, that they're co-parenting or whatever, but it seeps out of her pores, out of her pissed-off hair follicles, even her tensed fingers, which are pressed tight against the refrigerator door. It's kind of divorce textbook, I guess, but she would love it if none of us knew it. Then again, if she was really trying to protect us, she wouldn't have this conversation in the kitchen.

I get on my own case for the unkind thought. It's not like she has much choice when she has to get the cold things into the fridge before we go. For sure River isn't going to help her, and Forest? Well, he's four, so he's not even a real person yet.

But he *is* a thief. Which returns me to my original purpose.

"You want me out of here? I'd love to oblige but . . . Have you seen my gold sneakers?" I stage-whisper.

She shrugs, as if she doesn't know how much I need those shoes. I'm working on the dance routine for the cover song after school, and the last time I didn't have them, I about broke my ankle. That would slow things way down if it happened now, and I don't need them to slow down. I need them to speed *up*, which they will as soon as I graduate in—I steal a glance at the *X*'s counting down on the calendar pinned to the wall above the coffee maker—exactly one week. The path from here to stardom is as clear as can be.

One week until I board the on-ramp to the rest of my life, starting with my full-ride scholarship to Middle Tennessee State University. I'm going to be the first person in my family ever to go to college, and because of all the bruises and sacrifices, it's going to be *free*! So many musicians who inspire me have gone there too, and I'm going to make the most of it, follow in their footsteps. Plus Nashville is *right there*. Showcases, songwriting groups, open mics. Only a matter of time before I get plucked out of the crowd.

But none of that is going to happen if I can't find my shoes.

I point frantically to my socked feet.

"Sorry, honey, I haven't seen them," she says, rolling her eyes toward the phone. I can hear my father, his slow, raspy, Texas drawl, taking his time with every word he says, each one designed to ensure everything goes his way and nothing is his fault, like always.

Once he's done with this fight, no doubt he'll be at his favorite crappy watering hole at the stroke of eight a.m., getting lit with no kids to take care of and nothing to weigh him down, exactly as he likes it.

Which is why I don't drink. Why would I?

He does it enough for the both of us.

"Okay," Mom says, turning back to the call, "then what about the child support you owe me?" She waits, and when he answers, she lets her elbow fall onto the counter and her head collapse into her palm.

Mom tries to shoo me away again as she sniffles, but I'm not going anywhere now. When she lets him get under her skin like this, she ends up having to spend her one night off in bed with the door closed.

Or worse, she lets him back in.

That's where Forest came from. It was fun being a family again for, like, two-point-five seconds, and then Dad was gone once more and Mom was left pregnant AF.

"No, *you're* the ballbuster," Mom says. "You are. You have *no* idea." Her voice is so sad, so lost, I give in to my inevitable lateness and rest my hand on her back. She stands up right away though, shaking me off. "Go," she says. When I don't move, she says, "Love. Your brothers. Now."

I would probably ignore her except for the fact that Forest

chooses that moment to jet from his room into the kitchen, my sneakers on his feet, the shiny gold catching sunlight as he whizzes by. He shoots back down the hall, and I toss my bag on the ground as I take off after him. Forest speeds behind the couch, taking cover out of reach. Our other brother, River, sits on the couch, playing something loud and annoying on the TV that looks like *Call of Duty*, the game he plays instead of talking to humans face-to-face. His backpack is leaned against his knee like he's ready to go to school, even though I know he didn't brush his teeth. He has been a major douchebag ever since he turned fourteen, but I remind myself to focus.

"River, grab him!"

River barely moves his eyes in my direction.

"Can't. On a team."

I don't know why I even try. I creep toward the couch myself. "Forest." No answer. I soften my voice. "Forest, come on out. You know I need those sneakers."

Still nothing. I finally get close enough to see him, knees up to his chin, hand over his mouth to cover what I'm sure is the world's fattest grin. Pushing River to the side, I jump up on the couch, reach over it, and get up under Forest's pits in a swift movement I've perfected in my years of being a big sister, before laying him on his back next to River.

"Hey!" River doesn't spare us a glance, just pushes buttons, craning his head to the side to dodge us. "Not cool. I just got sniped!"

I hoist myself up to standing on the couch and pull at the sneakers, but Forest and his sticky little hands fight back with surprising vigor for such a little guy.

"I just wanted to borrow them and you *never* let me!" Forest shouts, grin gone. "Mom says we have to share and that means you *have* to share your shoes with me!"

I finally wrestle off the sneakers and clamber back to the floor. As Forest bursts into wails and runs toward the kitchen, River throws down his controller. "Can you guys ever shut up? I lost my game."

"This is the living room," I say as I tie my laces and wipe the smudges off my shoes. "You know . . . where people *live.* It's not your personal space. And anyway, it's time for you to get in the car."

"You're not Mom," he says, but gets to his feet anyway.

"Well, maybe you should think about helping out every once in a while so *you* don't become Dad 2.0."

I am halfway back into the kitchen when I hear him say, "That's low, Love, even for you."

I don't look back because it's not like that's some big surprise.

Let me tally it for you.

Mom hates Dad and Dad hates Mom.

Dad obviously has no love for us.

And Forest and River? Well . . .

Forest meets me in the hallway, face slathered in snot and tears. "Mom told me I should tell you about my *feelings* and I *am.*" He steels himself, balling his fists at his sides, then opens his mouth as wide as he can and screams, "I HATE YOU!"

My parents may have named me "Love," but I'm a lot more familiar with hate.

If you thought that might change once I get to school, you'd be wrong.

My high school is a gleaming stone building that got plopped down in a giant field (all the better for the football) in the eighties. It's in a community of pretty, bland, cookie-cutter McMansions, complete with pools and Chevy trucks and minivans. Riches abound . . . except for the Sweet Pea Mobile Home Park right at the edge of town, where we live. Mom rented the trailer instead of an apartment somewhere else because it's in this school district. She thought I'd get a better education here, but I guess she forgot what it was like to be a teenager. That high school is so toxic, you need a radiation shower at the end of every day.

The path to the front doors is more dodging-snipers energy than red carpet, but there's no other way into the main building. On rare occasions I make it through the gauntlet unscathed, but I can already tell that's not going to happen today. As I approach Bryce Prescott, who's sitting on a bench, manspreading aggressively, he shouts, "Waddup, Trailerina!" and all his equally annoying friends laugh.

The marquee outside the school reads "Congratulations, Graduates!" and graduation's so close I can taste it, so I march straight ahead, keep my chin up, and search for my best friend Patty.

My *only* friend, I should say.

Most people at school hate me because Bryce hates me and they are lemmings. What they don't know is that when we first moved here after Forest was born and I still had some new-girl cred, Bryce asked me out. When I told him no, he informed me and then everyone else that I was a trashy bitch, and that was that. I never even had a chance.

I know one thing for sure: A guy like Bryce never forgets a rejection, even with his girlfriend, Liberty, on his lap.

Fortunately, whatever insult he has planned next is interrupted as Patty, my Patty, runs over to me. She's glorious, curvaceous, with short wavy hair and a nose ring, and I'm obsessed with her freckles. She has saved me every day since I got here.

"Hey, girl," she says.

"Hey, Patty," I say, and give her a smooch on the cheek.

"Fatty Patty! Fatty Patty!" Bryce calls. "Lift her over your head, Trailerina! Do a duet for us!"

"How's this duet?" I say, sending up both middle fingers. "You like that?"

Bryce's cheeks redden for a second before his smirk returns. "You'd probably get more likes for those than for any of your cringe videos."

Liberty flashes me an apologetic look. But Bryce isn't done.

"I mean, you don't *actually* think that's going to get you out of the gutter, do you?" He tilts his head. "Wait . . . you *do* think that, don't you? Aw . . . poor little Trailerina."

"You know what—" I start, but Patty ushers me away.

"Not worth it," she says, so only I can hear.

"That's right, Fatty. Get out of here and take your trash with you."

Blood rushes to my face, but Patty gives me a pleading look, and we walk away in silence.

"You're so beautiful," I say. "Don't listen to them."

"Oh, I know," she returns, unfazed. "And you are *not* trash. I promise you five years from now I'm going to be opening my bookstore/skate park and they are going to be wishing they were back in high school when they mattered." She turns to me. "And you . . . you're going to be bigger than Taylor Swift."

My heart lurches with hope.

"Do we really have to do this?" Patty says, sighing as we reach the door.

"Graduate?"

"No," Patty says. "This week. Can't we just go now?"

I weave my arm through hers. "I'd say yes if we didn't have finals. If we don't stick it out for those, we'll subject ourselves to another hellish year."

"Yeah," she says with a sigh. "At least I didn't promise my parents I'd wear a floral minidress under my grad robe." She rolls her eyes. "LOL, psych, I totally did. I'm going to wear my Hello Kitty undies to counteract whatever terrible things are going to happen to me from shaving my legs."

Patty's parents are rich, conservative, and incredibly well-groomed. I don't even know where Patty came from but she's the opposite of all of that and her parents treat her as such.

Dinner at their house is delicious, but no fun. Trust.

"So close," I say sympathetically. "We're so close now."

The rest of the morning goes okay. Patty and I have all our a.m. classes together, so we form a barricade against the noise and focus on our physics and English finals. By the time it's lunch and I can see the light at the end of the school-day tunnel, I'm thinking about my dance lesson, putting the new moves, which I've been working on whenever Forest and River are busy with things other than torturing me, into practice. In those moments when the house is quiet, the lights are down low, and the living room floor is mine, I can almost pretend I'm already famous. That I'm center stage, dancing not to someone else's songs, but my own. Singer, songwriter, dancer. A true triple threat.

I repeat my mantra: *Graduate. Nashville. College degree. Connections. Showcase. Los Angeles. Stardom.*

"Spaghetti and terrible sauce accomplished," Patty says, bringing me back to earth. The cafeteria is peppered with round tables, and the lunch line winds its way into the hall while she joins me at our table, as close to the exit as possible.

Patty pokes suspiciously at the teensy bits of meat that dot the pasta.

"Don't forget iceberg plus gloopy ranch," I say. I'm a vegetarian so I can't eat the meat pasta and instead have tried to load up on as many veggies as I can from the salad bar, which equals tomatoes that taste like paper, the aforementioned iceberg lettuce, and three soggy cucumber rounds. Thankfully, I also have my reserve BiteRite protein bar and a Ziploc baggie of walnuts.

Patty swirls her pasta onto her fork just as Bryce and his asshat friends walk past us, heading for their table by the salad bar.

Bryce slows and lets his bulky butt take up the whole pathway to lean over right into Patty's space and says, "Lighten up on the carbs, Fatty Patty."

This motherfucker will *not* leave us alone today, and once again Patty is in his sights because she's my friend.

"Sorry, Bryce, we can't all survive on a diet of Muscle Milk and human misery," I say, directing his attention back to me.

Of course he takes that as a compliment, flexing unsubtly. Not exactly my intention, but it soothes his ego enough for him to turn his attention to the girls at his usual table, who are very much watching the flexing. He struts over to them and plops his vanilla Muscle Milk down with a thud, spreading himself into his seat like a lord.

"He's so heteronormative, it actually makes me want to vom," Patty says. "How messed up is it that the rest of our class voted for him to give a speech at graduation? Like we need to hear any more out of his mouth."

"Assholes love assholes," I offer, as Bryce and Noah chest-bump, congratulating each other on their existences.

"I didn't know he was capable of original thought."

"Oh, I'm sure he'll go for something real deep, like 'cherish the memories' and 'you're all the leaders of tomorrow.' Like, at best."

Patty chews a hearty bite of pasta before she says, "I wish, just once, someone would give an honest graduation speech."

"Oh yeah? What would yours be?"

"'I hated you all as much as you hated me and I hope you rot in hell. Thank you!'"

That makes me laugh, harder and louder than is allowed for subhumans like us. I'm immediately rewarded with a whack to the head. An empty Diet Coke can lands at my feet, and the same anger that reared up when Forest stole my shoes overtakes me. My forehead starts pulsing. One look at Bryce's table and his stupid ugly smirk, and I know that's where it came from.

I try to grab the spork off Patty's plate, but she pulls it away from me. "What are you going to do with that, Thompson?"

"Gouge an eye out?" I suggest. "Slowly slice off a single ball?"

Patty eyes Mrs. Vasquez, the lunch monitor on duty today. She's walking around, arms crossed, stopping to chat with students here and there, like a beat cop trying to be friendly with the neighborhood riffraff. Patty gently pulls my hand back down to the table. "Dude, ignore them. Four and a half days."

"Yeah," I say. Except I'm not going to ignore them. I'm not going to shake it off. I'm going to swallow it, and feel it burn in my stomach. I'm going to let it drive me. I am going to turn this anger into rocket fuel and use it to launch me to my destiny.

Wherever that is.

Because yeah, I know a whole hell of a lot more about hate than I do about love.

But someday, that's going to change.

When the heinous school day is done, I take the bus into Austin, where the Sugarplum Dance Studio lives. Danny Roth runs the most desirable program in Texas there and I think he's the only person besides Mom and Patty who actually believes in me. Danny is from Dallas but moved to Austin ten years ago because of his husband's work. He says he found himself here and then he found me.

"Oh," he says as I blaze past him and take my spot on the floor, the first one there like always. "Hard day?"

I nod. "Would you mind if we didn't talk today? I would really like to just dance."

"That's my girl," he says, lips shiny, green eyes piercing. He nods toward Raven, his assistant, a goth girl who definitely renamed herself. "Play something loud, would you, darlin'?"

As soon as the music starts, I feel the day start to metabolize. I draw each memory to the surface, spin it around, look at it for all it is and everything it means. I don't try to make it go away; I transform it. My dad, Bryce, the school system, Trailerina, and Fatty Patty—I use it all. I make it work for me, burn it until I fade into the music and pain loosens its hold so that what's primal and free takes over. By the time the other dancers arrive and class begins, I feel like I belong.

After it's over, I stay for a private lesson to review the choreography for my next video. It's complicated yet plays to my strengths. Danny works from what he knows I can do, then refines it to show off my best. He's hard on me, stretching me to the edge of my abilities, tapping and clapping to the beat until I get it right, but I wouldn't have it any other way. By the end, I've sweated through my clothes and still he has me run through it again. He disappears into the shadows at the back of the room so I can totally get into it, imagine it's just me, and that the only people watching are the ones who can help change my life. When I finish the combination, Raven kills the music and the words ". . . get it to you next week" rip through the room at full volume.

My peace evaporates as I turn, chest still heaving, and see my mom at the back of the room, in pink scrubs with little hearts on them, mouth dropped open in surprise. She's glancing toward me worriedly as Danny puts a comforting hand on her shoulder. His expression is strained though. Danny has me here on a partial scholarship, but he's the best, and even with that assistance the classes aren't cheap.

When we walk out after, the cool night air blows on my skin soothingly, but the guilt still has me. My mom has given up everything to give me everything. I've worked since I was old enough to get a job to pay for lessons, to pay for shoes, but at a certain point we realized I couldn't go to school full-time, work, *and* develop myself as a dancer or a singer well enough to get to the top. We had to make a choice. She is betting everything that it was the right one.

When we get to the car, she wraps her arms around me and says, "This is going to be so good, baby. You'll see. You're special, Love, and the world is going to turn out for you."

I look at her, really look. Forty, nails and lashes done, lips plump with gloss, but plagued with an exhausted slump. There's a direct line between that look and the life she's made for me, all the lessons she's invested in instead of doing anything for herself.

My determination returns as I glance up at the full moon. Someday she's not going to have to work anymore. Someday I'm going to take care of *her*. Make this all worth it.

"When I'm famous, I'm going to buy you a house," I tell her, voicing for the first time the thing I usually think in secret. "And a new car, and a whole new wardrobe."

"Oh, hon," she says, "you don't have to—"

"Yes, I do. I have now promised that big full moon up there." I pause. "You watch me."

Hours later, after a silent car ride home and when I'm done with the very last of my high school homework, I open my school laptop, the one I'll have to give up in a few days. I slide on my headphones and pull up YouTube.

I type in the letter *M*, and the algorithm knows me so well, the song "Me Without You" by Lil' D pops up first in the list of suggested videos.

I select it and wait, ready to watch and get inspired for my own upload.

There's something about him. He's . . .

Talented.

Perfect.

Successful.

Confident.

He's everything I wish I was. No one would throw a can at *his* head. Everyone loves him.

But . . . he's raw, too, in a way that makes him feel almost familiar to me, like I know him.

Salt on my lips reminds me of you, babe

Sun in my eyes makes my heart ache

He walks along the beach with a girl, wind tousling his blond hair. Beautiful, with his brown eyes, long muscles covered in tattoos. The lyrics might be a little cheesy, but there's something in those eyes, a hunger that aches inside me, too. I do a rough blocking of my dance steps in my room, make sure I have the space I need, while I hum along to his words, warming up my throat.

Blue skies, all I see is blue eyes

Me without you is life without highs

Damien kisses the girl in the water. For just a second I can imagine it's *me* he's holding, *me* he's singing to, telling me I belong there. That I'll get there.

The house still smells like the eggplant we ate for dinner, River is still *pew-pew*ing in his room, and our neighbor's dog Sundae is outside, howling at the moon by the Adirondack chairs like she always does when it's full. But things won't always be like this.

In the meantime, I set up my phone, turn on the softbox lights I bought last summer, and get ready to hit Record.

CHAPTER TWO

Love

"I will cherish these memories. And don't forget, you're all the leaders of tomorrow. Thank you!"

Bryce stands at a podium in his cap and gown, while the faculty and staff sit behind him, pretending to be oh-so moved.

The audience claps, including Mom, who is recording the entire graduation ceremony on her phone. Patty spins around in her chair, mouth dropped open, and gives me the biggest eye roll. We're still sitting, but it's almost time for us to mount the stage, get our diplomas, and flee this place forever.

Mrs. Messerole takes Bryce's place at the podium.

"Thank you, Mr. Prescott," she says. "Excellent job. All right. Is everyone ready?" Howls and whistles go up among the seniors. The parents chuckle. "Please rise."

We shuffle with excitement as "Counting Stars" by One-Republic starts to play and we get in line, just like we practiced. Everything seems good. We're here. We've *arrived*. But as Bryce goes to find his place in alphabetical order, he bumps into Patty. Something doesn't feel right, and when he moves along, I see a sign stuck to the back of her gown. I can't make out what it says because I'm all the way back in the *T*'s, but whatever it is, it can't be good.

"Patty," I hiss, but the music is too loud. As we walk down the aisle toward the stage, I call out to her again. "Patty!" This time she looks over her shoulder, forehead creased in confusion. But she's passing in front of her parents, and before I can communicate, her head whips forward again, her shoulders tensing as she hyperfocuses on them. She's not going to listen to me now. She's wearing a dress. She shaved her legs. She is *trying* to be the kid her parents want one last time.

And now I'm not going to be able to stop whatever final insult high school has to deliver to her.

As we climb the stage, none of the teachers seem to notice the piece of paper flapping on Patty's back or Bryce high-fiving his awful friends. I try to repeat my mantra about getting out of this place and everything Patty and I are going to do with our lives while these jerks melt slowly into their couches, but this time it doesn't work.

Mrs. Messerole calls out, "Blake Armstrong."

Oh God, Patty is next. She's about to be in front of all these people, in front of her parents, with whatever is on her back visible to all of them.

Mrs. Messerole announces, "Patricia Avalos."

It's like everything is moving in slow motion. Patty walks carefully to center stage, tottering a bit on her shoes. Now I can clearly see what the sign on her back says: Fatty Patty. Complete with a crappy doodle of a pig. A swell of laughter rises from the audience and Patty freezes, then looks around. She finally realizes something is flapping off her.

I leave my spot in the line, rushing toward Patty. Miss Jenkins calls out, "Love! Love, where are you going?" and tears after me, probably to corral me into place rather than help the person who actually needs it. I dodge her as Patty desperately tries to pull off the sign, but her arms can't reach it.

Patty scans the crowd helplessly, and as I near the stage, I'm caught between bravery and the knowledge that my mom and brothers are in the audience, that my mom is recording this for posterity, as are hundreds of other cameras. Patty tries and tries again to get the sign off her, and finally just pulls the gown up over her head, revealing the sweet floral baby-doll dress she agreed to wear today. I watch in horror as Patty's dress gets caught on her mortarboard, the one she decorated with block letters reading, Byeeeeee! And then, as if the whole universe is conspiring against her, she slips and falls flat on her stomach. She hasn't smashed her face, but there for everyone to see is her epic, lucky Hello Kitty underwear.

This is a travesty beyond imagining. Patty *loves* that underwear. It is a beautiful reminder of everything that is badass about her: her spiky spirit, her playful nature, who she is when she's not here. And her beloved undies will now be forever polluted by this event. This isn't just another prank or insult—it's a social assassination designed to follow her well beyond this botched graduation.

My eyes skitter to her parents, who have both blanched and are scanning the room for some kind of exit strategy, I'm sure. I suspect our plan of lounging in Patty's pool eating Doritos for the rest of the day is off the table. They won't be kind about this. Oh, no they will not.

The laughter goes monstrous. I mean, grandmas, younger siblings, even teachers . . . everyone is howling and hooting. The level of glee is insane. Our class, however, is dead silent. Not out of pity, but I'm pretty sure everyone is thinking about their imminent walk across the stage and praying to some lesser God to have mercy on them, to make Patty the day's only victim. My throat locks up, and my heart is beating so hard, I can barely breathe, everyone in the audience blurring. But I can't let this go on. I. Can't.

I run up onstage and rip into action.

That action turns out to be some combination of a twerk, an interpretive dance, and an avant-garde burlesque routine. I feel possessed, burning with energy. It's like I'm making up for eighteen years of only being myself at Danny's dance studio, for eighteen years of stress and anger and loss. I take everything that just happened and the past four years of hell, and I use it to distract attention away from Patty.

"Love Thompson!" Mrs. Messerole says. "Love! Oh God, no. Not graduation. Love . . . please get back in line?"

In my peripheral vision, Patty clambers to her feet and grabs her cap and gown, then takes her diploma from the principal's hands as quickly as she can.

Once I know she's made it offstage, something shifts. I'm no longer jerking around to distract the audience from Patty's embarrassment. I'm in the music, just like in dance class. So I keep going. I yank off my own cap and gown and throw them to the side, revealing my cropped lace blouse and black pants. I am not warmed up but I drop into the splits anyway, and start popping my booty like I've been practicing. The teachers approach, but I'm already back up, prancing upstage. I grind my body close to Mrs. Messerole; then I spin and twirl her, making her my partner.

The auditorium goes *wild*. This time though, they're not laughing. They're screaming and yelling and it sounds like . . . applause. Like they actually like what I'm doing. Teachers aren't allowed to touch students, so even as they form a half circle around me, trying to block me from view, I know they can't actually force me offstage. I pretend they're background dancers, and weave around them until the song finally comes to its triumphant end and I bow, sweating hard.

When I bring my head back up, everyone is on their feet. Even my mom is jumping up and down, phone still raised and recording. Quickly, I dash past the teachers and over to the mic. "Thanks so much to Mrs. Messerole for allowing Patty and me to flash-mob at graduation. Haha . . . pranks rule! And now, please return to your previously scheduled graduation ceremony."

I jet back into the line and wait to see if I'm going to be in trouble, if they'll hold back my diploma, or worse. But Mrs. Messerole just gives me one intense look that tells me we'll be having a nice long chat after. Once the crowd begins to quiet, she says, "Our next graduate is . . . Dante Brown. Come on up, please."

The recovery is instant. Everyone settles back down. But my performance is still in the air, and the auditorium crackles with energy until every last diploma has been conferred. And I know something has happened, something irreversible.

I have come to life.

CHAPTER THREE

Austin

Fred, the nice man from the Jewish funeral home, knows what he's doing. I watch him as he speaks to his employees in a hushed tone, swooshes back and forth busily in his corduroy jacket and button-down shirt that strains slightly over his belly. He does this almost every day, I'm sure.

I mean, people die.

All the time.

Can't be stopped.

If anyone has job security, it's Fred. He seems genuinely kind, but I don't know. Can you *really* care about every person's loss all the time? Or do you stop seeing people individually after a while and learn how to wear a convincing mask?

I know a lot about convincing masks. I've been wearing one since I was here a few months ago, when Dad's numbers started going steadily in the wrong direction. He made me come along to make his own funeral arrangements while he was still strong and clear enough to make decisions for himself. The whole time I didn't know what to say, and Dad didn't ask me to do anything at all until Fred went to the printer in his office to get the hard copy of the plan. That's when Dad put his hand on my shoulder and said, *This way, your mother won't have to deal with it. You're going to have to hold steady for her, bud. She's going to need that.*

I didn't understand then because my mom has always been so tough. Both my parents have.

But over the last few weeks, I've started to get it. So today I'm trying to be there for her and my little sister, Zoe, putting on a convincing mask of someone who can hold them together, even when I feel myself falling apart.

I can't believe it was only yesterday morning that Dad took his last breath, the IV bag dripping morphine through him as all of us told him what a great job he'd done being a dad, a husband, a man. After a week of the house being full of people from the neighborhood, the family, the diner, all taking turns saying goodbye and dropping off food in the kitchen, at the end it was just me, Mom, and Zoe. Even though we knew it was coming and had made all the preparations, when he took that last breath, it didn't feel real.

Not until they came and took him away but left the hospital bed and the machines that had kept him alive stacked in a corner, haunting the living room like unemployed poltergeists. Even though it'd been a few days since he was conscious enough to speak, the space he took up, just his existence in the house, made us all feel like we were still in a world we could recognize. Now everything is as new and painful as shiny, burnt skin. None of us can really believe we're here, about to have his funeral, about to say goodbye to his body forever and be left with . . . what?

Dad is everywhere. Dad is nowhere. I can smell the clean lime of his aftershave, the mint of his toothpaste. I can feel his hand on my shoulder, encouraging me to be a man, to face this with as much dignity as he did. So I steel myself as Mom and I wait in the funeral home's comfortable easy chairs. Tears streak her cheeks, falling so continuously, she's stopped trying to brush them away. They leak down her shirt, past the pendant Dad gave her for her birthday, which hangs at her throat. My parents met in high school, and they loved each other like they were sixteen every day of their marriage. I think right until the end, that's how they saw each other still. Then, not now.

Fred comes padding over to us, the plush carpet absorbing the sound of his steps, his face fixed into an expression of empathy, but without the pity I've seen on so many others. He takes a look at Mom, then at me, and decides I'm the one to address. "We're ready to close the casket to begin the service." He clasps his hands and his voice is even, yet filled with emotion. It sends me back to Dad at the very end, when he finally gave in to the tears.

It takes a lot, Dad said, *to let go of this life.*

"Would you like to say goodbye, first?" Fred asks now, pulling me back to the present. "This will be your last opportunity. There is no rush, but we are ready to proceed if you are."

Panic creeps up my throat. When we leave here, we will go to the grave site. All the people who have come in and out of the house will be there, dressed up, ready to pay respects. We will lower my dad into the ground, and then I will have to face everyone who loved him. There will be many people whose hands I will need to shake and whose condolences I will need to receive.

I feel ripped apart but also oddly and intensely alive. Like everything that happens is important and I should remember every second of it. I feel like my dad is giving me a tailwind from beyond.

"Where's your sister?" Mom says, sniffling, blinking like she just woke up. "She needs to be here. We have to . . . we have to do this thing."

Zoe. I didn't even notice she never came back from the bathroom.

"I'll go get her, Mom," I say, getting to my feet. "You go be with Dad and we'll be right back."

"Okay, honey." She comes over to me, raises her hand, and touches my cheek. "You're so handsome. You know that? You look just like him. He would be so proud of you."

I don't know what to say to that, the pressure in my chest is too much, so I just take her hand in mine, squeeze it, and then let it fall.

When I knock on the bathroom door, there's no answer. I check out the window and there is Zoe, crouched down on the steps, a little ball of black clothes, her curly brown hair pulled back into a ponytail. The day is crisp. It's May and the tulips, daffodils, and azaleas are in full bloom. A row of black locust trees casts shadows across the grass, white petals dropping to the ground like snow. It would be a beautiful day to be doing anything else.

Zoe's only eleven, and was still always in his arms until he got too sick for it. At least I got Dad until I was almost grown. I open the front door gently, and see that she's curled over her phone with a distant smile on her lips. I pause for a second, not wanting to take that smile away.

She lets out a little giggle, responding to whatever she's looking at. I haven't heard her laugh in weeks, and Zoe loves to laugh. It's so familiar, for a second I almost feel safe.

"What's so funny, Zoe?" I ask, taking a few steps toward her.

"Nothin'," she says quickly.

I can tell she's embarrassed I caught her experiencing joy when we're supposed to be sad. It's the opposite of what I meant to do.

"C'mon. Don't be stingy," I say. "Really. What is it?"

"It's so stupid though." She tucks her screen under her arm, where I can't see it.

"The stupider, the better." I sit down next to her, nudge her softly, until she takes out her phone again and places it between us so it balances on both our knees.

"I'll put it back to the beginning." She slides her finger along the screen. "Some girl in Texas turned her principal into a stripper pole."

In the background, a girl is lying on her face and it looks like her dress is up over her waist. Another girl bursts onto the stage and starts dancing. The attention shifts. The principal is tall and boxy with a prim bob, and the dancing girl is tiny by comparison. Teachers chase her across the stage as kids in caps and gowns look on, and this girl . . . she does not care at all. She just slides herself up and down the principal, using her as leverage to kick up her legs and then slide down into a split.

"See, I told you," Zoe says. "Stupid. Just some girl being chaotic."

"Watch it again," I say. "I think she was trying to help someone. I think her friend was in trouble and she was taking the heat."

Zoe drags her finger across the screen and pauses on the girl in the background. "You're right," she says. "Huh."

"What?"

"Just figured everyone does everything to get attention. Especially on the internet."

She lets the video play through again and I cannot take my eyes off the dancer. Someone else would have made this whole thing seem super trashy, but instead there's something, like, . . . rebellious about it. She's super cute and super alive, and I find myself laughing too.

"Thanks for that." I sling my arm around Zoe's shoulders. A breeze kicks up, sending swirls of petals into a mini cyclone.

"There's another funny one where a cat is stuck in a laundry basket," she says.

"Maybe you can show me when we get home."

At the mention of home, we both get quiet again. Home means something different now, without Dad. Which reminds me why I came outside in the first place.

"Z, they're closing Dad's casket in a minute. You want to come inside?"

Zoe stiffens and then slumps over, leaning her head into my shoulder like it's too painful to speak. But I understand anyway.

"I don't want to say goodbye either," I say.

"Yeah," she says. "This is a bad day."

"It is," I say, "but at least we know it can't get any worse."

It can get worse, and it does. I thought I was prepared, but there's something about them lowering that casket that feels so . . . final. So horrible.

Mom throws in the first handful of dirt. Zoe and I are next, and then a whole line of mourners follows. Fred guides Mom and Zoe and me like a mama duck to form the receiving line, where we have to listen and say nice things back to everyone we know—all the guys from the team, all the regulars from Nathan's, so many people—like we didn't just have to do the worst thing imaginable.

When it's over, Mom and Zoe begin to retreat, while the undertakers continue to shovel dirt into the grave. Mom looks back at me. "You coming?"

"In a minute," I say. I'm not ready to leave Dad with strangers. I still need his strength, especially for what's next. Not just the days and weeks to come, but because I've made a decision:

I'm going to finally tell Emma that I love her.

I've never done that before. My family is all about love, but we don't *say* it. Or at least we didn't until it was almost too late. I don't want to leave anything unsaid anymore. Life is too precarious, too much like . . . well . . . this. You never know what the future will bring.

Dad always said the best time to do anything is now.

So now, it is.

Like she can read my mind, Emma—who has been hanging back with Chad and Tyler and Paige—slips her hand into mine, grounding me just when I need it most. It makes me even more sure I've wasted too much time already. We've been together a year and a half and I've hesitated so long, it feels like a decision I didn't even make. The world has just been *happening* to me. I have to live in it now. For him.

"It's hard to say goodbye," Emma says, giving my hand another comforting squeeze. "Especially when it was all so fast."

"Fast and slow. A fat dose of each. This whole shitty year felt like one nonstop do-or-die."

She furrows her brow adorably as she tucks a loose strand of hair behind her ear. "Say more."

"Sports analogy incoming," I say, half smiling. She always gives me a hard time for those, but today she just nods, waiting.

"You ever watch a baseball game, bottom of the ninth, two outs, two strikes, and your team is down by one? We call it 'do-or-die.' It's this moment where the only way to win is to do the near impossible. You have to hit a three-inch ball moving at a hundred miles per hour out into the stands. Time slows down—adrenaline floods your veins, but you need to stay so calm . . . it's exhausting."

Emma nods again, but I'm not sure she really understands.

"My dad getting sick . . . it was literally do-or-die." I inch a bit closer to her. "You convince yourself you can hit a home run even with the odds against you, but this time the game was rigged, you know? With the kind of cancer he had, by the time they found it, he was too weak to even swing the bat."

"You did everything you could, Austin," she says. There's a glimmer of something pained behind her eyes. "I was there. I saw. Your whole family was amazing, but you especially."

"Because I had you in the stands."

Emma smiles. Her hair is black, long and glossy, and her lips are red and chapped, raw where she chews on them in that cute, nervous way. Her nails are short and clean, her eyes blue and wide open. She is familiar and loving and always there when I need her. She was at every important family gathering . . . anytime I asked her to be somewhere, she was there. She and her mom organized a food train and took care of the whole thing. And when it got really bad and we stopped having people over at all, Emma FaceTimed me every night to check on me. I've leaned on her so much this year and I can't imagine not having her by my side. For graduation. For college. Hopefully for everything after, like Mom and Dad.

Dad's voice echoes again. *The best time to do anything is now. Now, Austin.*

"Emma, I—" I begin. It's like approaching a gate and on the other side of it is everything I've ever wanted and been too afraid to reach for.

Finally, I walk through it.

"I love you, Emma."

I expect to see her features soften at the words she's been waiting to hear from me.

But instead her face pinches.

I wait, my stomach on a plane plummeting to the ground. I don't know what I thought was going to happen, but not this.

Not this . . . nothing.

I glance around. This was not the best time; I see that now. It was the worst.

A graveyard on the day of my father's burial? Now she probably thinks I'm a dick.

Oh God.

"I'm sorry . . . I know it's not the most romantic place to say it. I should have done something creative. It was a bad call." I rush over the words because I can't take another second of silence and because I'm still hoping for some glimmer of reciprocity. But when I frantically search her face, I find only fear.

Fear is something I'm familiar with, that I might be able to make better. Take it away from her the way she has from me. "You don't have to worry. I'm not just saying it because of . . ." I stare at the grave site again for a few seconds before turning my attention back to her. "It's true. I love you."

Her eyes fill, water poised at the edge of her lids. At first I think they might be happy tears, but when she still doesn't say anything, my stomach drops again. We're still standing here and she is her and I am me and nothing has changed, except it feels like everything has and I don't know why.

She pulls her hand out of mine and stares straight ahead for a moment, breathing shallow. "I . . . I was going to wait, but I can't. It's not fair. I can't do this anymore." She's talking speedily, the way she does when she's nervous, and my body sends up even more red flags.

"Do what?" Something new spirals in my solar plexus, water circling a drain.

"Us. It isn't feeling right anymore. I mean, you're amazing. Hot and smart and all of that. You'll always be my first and I'll always be yours, but . . ."

"Not feeling right?" I'm dizzy, like the time I got knocked out by a fly ball in third grade. Except worse. "So what does this mean?" I ask, as if somehow I might get a different answer that undoes everything she's just said.

"I really care about you, but . . . not like a boyfriend."

Oh God. Oh *God*. "Why didn't you . . . How long have you felt this way?"

Her face falls even further and she hesitates like she doesn't want to answer, but finally she does.

"Since homecoming."

"Nine *months*?" We've been through birthdays, holidays, New Year's Eve, Valentine's Day, dances. She's played with Zoe and helped my mom out at the diner. We've had sex . . . kind of a lot actually. I don't know why my brain careens down that path, but it does and I'm assaulted by images and memories, all in soft focus, of us in shadows, and . . . I don't know . . . what seemed like passion? What seemed like love. And during all of it she was feeling this way? Like I'm her *friend.* I am burning—with anger, with sadness, but mostly, with humiliation.

"I was going to talk to you about it after the dance, but that's when you told me your dad's prognosis. And then . . . I know it sounds horrible, but I didn't want it to seem like I was breaking up with you because I didn't want to deal with it. Because I wouldn't do that. I'm *not* that kind of person."

"Right." So much of what I thought was true these last nine months has been destroyed in the last five minutes, but that is one thing I'm pretty sure of. "I know you're not."

"I couldn't figure out what to do, what would be worse. So I decided to stick by you. But, you saying you love me . . . I can't honestly say it back and . . . I realize I chose wrong, I guess."

"So you don't love me . . . at all." I say it out loud to make myself realize it's the truth: I've been a pity boyfriend this whole time. But as I do, it feels incomplete. A new whisper is getting louder in my brain, coming to deliver another new and painful dose of reality. "And?"

"And what?"

"And there's something else you're not telling me . . . isn't there?"

"No!"

"Em . . ."

Her shoulders slump. "I . . . I've had feelings for someone else for a while now." She pauses, like she's said too much.

"Did something happen?" I ask, trying to make sense of everything that's going on right now.

"No. You didn't do anything wrong, really. I didn't want to hurt you. I would never want to hurt you, Austin." Her tears spill over and she turns her body away from me.

"Who?" I say. "Just tell me."

"Chad."

The word lands with a thud. Chad. One of my best friends. Who conveniently disappeared from the grave site right before we started this conversation.

I finally pull away from her.

"I'm sorry. You're a great guy. I know you'll meet a girl who really loves you. You'll forget about me and—"

"Yeah," I say, looking away. "I'm sure the perfect person will fall right into my arms."

"I'm sorry, Austin," she says. She still looks beautiful, even after breaking my heart. "I really am. You deserve better than this. Better than me."

I have to get out of here. I speed toward my car, the white petals dancing around me again, floating through the air. Better to be like them, just going along with whatever. Dad was right about a lot of things, but not this.

From now on, I'm just going to keep my head down. Do what has to be done. No risks.

What's the point of wanting anything more when it all just ends anyway?

CHAPTER FOUR

Love

I'm in my bed, asleep until morning light seeps through my blinds. I feel like there's something I should remember, but I don't know what it is.

Forest? No, the house is way too quiet for him to be lurking about, looking for stuff to steal.

River? Also no, it's Sunday so he'll be sleeping literally all day.

I pull the covers up over my head so the sun doesn't burn my eyeballs out of my head, and try to sink back into the dream I was having, until it comes to me.

My phone buzzes on my nightstand and I sit up, wide awake.

My God, I gyrated on Mrs. Messerole.

In front of everyone.

I grab my phone, expecting to see a text from Patty, but my screen is filled with so many messages, I can't even begin to sift through them. There's an announcement from Lil' D that he's making something special for fans of "Replay," which would normally spike my blood pressure, but something else hits me even harder. Up top is a notification from TikTok: "You have 300,000 new followers!"

I throw the covers off me and open my messages and sure enough, Patty did text me—

call me when you're up

like srsly

you're blowing up bitch!!!

I tell the phone to call her, knees tucked up to my chin. Yesterday I had 922 followers. How could I now be in the *hundreds of thousands*?

"Well, hello, Your Grace," Patty says.

"The hell does that mean? Can you please tell me what's going on?"

"Of course, Your Grace—"

"Quit it," I snap as I hear the sound of cans being shelved. "And why do you keep calling me that?"

"Because you're, like, the queen of the internet now. Open le TikTok and you'll see."

I open TikTok and number one on trending is #gradgirl. There are thousands of posts and reaction vids and comments. It started yesterday a few hours after graduation. Someone who was there got the whole thing on her phone and tagged me when she posted it. It was funny, so I reposted it and it got a little bit of traction, but nothing like *this*. A lot happened while I was sleeping, I guess.

There's silence on the other end of the phone, and I can tell Patty's not shelving anymore. I picture her sitting on a crate, surrounded by beans. "You took a bullet for me up there, and people love you for it," she says. "I guess karma's real."

I let this settle. I *want* it all to be real, but I know how the socials are. This happens to someone every day. I mean, there's a dog with an Italian accent who is definitely going to start talking in full sentences any day and where will that leave me?

"I'm sure it will blow over after my fifteen minutes of fame," I say, trying to slow my heartbeat.

"Or blow *up*!" She pauses. "You're special, Love. There's a reason people are reposting it. You didn't just make a distraction—you put on a full-blown *show*. Who else could do that? Think about it: I have never once in all my days wanted to be famous. I want to be with the books and the skateboards and live in Austin forever and mostly not be fucked with. But you . . . this is the chance you've been waiting for." Her voice gets muffled and I can hear her saying, "Yes, Amir, I will get up off my ass in a second but for right now, shoo. I have something I must share with my bestie." She turns her attention back to me. "I found out something today."

"Tell me," I say, welcoming the pivot from my own bullshit for a second.

"Remember how I got wait-listed for BU? Well . . . as of this morning, I have been un-wait-listed."

"Oh my God!" Patty has wanted to go to Boston University as long as we've been friends, and I thought she would never get over what she saw as a total rejection. It wasn't though. "I'm so happy for you."

"We're both getting out of here," she says, and I hear more clinking in the background. "Anyway, I am but a simple peasant and must take my leave to fill the storehouses. Fare thee well."

"Bye, Patty," I say. "And hey . . . you're the best person who ever lived, okay?"

"Yeah, okay. Life is gonna be great, you know?"

"Yeah?"

"Yeah. *Salud*, buddy."

"Salud."

I put the phone down and look around. It seems like *something* should be happening. River and Forest should be in here giving me shit, or Mom should be gushing or fretting, or something inside me should be changing. But the room is still sweltering as usual, the sun is shining right on my cheeks, and the only thing different is the way my phone buzzes and buzzes and buzzes with clusters of notifications I can't hope to keep up with.

Then it starts ringing with an unknown number. Los Angeles. I freeze. I have never gotten a call from *Los Angeles*. It could be a spam call about my taxes or the warranty on a car I don't own. It probably is, but I answer anyway.

"Hello?" I say. My hands tremble.

"Love!" a chirpy voice says. "This is Christine Ryan. I'm a talent manager at Impression Partners, and I'd love to—"

"Talent manager?"

"Yes, as in the person who is going to make all your dreams come true." Her voice is clear but pressured, like she doesn't have time to explain herself to anyone, ever. "Your dreams of fame and fortune?"

"Oh," I say, getting to my feet. I open the door and look down the hallway, but the house looks silent, asleep. "I don't know if I should talk to you."

The voice gives an indulgent little chuckle. "Oh, I don't want to talk, babe! I want to meet! Check your email."

I put her on speaker so I can access the screen, and I open my mail app. Right up top I find a confirmation for two business class tickets for Mom and me from Austin to Los Angeles. I get a weird out-of-body feeling. How did she find my email? How did she already do this?

Then I see the dates.

"Wait—" I say. "These tickets are for tomorrow. I have two brothers and we can't just leave them."

"Already talked to your mom. Hired a nanny service. NBD."

NBD. I think of all the times my mom has wanted to go out or do something while I had practice or auditions and the way it's been a very big deal. She's had to contort herself to find someone to hang with the boys, because River is not exactly nurturing and Forest is not exactly independent.

I can't think of anything to say. Everything is moving so fast.

"Hello? You still there?" Christine says.

"Why would you do all this for me?" I ask, slipping my feet into pink fuzzy slippers as I walk into the bathroom.

"Because I saw your video. You're a star. And you should be treated like one."

I let that sit for a second.

"Hello?" the voice says. "Love?"

I thought my dreams of going to LA were like the final-boss battle. That I would have to go to school first, level up awhile. But this could be the cheat code I need to get me there so much faster. *Tomorrow.* I try to push down the panic. I don't want to get too excited or read too much into it. What I said to Patty is still true; my fifteen minutes could be up like that and this could all go away. But even so, I feel a tiny twinge of hope.

"Love?" Christine repeats. Her voice is still sweet, but tinged with a warning, like an hourglass sitting nearby is running out of sand.

I give myself a nice solid stare in the full-length mirror. *You ready, girl?*

"Yes," I say to both my reflection and the phone. "Great. As long as we can really leave the boys, we'll be there."

"Excellent." She lets out an almost manic laugh. "And do me a favor, Lovebug."

"What's that?"

"Don't talk to any other agents or managers until we get the chance to connect. Deal?"

As if summoned by her words, my screen is blowing up again, beeping with another call coming in from LA. "Totally." I send the call to voicemail. "Thank you."

"No," she says, a little breathless. "Thank YOU, Love. This is going to be great. You'll see." She squeals. "So. Exciting!"

After we hang up, I go through my morning routine: smear the toothpaste on my toothbrush, slide my headband over my ears, and start warming the water so I can wash my face. It's all so normal.

And yet, everything just changed. Maybe just for fifteen minutes.

Or maybe not.

Maybe forever.

CHAPTER FIVE

Austin

Two days after the burial, we hang a big picture of my dad on a sandwich board at the front of the diner for the reception to let any random customers know what they're walking into. But that isn't really necessary. We're a tight neighborhood and I can't think of anyone who doesn't know what happened to him. He also sort of *is* the design of the place—pictures of him and friends and family through the years are all over, plus his favorite old records hang on the walls, and the genuine mini jukeboxes he loved so much when he was a kid sit on every table. It's like we're inside his spirit, even though we've left his body behind.

Mourners pack the restaurant, eating and drinking, as the kids from around the neighborhood we hired for the day carry food from the kitchen. I knew being with everyone would be overwhelming, but throw in the fact that my now ex-girlfriend is slouched in a booth with my friends, including Chad—just right here in front of my face—watching the viral video of that girl saving her friend at her graduation on repeat, and it's actually impossible to be here. I've been mostly hiding in the back, cooking and assembling platters of hot dogs, Chicago-style (NEVER KETCHUP). When I finish a fresh batch, I grab the tray and head out onto the floor. At least if I'm busy, I don't have to look at Emma or anyone else.

Zoe is sitting at the center table with her friend Shelby, whose blond hair is tied back in a pink ribbon that matches her freckles. Their nails are both done in fuchsia with rhinestones, and they both fix me with equally disappointed, judgmental squints.

"Shouldn't you be *getting* served?" Zoe says, pointing to the tray. "You know, as the dead guy's son? Don't you want to, like, hang out with your people?"

I don't want to talk about Emma in general and I *definitely* don't want to talk to Zoe about Emma, so I reach for an excuse. "Only I know how to make the hot dogs like Dad did. They're beef. You gotta put them on a skewer—"

"—and cut a spiral through them. I know, I know." She shreds her napkin before looking up at me, jaw set.

"It's what Dad would've wanted." I ruffle Zoe's hair, then head back, hoping I sounded adequately big brotherly. I pass Emma and Chad, and Tyler and Paige, avoiding eye contact even though I can feel them watching me, wondering why I won't sit down with them. When I get in the back again, I slap the tray down, pull some hot dogs off the grill, and rotate the rest. I focus on watching the grease pool at the dogs' edges, trying to keep myself together, when I hear a sound coming from the office. A thump. There's a pause, and then another thump. What the hell?

"Can you keep an eye on these for me?" I ask Dave, one of the kids from school.

"Sure thing," he says.

When I step into the office, Mom is holding a folder. Three cookbooks are on the floor, splayed open, and she is looking into the middle distance. It's like she doesn't see me, even though I'm standing in front of her.

"Hey, Mom," I say gently, waiting for her to focus on me. But she looks like she's lost in a hurricane. "What are you doing?"

"Oh." She snaps to attention and breezes past me. I follow her small, determined footsteps.

"Mom, what is it?"

"I was getting something for the memory table and I needed the old inventory reports," she says.

"That's a weird thing to put on a memory table."

She doesn't slow down. "It's for your uncle Noah. One of his clients is a culinary group out East and they're thinking of expanding to Chicago. I don't want to talk business at a funeral, but I'm not sure when's the next time I'll get to see him and . . . it's a little urgent."

Wait . . . does this mean . . . "Mom . . . ," I say, but she just keeps heading toward the door to the kitchen. "Mom, stop!"

She stops and spins on her heels. Her hair is feral, and I realize for the first time that some gray is appearing at her temples.

"You want to sell Dad's diner?" I ask.

"I don't *want* to," she says shakily, "but I'm not sure we have a choice. It's not his fault. Nothing's his fault, but when your dad got sick, we had to hire extra help and . . . cancer is expensive. I didn't even really have the chance to track it until now and . . . I don't want to stress you out, but it's not good. It's going to be even more of a struggle for me on my own." She puts the folder down on the counter and shakes her head.

"But what are you going to do with the place closed? I mean, what did you do before you guys opened Nathan's?"

It's a trick question, one I know the answer to. Mom was an English major who got pregnant with me right after college. She has always been our mom and worked here with Dad. That's been her whole life.

She gets that out-of-focus look again before shaking her head. "I don't want you to worry about this right now. You've got enough on your plate as it is, and Noah can help. At least we could get out of the hole . . ."

"We don't need Noah," I say, with more conviction than I feel. "I can help you figure everything out." I put my hand on the folder and try to take it, but Mom won't let go. "I'll work with you all summer, longer if we still need it." I see a sliver of sunlight pierce through her glassy eyes, so I push harder. "I can cook and wash dishes, and if you wait tables, we can make it work. Let's try at least. Please."

Mom taps her finger on the folder and levels her eyes up to mine. "This is not an easy thing to say to you. A person should be able to raise her kids without so many hard lessons at once. But, honey, I have to be honest with you. This place may be beyond help. It's nobody's fault. We know how much it meant to your dad, but restaurants are tough."

I lean back against the wall, tired. So, so tired. It's not like I didn't know we were scraping by, but it never felt like the end. Another ending. I can't.

I reach through my dread and give her my best, most convincing smile, the one I know she needs from me right now. "You know I always deliver in the clutch."

Reluctantly, Mom takes her hand off the folder, and I open it. A flood of purpose washes over me. I can do this. I can make one thing that is wrong in the world right again. For my family. For Dad. And I won't be mad about a summer of hard work away from Emma and Chad.

"Okay," Mom says. "As long as it doesn't interfere with your schoolwork. Or college applications."

"It will not." I kiss her on the cheek. "Anyway, I'm sure we'll be fine by the fall."

She marches the rest of the way to the kitchen doors.

As she enters, Dave hands off the newly plated burgers to Mom, plus a basket of fries, and Mom pushes open the door to the dining room. She stops and looks back before walking through though. "You're a good boy," she says. "Your dad could not have been prouder of you."

And like the amazing mom she is, she's gone before she can see my eyes redden.

Because amazing moms know when to look away.

"I think that's it," I say to Dave. "Thanks for your help, man." I try to say it with authority, like the boss I guess I kind of am now.

"No problem. And I'm real sorry about your dad."

"Yeah," I say. "Me too."

Once the door has stopped flapping behind him, I go back into the office, pick up the books from the floor, and sit down in my dad's orange desk chair to start studying.

Like that girl in the video, sometimes you have to take the stage and do something bonkers just because it's the right thing to do.

CHAPTER SIX

Love

When we get off the plane at LAX, I overhear a woman in big sunglasses and a silk maxi dress say, "I'm telling you, Venice, saffron lattes are the way to go. Incredible for anxiety and inflammation and only ten dollars each at Erewhon. Really reasonable."

Mom's in her skintight jeans, a salmon tank top, and a gray hoodie. With brown cowboy boots on her feet, she looks like a shot of whiskey at a green juice bar. I'm wearing my dancer blacks. They're comfortable for flying and I'm not sure if I'm going to an audition or what. According to the itinerary we are going straight to meet Christine before any sort of hotel, so I need to be ready for anything. I've got my heart-shaped shades and my gold sneakers on, and my third coffee in hand when we walk through baggage claim, past all the people who are clearly no strangers to lip fillers and facelifts, duffel bags over our shoulders.

"Where do we go now?" I ask.

Just then, a girl with amazing brown hair waves to us like we're old friends, consults her phone, taps something into it, then waves again. "Hey!" she calls. She's in a green sweater-vest and brown cords, and her makeup is flawless. She has one gold hoop in each of her nostrils, which makes her look chic and, well, everything we're not.

I point to my own chest and she erupts into infectious laughter. "You're so silly. Come on, let's go!" She leads us outside to a black Escalade.

"Is that for us?" Mom says, looking over at me worriedly. "Christ almighty, what is going on?"

The girl looks at her watch. "Come on—we're on a schedule. Christine is going to flip!" We follow her into the car. Am I imagining that she gives my blue Walmart duffel a judgmental squint? "I'm Fiona!" she says. "I'm so excited to meet you."

"You too, darlin'," Mom says.

"Oooh, 'darlin',"" Fiona says, flashing her brilliant smile again. "I love it. So Texas."

Mom smiles, but this one is more forced and I feel her nerves from across the seat.

"Buckle up," Fiona says, tapping her black manicured nails against the wheel. "It's going to be a hell of a day."

Once we arrive and walk from the museum-like lobby of the office building to our own private elevator, Fiona leads us at a clip toward a pair of glass doors. "You ready?" she asks.

But I can't concentrate on her or anything else, because *Colin Farrell* is literally sitting on the cream couch in the lobby. "I loved *The Penguin*," I say, because I cannot help myself.

"I loved what you did to that principal of yours," he says, after glancing up from his phone. "Good on you for taking care of your friend."

My legs go weak. Because Colin Farrell, *the* Colin Farrell, not only recognized me, he just gave me a compliment. A wave of sparkly intensity comes over me. If nothing else happens, ever, this will still be a day I'll never forget.

The receptionist, wearing a complicated bun and a pencil skirt, stands up from behind her desk.

"Do you need anything?" she asks Fiona.

"Nope. They're just meeting Christine for the *first time ever*!"

"Oh yay!" the receptionist says, her face relaxing. "I'm Shayla. *Love* your work!"

"Right this way," Fiona says.

We clack down the hallway, where meetings seem to be afoot in every room.

"In here," Fiona says, after we've turned and turned again. I'm so lost, I would never be able to find my way out. I would die in a random hallway, and no one would ever find me. So I guess I have to hope they don't turn me away just as quickly as I've arrived.

Before I can worry any further, Fiona slides open the door.

Behind a raised glass desk, a Black woman with a fractured afro in crisp white athleisure is toggling between three different desktop screens while maintaining a speed-walk pace on a treadmill pad.

"Hey, Chris," Fiona says. "I've got Love and her mama here to see you!"

When Christine doesn't immediately respond, I'm worried she is going to give me a blank look and send us on our way, but after she types something and then hits the Send button, her face opens into a wide, warm grin. I've never been anywhere this important or met anyone this important. And she's looking at me like *I'm* important.

"Oh my gosh, here she is in the flesh, and more beautiful than I could have imagined," Christine says, talking to Mom, which is a good move. She hits a button on a white remote and her walking pad slows to a stop as she motions to the sofas in her giant office.

Somehow, she hasn't let out a bead of sweat. "Welcome, guys! Take a seat. Please. Espresso? Cold brew? Matcha?"

I'm jittery from my many coffees and Mom is quiet as we sit, so I say, "We're good, thanks."

"You can go, Fi," she says. "I'd love it if you'd pick up my lunch smoothie."

Lunch *smoothie*?

"You got it," Fiona says. "It was so great to meet you both."

When Fiona is gone, the door shut behind her, Chris sits across from us and scrutinizes me. I swear she checks out my boobs, my waist, thinking, thinking, before meeting my eyes. "Let me cut straight to the chase," she says. "I love you." She turns to Mom. "I love your daughter. Love her."

"You and me both!" Mom says, and I can tell she's charmed. And I mean, all this is amazing, like, super, ultra-amazing, but we've only been here a minute. She doesn't even know me.

Christine seems to read my thoughts. "I mean it," she says. "You're that rare combination of talent and authenticity that everyone's looking for. It took a lot of guts to stand up for your friend like that."

"And Colin Farrell thinks so too," Mom says, nudging me.

"Thanks . . . ," I say, after a beat.

"So tell me, who else are you meeting with while you're here?"

"Umm—" I panic, looking at Mom. Christine took care of

all our expenses, put us up, and sent Fiona, but a couple of people from CAA and WME also called and Mom said it would be stupid not to at least hear them out. And Christine technically only said not to meet with anyone else until *after* we met with her.

"A couple other people," I manage, thinking again she's going to throw us out.

"Good girl," she says instead. "Always do your due diligence. I knew I wouldn't be the only one who saw your star power. And you deserve it. This is a serious decision. A manager is like family . . . at least a good one, and I am a very, very good one."

"We have no doubt," Mom says politely.

"Okay," Christine says, going from sparkly to no-nonsense. "Then I'll keep my pitch short and sweet. You should sign with me because I can make your dreams come true in such a way that you'll never wonder about my intentions or my attention. I will be here for you every step of the way."

"You don't know what my dreams are though," I say softly. "They might surprise you."

"Okay," she says, leaning back. "Why don't you tell me?"

"Honey, you can show her your vision board." Mom leans over to her bag. "I've got it right in here."

The blood rushes to my cheeks. Even with those guys calling me Trailerina, I never thought of myself as a bumpkin, but I sure do feel like one now.

"Mom . . . please don't," I say. The room settles into a deep quiet. I think about what I want to tell Christine. She said she was pitching me, but actually, this might be my one shot to pitch her. "I guess—" I start, "I want to be, like, a singer-songwriter." It's like I just put my heart on a plate for her to eat. That video was all dance. What if she's not interested in another singer?

Sure enough, Christine's face puckers. "Then all you have to do is get a SoundCloud."

I wince and sink back into the sofa as Christine leans forward.

"What I mean is, you're thinking small. You're being *shy*, Love."

"No, I'm not."

"You are. That's understandable. You're from a small town. And in small towns, people dream small dreams. Because if they dreamed any bigger, everyone in that small town would cut them down. Am I right?"

Trailerina! Trailerina!

"You're . . . not wrong," I say.

"But you're in LA now. *No one* here is shy about what they want. No one's going to look at you funny for having desires. And I saw plenty of those in the way you danced. It's your longing, your passion, your bravery that caught everyone's attention."

I'm a little breathless. Maybe she *does* see me after all.

"So what is it, Love? What's that crazy thing you want that you can't even admit?"

"I want to dance . . . ," I start.

"Mm-hmm. And . . . ?"

". . . and sing, and write, and act. I want to do it all." I feel a surge of kinetic energy and a dam inside me bursts. "I want to be the next Lady Gaga," I blurt, then gasp and slap my hand over my mouth. "Holy shit, that's nuts, right?"

But Christine only smiles. "Now we're getting somewhere."

"You really think that could happen for me?"

"I do," she says firmly, like she is one hundred percent certain.

"How do you know?"

"Well, for one, I've done it before. I rep Sabrina Carpenter, Addison Rae, Damien Hunter—"

Now she has all my attention. "You work with *Damien*?"

It's obvious I'm intrigued, and she eyes me like an iguana about to lick up a mosquito, but this time I'm not wary, just excited. *This is meant to be.*

Christine gets to her feet. "Let's go on a little field trip."

Mom and I look at each other behind her back while she's gathering her things.

What is happening? I mouth.

Mom shrugs. "We're on this ride, sweetie pie. Let's hold on tight!"

Christine swings her black BMW through a gate with security and into a lot where people are loading trucks with furniture and boxes. She parks next to a truck and we all get out.

"Is this still LA?" I ask. It looks completely different, like its own world.

"Oh yeah," Christine says. "The most LA part of LA, in my opinion. This is where it all happens."

"Where's the beach?" Mom asks.

Christine laughs, patting Mom on the shoulder. "You're about to see what really makes this the place to be." She heads for the entrance to a warehouse, and we follow behind.

A security guard stands by the door and waves us in. As soon as we cross the threshold, I see I had it all wrong. This isn't a warehouse . . . it's a set. For a music video. It's decorated like a high school gym at prom. Crews position cameras and adjust lights, dancers mingle under a disco ball . . . and then there, *right* in front of me, is real, actual, even-hotter-in-person Lil' D. He's talking softly to his makeup artists; then he lets out a raspy, *sexy* laugh as he tilts his chin upward for more contouring.

He notices us standing there and smiles at me. Me! I try not to blush any more than I already am as I smile back.

"Like I told you, this is where wishes come true," Christine says, waving to Damien before continuing. "And I'm the genie who can make it all happen."

I'm so focused on Damien and his xylophone abs that I almost forget why I really came here. I turn my attention back to Chris.

"If I were your manager . . . ," Christine continues, pinning me with her intense gaze, "I would start by saying you should dance in this video."

"*This* video?"

Christine folds her arms across her chest in a clear challenge.

"I—I don't know the choreo." *I just got here,* I want to say. *You tricked me. I need time.*

Once again, it's like she can read my thoughts, and for once her face softens kindly. "You've got ten times the talent of these girls," she says. "Like I said before, you're a star. Stars improvise. We've already seen that *you* can improvise. Pretend your friend is showing the world her drawers again if you have to. Just . . . go."

Mom's eyes are already brimming. I watch her struggle to push past her own emotion to say, "Make 'em feel something, Love."

I want to do what Mom said, but something is off. I just got here and I'm already in the room with one of my idols. This feels almost too easy, like some kind of trap. Is Christine sending me to my doom, messing with me the way Bryce did Patty at graduation? I am not going to wind up a fool on the internet.

I'm also not going to run away.

"Okay," I say.

Christine breaks into a genuine grin. "Carlos!" she calls to a man sporting a black tee, cargo pants, and a thousand-mile stare standing a few feet away. He carries an iPad and a can of Monster Energy that's bigger than my head.

"I've got another dancer for you," Christine says.

"Great," he deadpans, making a whoopee swirl with his pointer finger, then motions to me in a way I assume means I'm supposed to follow him.

"Where are we going?" I ask.

"Costume department," he throws over his shoulder. "I.e., the trailer right outside. Come on. Everyone else is on lunch and we need to go as soon as they get back."

"Do you get a lunch?" I ask, hustling to keep up.

He looks back at me, eyebrows raised. "Do you actually give a shit?"

Seems like a trick question, so I say nothing.

After about thirty minutes of being primped and manicured, I slip into a slinky cutout prom-ish minidress (they let me keep my sneakers), and I follow Carlos back to the stage, where he leaves me with about ten other dancers. They are all tall and skinny, with fake lashes and puffy lips. I am so small compared to them, it's ridiculous.

"Is it supposed to be special ed prom?" one says. The rest of them laugh.

Scratch everything I said before. This is exactly the same as Texas. Which means I know how to handle it.

"Mean-girling is so over." I blow her a kiss. "I hope you'll be happier in your life soon."

She drops her mouth open as the other girls laugh again.

Carlos zips past me and I scurry up next to him, shivering as the AC blows the place into an icebox. "Can I talk to the choreographer?"

"Choreo—no, she's working with D." He stops, sighing loudly, like I'm the worst. "Just dance sexy when they call action, okay?" He rushes over to a group of people—two guys and a girl—and says, "You ready? First team coming in! Quiet on set!"

A woman, long, lean, and pretty herself, even without makeup, leads Lil' D past me and over to the backup dancers. That must be the choreographer.

I try to plan some steps in my head, but my brain is shorting out, being this close to Damien. Thoughts are heartbeats I can't catch, going too, too fast.

"Let's hear some playback!" Carlos yells.

The music starts and then there it is. "Replay." Oh man, this is what Lil' D meant when he said on the socials he was making a present for the fans of this song. And now I'm here for it!

I'm not just a fan anymore. No more pretending I'm the girl on the beach. No more me watching them from far away.

This is me . . . here.

I can do it. I can.

The backup dancers fan out behind him, and I join them. I bob my head to the music. I can't help it. It's genuinely such a banger.

"I love this song!" I say to the dancer closest to me.

She glares, before spitting, "We're about to roll, bitch."

Right. *Just dance sexy.*

They run through the choreo quickly, thankfully. Damien pumps his arms to the beat, and the backup dancers copy his moves. I mimic them as best I can, but they're speeding around and it's impossible to nail it down in one go. I am going to fail so hard.

"Roll sound," Carlos says. "Roll camera."

"Rolling, rolling . . . ," someone else says. The lights are on and they're *hot*. I see now why they have to keep it freezing.

"And . . . ACTION!"

The cameraman swoops in tight on Damien, and he starts to sing:

When I'm with you, I don't need a selfie

All my pics are just you and me

The lights . . . the crew . . . the girls . . . my rock-star crush five feet away from me . . . It's overwhelming. I force myself to think fast. I am not going to be able to keep up, so that means . . . I shouldn't try. I'm going to have to do something else, something that's just me. Improvise, like Christine said. I close my eyes and focus on his voice and my movement, how to bring them together.

His voice.

My body.

His voice.

My body.

The other girls, they all fade away

You're stuck in my head, you're on replay

The words send shivers up my spine, and I channel them into

a body roll, and then another. Finally feeling the beat, I crisscross my legs and go into a spin. I'm not doing what the other dancers are doing, but going for it—feeling my way through is what got me here, so I have to trust it will work here, too. The track moves into an instrumental, and Damien turns to face us.

I see him notice me, size me up. *The other girls, they all fade away,* he sings, and I believe him.

His eyes on my skin feel incredible. And then it's not just his eyes. He pulls me up against him, and it's the best thing that's ever happened to me. I throw my hands up over my head and make room for him to come closer. I should be nervous, but I might never see him again. And if that's the case, I'm going to make him remember me.

I sing along with him, the words so imprinted, I don't have to think. He seems to like it, so I keep going, and it's like it's just the two of us. *You're stuck in my head, you're on replay.* We're body-to-body as he runs a hand up my vertebrae and it lands at my neck. He leans toward me and, oh my God, I think he's going to . . . kiss me.

"CUT!" a male voice calls from somewhere in the dark.

He loosens his grip on me, but not all the way. When the music stops, we let each other go, but he's still staring at me. As the director—a guy in rolled-up jeans, a big T-shirt, and dreads—comes over, the silence suddenly feels uncomfortable. I slip back into the line of dancers and every single one of them stares me down, but the director gives me a curious glance. I can't tell what he's thinking. Did I ruin it?

"We got it!" the director says, clapping Damien on the back. "That was *fire*, man."

"Cool," Damien says, and a thrill pulses through me.

"That's a wrap!" Carlos calls. "Good job, everyone!"

Like an army on the move, the entire set takes off in every direction. I stand in the center of it, watching Damien get swept away before I can even say anything to him. The stage lights go down and when the overhead lights come up, I run over to Mom and Christine, who are both beaming at me like I just did something spectacular.

"I'm so proud of you, honey," Mom says.

"Is that . . . am I actually going to be in this music video?" I ask.

"Maybe," Christine says.

"That's the best thing that's ever happened to me. So thank you, really."

Christine is already on her phone, getting to work posting a behind-the-scenes clip of me dancing with Damien, as if I'm already her client. She looks up, like she's surprised I said something nice. "You can go get changed, Love. And don't you worry. There is so much more awesome to come."

Later that night, we're in the Beverly Hills Hotel in the plushest room I've ever seen in my life. Stripes and pond fronds are everywhere. The luxe bed with the hanging chandelier gives me full princess vibes. Mom is just out of the shower and has a towel wrapped around her body and another on her hair. She comes out of the bathroom, bringing the steam with her, and pulls her phone off the bedside table. She wipes it on her hip, unfogging the screen.

"You and that singer are all over the internet!" she says. "I mean *everywhere*. Like, if I didn't know you and you weren't my daughter, I would know you now."

She's right. #gradgirl is trending again, and it's me and him over and over in every square.

"You have more than eight hundred thousand followers now," Mom continues excitedly.

"I know, it's wild!"

"People love you, Love."

"Maybe," I tell her, but the more I scroll, the less sure of that I am. "But . . . they also hate me. Have you seen some of these comments? 'Trailer trash,' 'short stack,' 'Oompa Loompa.' It's just like high school. Except now it's the whole internet."

Mom trades her towels for a hotel robe and cinches the waist. "Oh, baby. That's hard. It really is. I'm sorry. You did get those short genes from my side of the family. And the trailer thing? Well, you get that from me too. But I can tell you that it makes you strong. Makes you solid where other people get knocked down."

"Yeah?"

"Yeah, honey. You have to take the bad with the good. Comes with the package."

"Looks like a lot of bad though, and I'm just getting started."

She sits down on the bed and pats the spot next to her. I sink down and wait.

"You know, when I was doing competitive cheer, the things girls or coaches would say were brutal, but when we won, none of that mattered anymore. It's all part of the journey."

"But then look what happened. You got an injury and they forgot about you."

For a second, as we sit in the silence, I'm afraid I've gone too far, poked at something I know is painful for her, but she only shrugs. "I went big that day. Bigger than I ever had before. Sometimes it pays off, but that day my knee just wasn't in the mood. That was the end for me and cheering, but I don't regret it. People knew me as the girl who was almost special, and that hurt, but I know I'm more than that. I know I tried. And when you get to be my age, the only thing that's going to matter is whether you took the opportunities you had and did the best you could. The rest is up to fate." She takes my hand in hers. "Do things now that you won't regret later, so you can look back and be proud." She pauses and gazes at me. "You understand what I'm saying to you, baby girl?"

I do, but I'm not sure she's right. I'm going to be putting myself out there on the internet, and now that people are actually watching, that feels like a big deal. It means if I take a big swing and miss, like Mom said, I won't just be the girl who never got back up again. I'll fail in front of the whole world, where it'll live forever. Follow me forever.

"There might not even be a later," I say, thinking maybe that would be the best thing for everyone. "This is my fifteen minutes. That's it. I don't want to get my hopes up that it's anything else."

"You didn't see yourself today. You stood out in the best way. Even that Lil' D noticed."

Damien really did notice me, but only for a minute. As soon as the floodlights came on, he disappeared. "I thought he was going to kiss me, Mom. But then he didn't even ask my name. I'm still a nobody."

"Oh, Love . . ."

Mom hugs me tight and her hair wets my cheek. But then a loud rumble comes from right outside the room, which makes us both jump. Mom pops up and opens the curtains, then closes them again quickly, wearing a huge, mischievous grin.

"I don't think Damien forgot you at all. I think you made an impression."

I dash over to the window and wedge myself in next to her. Damien is right there, closing the door of his Mercedes G-Wagon.

It could be a coincidence. I mean, this is the hotel for the stars. But what if maybe I was right? Maybe we are . . . fated?

I don't know. But I'm going to find out.

CHAPTER SEVEN

Love

Damien was at the hotel for me.

Me!

It wasn't a coincidence.

Damien's Mercedes G-Wagon is bright red and perfect inside, unlike our minivan at home, which is covered in Forest droppings: Cheerios and Pirate's Booty and Goldfish, even little pieces of carrot and apple. This is slick, sleek, and he maneuvers in and out of traffic on Rodeo Drive with ease, like even his driving has charisma. And he hasn't let go of my hand, except to open my door.

After parking, we walk past CHANEL, Bijan, Louis Vuitton. Each window is art. Everyone walking has style, and it feels like nothing bad can happen. A warm breeze falls over us as we follow the pace of everyone else on the sidewalk: slow and easy, no stress. He seems to be watching me watch everything, and the fact that he stays silent makes me feel like he understands, like he wants me to absorb it all.

"You were fire on the dance floor," he says finally. "Where'd you learn to move like that?"

"About four hours in the studio, every day, since I was five, with an amazing teacher."

"Since you were—what?! That's insane!"

"Yeah, people back home think so too." I wonder what all the people with "Trailerina" on their tongues are doing now. Nothing *this* amazing, that's for sure. But I think of the online haters too, and the doubt creeps back in.

"I mean, like, good insane," he says, squeezing my hand. "Insanely dope. People love to shit on people who try hard, but those are the only people that get anywhere."

"Exactly," I say.

Damien rubs the back of his neck. Thinking.

"I was surprised when Chris told me you're on the fence about moving out here, trying this out for real?"

"A little. I just want to be smart about this."

"Fair, fair. I totally get that. I just want you to know Chris is the bomb. I can't even express what she's done for me and my career. That's why when she told me she was bringing in a new star on the day of the shoot, I trusted her. She's like that. She just knows. And she was right."

"Yeah, from everything I've seen, she's scary good," I say. "But still . . ."

"But you still have doubts?" he says as we pass a huge, beautiful palm tree.

"About myself," I say. I don't know why I feel so safe with him. Maybe it's because I feel like I already know him—like some part of me knew, even when I was just watching on my computer, that I was always going to end up right here, holding his hand.

"What? Come on! You've got that thing everyone is looking for. Truth, I swear." He drops my hand and looks at me like he genuinely can't understand why I would be freaked out.

"You're nice to say that, but . . . I've always had a plan." We arrive at some rows of green benches separated by baby palm trees and sit. The sun is starting to set and everything feels so slow and easy.

"Tell me," he says.

"I have a full-ride scholarship to college. I'd have to give it up, you know? LA has always been the end goal, but I never expected it to be right out of the gate."

He gives me a huge smile. "So college, classes, papers, all that—and then real life starts in four years?" It sounds so silly when he says it. "*Or* you could skip the middle and go straight to the coming-out-here success part."

"Yeah, it's also like, say 'no, thank you' to college, free money, and to making my family proud in that way." I tuck my knees under my chin and wrap my arms around them. "And I don't know if I'm capable of a whole-ass career at this point. You saw me dance for five minutes."

He spreads out and slings an arm over the back of the bench, easy with himself, easy with me. "This is gonna sound cold," he says, "but I've danced with, like, a thousand girls. And not one moved the way you move. For real." He looks over at me, his eyes softening, his arms tensing. "Every one of those girls would've told me how amazing they are. The real artists, they have that imposter syndrome, like you. Like me . . ."

"No way you feel like you're not good enough," I say. That cannot be true. He is perfect. Fully incredible with real, dedicated fans to prove it. How could he ever think anything different?

"Seriously!" he assures me. "The only reason Bieber listened to my demo was because my dad is Travis Hunter, 'Mr. Rock

Star.' Being a nepo baby isn't as glam as everyone thinks. I had so many haters at first. Honestly, it's kind of exhausting. I had to prove myself. I'm still proving myself every day."

All those nights I spent in my room, watching his videos . . . I was right. We are similar in all the ways I thought we were. So I know I'm safe to tell him the truth. "I've been dealing with haters my whole life," I say, letting my feet fall back to the ground. "I've always had rhino skin about those dummies, but this is a new level. I don't know if you know, but I have a post that went viral and some of the comments are . . . brutal."

"Yeah," he says, "I know all about that." He turns his body to face mine and I feel like we're in our own little cocoon, like we're here together, protecting each other somehow. "But remember: The people bringing you down? They're already below you."

I'm about to tell him I love that, that I imagine Bryce as a tiny little dot at the bottom of the ladder I'm climbing, but we're interrupted by Damien's song, the one from the video, playing from a nearby store. We glance over and see that it's no coincidence. The women working inside have spotted us on the bench and are smiling intently, phones raised. He smiles and gives them a half wave before turning back to me, sheepish.

We listen as the song plays. *You're stuck in my head, you're on replay.* I feel that same shiver, the spark I felt while we were dancing together. I think maybe he feels it too. But instead of leaning toward me, he groans, pulls his arm off the bench, and puts his face in his hands.

"What's wrong?" I ask, my stomach icing over.

"Flashbacks." He rubs at his chin, and shakes his head. "I feel like an asshole. One of the reasons I came to find you is . . . I need to apologize for, uh, almost kissing you on set. It was around this part, right?" he says, tilting his head toward the store, and I nod. "That was way outta line. I don't know what happened. I got caught out . . . caught up. I should not have done that. No excuse, truly."

"It's okay," I say. "I was caught up too. I was there with you. And . . . I mean it. Don't worry," I say, my voice getting breathy, winded, even though we're just sitting here.

"For real, I think you're amazing. I even kinda think I might . . . need you."

"Need me?" The words spill from my lips, more dreams turning real than I can count.

"I would love to team up, if you would want to work together. I mean . . . if you think we're a match." Damien looks down, then back up, and when he does, he holds my gaze. I feel it all the way at the base of my spine, where he touched me before, when he ran his finger up my vertebrae, laid his hand on my neck. And it sounds like he's asking for more than just a professional partnership.

"Yeah." My lips are already buzzing. "I would really like that."

"So . . . ," he says. "Does that mean I can I make our almost-kiss a real one?"

I let the ice in my stomach melt, let the waves wash through me, and this time it's right. I don't feel like a little kid about to make out with an imaginary person. I feel like I am the girl he wants, like I actually do belong here with him. At least right now, and that is enough.

"Yes," I say, my doubt draining away.

He leans in, making sure I'm still okay, eyes searching before they flutter closed and his lips brush mine. I wrap my hand around the back of his neck and pull him in closer as he traces my spine again. His mouth presses just enough to send tingles flying through my body. I want him even closer. I grab his shirt sleeve and kiss him harder. He returns my intensity, and finishes with a tiny bite on my lower lip. My breathing is fast now. I want so much more of that, of him, of all this.

It's like he's kissed me to my senses. I'm moving to LA as soon as possible.

I'm not going to let my fifteen minutes run out. I'm not going to let stupid, life-stealing fear control me. I have waited so long, worked so hard for an opportunity, and now that it's here, I'm not going to waste it.

Now my life finally begins.

Ten months later . . .

MARCH 22; 80 MILLION VIEWS
VIDEO TRANSCRIPT:

Hi, Lovelings!

Thanks for tuning in! It's me, your girl, Love. Wow, it's been a *time*. Wild! I just found out that as of this morning there are forty million of you wonderful people following me, so I'm sending forty million kisses your way.

For real, but it has been a dream come true for me and for Lil' D, too. Thank you for watching all our videos, for learning all our dances, and for coming to our shows. You made so much possible and . . . oh God, I know I'm getting emotional now . . . but maybe the best part was being able to buy a house for my mom and my little brothers back in Texas. Mom, Riv, Forest . . . I love you guys, wish you were out here with me! *sniffles*

So thank you all, thank you to my manager, Chris, who was the first to believe in me, and thanks to all the brands who've supported me. But also, thank you to my guy, Damien. I want you to know meeting you was the best thing that ever happened to me. I'm so happy to be your girl. *smiles*

But anyway, a video isn't enough to express how grateful I am, so as a special, special thank-you, I'm excited to announce I'm going to be making some visits to perform at twelve malls across the country. All you have to do is like this post and I'll send you a special secret alert about where I'll be. I love you guys so much. Can't wait to see you there!

April 15, 10:21 AM

Patty

Yay, you're going to be in Boston!
I'm feeling the love!

Love

OMG so busy! Miss you! Come to the show.
It's one song and then we can hang!

Do you want to get dinner?
Can you come see my apartment?

Okay haven't heard from you but you're probably busy being all famous! I'll be there!

April 21, 11:47 AM

Hey, that was really great.
Your manager said you have to go back to the hotel?

So many people here. You have a fangirl army.

I'm leaving. Waving at you from the back!

April 22, 1:32 AM

Patty girl, I am so sorry.
The schedule is hectic.
Let's find a way to get together soon, okay?
I'll fly back or something after I record my single.
LYSM!!!

April 22, 8:41 AM

Sure. Next time. Good luck, Love.
I hope you get everything you want.

CHAPTER EIGHT

Love

I am so tired. I feel like I have a bowling ball in my stomach, my head is pounding, and we had to drive from New York to Chicago overnight after all flights were grounded because of a freak May hurricane. We drove through it pretty well, thanks to the nice man who is currently taking us down the freeway in a black Lincoln at a leisurely eighty miles per hour. We have to get to the next location on time for the surprise/not surprise performance we're doing at the stroke of 11:11.

Even if we hadn't driven through the night though, I would still feel like crap. My feet ache from all these performances and every single muscle hurts because I have also been keeping up with my two-hour daily workouts from my new trainer, Jamie.

I miss Danny and tried everything to get him on my team. But Chris said I needed a pro, someone at the highest level, "experienced hands."

I guess it's true that Jamie is full-service. He even sends me messages through an app about what I am allowed to eat: smoothies, protein bread, salads, tofu, and the occasional bean or grain of rice, plus a damn *gallon* of water every day. Meaning I pee all the time. I have to pee right now. Not to mention I have wicked PMS. It's like, everyone forgets I'm a person living in this body, you know?

I feel a hand on my shoulder, interrupting my feeble attempts at sleep. Light and long fingered. So not D, who was fully crashed out, last I checked. I keep my eyes closed. I'm not ready to do this again.

"Love. Love," Chris says, her voice calm and smooth but in a practiced way. "We're here, hon."

"Here where?" I mumble.

"Highland Park, Illinois. According to our data, you have a full litter of Lovelings here."

"I hate that name," I say, embarrassed. "It's so silly."

"Well, they love it. And they love you," Chris says sternly. "That's the most important thing. The *only* important thing." She sighs. "Haven't you heard that saying? To whom much is given, much is expected? You have fifty *million* followers, Love, and the numbers keep rising. I mean . . . this is huge."

The truth is, I can't even conceive of fifty million people. Ten million more than since we started this tour. Meaning it's doing exactly what Chris said it would. And I know I should be grateful. I mean, I *am* grateful. But sometimes it's hard when thousands of thirteen-year-olds are running your life. What I eat, when I sleep, which song D and I perform over and over and over again—all revolves around them. They comment on what I wear, the makeup I use, the jewelry I buy. And every move Damien and I make together too. They want us to post every party we go to, everyone we chat with, even every kiss.

I guess I just didn't know it would feel like this: taking pictures and making reels for brands I don't really care about; backup dancing for Damien to the same song every day (on repeat and repeat and repeat). Barely any time for myself, for writing new material—I can't even remember the last time I sang a whole song. And definitely no time to visit my family.

I miss my mom. I miss Forest and his little attitude. I miss River, too, even if he is probably secretly a serial killer. I would give anything to just sit next to him doing nothing while he beeps and boops on his PlayStation for an hour.

"Anyway, it's the last stop of the tour!" Chris says, and even her irrepressible enthusiasm sounds forced this time. I wonder if she's as relieved as D and I are that this is almost done. She's got other clients to deal with after all.

We've performed at malls on the outskirts of LA, Seattle, Sioux City, Boise, Salt Lake City, Phoenix, Boston, Bangor, Bethesda, Jersey City, Brooklyn, and now here we are somewhere outside Chicago. All that in six weeks, just me, Chris, and Damien, twenty-four seven. Every time it's the same thing. Chris sends a message alerting the fans where we'll be next, giving them a two-hour lead-up. The mall puts up the Feel the Love banner at nine a.m. The fans gather. At 11:11, Damien's song comes over the loudspeakers, and we dance at the top of the escalator (with Damien lip-syncing, of course). Then we do a meet and greet. That's the important part because while everyone waits in line, we have a convenient merch table set up where they can buy Damien's album and Loveling and Grad Girl T-shirts, key chains, hoodies, fanny packs, and even a book that Chris had churned out a few months ago about our love story called *Lil' D and Grad Girl: A Match Made in Dream City*.

Chris has us stay until every last tween has gotten a picture or an autograph or both, and then if we're lucky we go to our hotel, where I am served my lettuce leaf, and then Damien and I upload our newest videos from the stop, run to the hotel gym to do Jamie's workout of the day, and flip through the socials to find out how we're trending and what's going on with the competition.

Then we're on to the next place.

Inside every mall, it's always the same, but each is a little more crowded than the last. Our fan base is growing, so at least it's worth it. But I can't quite figure out why it's working when all we do is the same thing over and over, and then let the lovers and the trolls battle it out in the comments section.

That's my life now. That, and being Damien's girlfriend. Which would be awesome if we got more time to actually *be* a normal couple instead of performing as one.

"Come on, Love," Chris says, a little more forcefully this time, like she's irritated by my weakness. "You gotta get up."

I peel open my lids, sit up straight, and look over at her, feeling grumpy. I have no idea how she keeps it together the way she does. I have studied her and found no sign of humanity. Damien and I are pretty sure she's possessed by a demon, because she walks faster than any other human I've ever met. She's from New York, but still. We've never seen any signs of a partner, children, or family, not that we would know though because she doesn't share anything, despite knowing everything about us. Like, does she have a mother? Or did she just crawl out of the earth fully formed and commence clacking around the planet? That, I haven't figured out yet. All I know is she runs on caffeine, is always on her phone, doesn't seem to sleep or need it, ever, and even with all the stress, all the running around the country, is always impeccably dressed, like today's white pantsuit, paired with gold chains hanging down her chest and stiletto boots to match.

Meanwhile my cheekbones are sharper than they were when all this started, my hair is a little greasy at the top, and I'm sure I still have the bruisy crescents under my eyes that I had last night in the airport.

I can already picture the comments:

Grad Girl is working too hard.

Grad Girl is so lazy.

Grad Girl isn't eating enough.

Congrats on the baby bump, fatass!

I pop a stick of gum in my mouth since I can't brush my teeth, as Chris claps her hands. "She's up. One down, one to go."

I glance over at D. He's in his black hoodie, sunglasses and double nose rings on. He sweats sweet, somehow still emanating a smell kind of like sugar cookies, and he looks like a star, even unconscious with his mouth hanging open and a little drool pooling at its edges. After a year of building a whole new life together, it's still sometimes hard to believe he's mine.

I pull out a #feelthelove compact and confirm that, unlike D, the state of my face has indeed gotten worse since last night. "Oh, ugh," I say. I don't want a #freebritney situation. "I look like hell. Can we stop somewhere so I can at least do something about this?"

"Aw," Chris says, patting me on the leg. "No time, but you look great! It's giving Courtney Love but, like, after Kurt when she got it together. Do you even know what that means?"

I give her a look. Like I wouldn't know Hole.

"You're so young, you'll be able to shake it off. Trust me—when you get to be my age, every mistake you ever made trots across your forehead. Give it five minutes. You'll perk right up."

"Don't you do Botox for that, Chris?" Damien says, stirring to life next to me.

"Not the point," she smile-hisses.

Damien pops up and looks around, then squeezes my knee. "What's with the negativity in here? The vibes are way off. You better hit that glitter, baby."

He's right. Some highlighter and a little sparkle wouldn't hurt right now.

"Look," Chris says, "after today you can take a week off, freshen up the spray tans, drink some green juice, and you'll both be all back to yourselves, inside and out. This is hard work, I know it, but you gotta persevere."

Even in my sleepy haze, I can feel how much of a brat I'm being. This is the life I wanted, that everyone wants.

But I can't silence that voice inside me that says *Not quite.*

The day I met Chris, she promised she would help me get a recording deal. And she keeps . . . not doing it.

I want to be an artist.

A Chappell, an Ariana, a Billie.

Right now, I'm just an *aspiring* artist with a lot of followers, and people care more about the social media numbers and the platform than they do about the music or the dance.

I wanted to change my family's life—it's true. I wanted to make life easier on my mom, and I'm so proud of doing that. But I'm also about the *art.* Or at least I want to be. So does D. But somehow we're both twisting through the same meat grinder instead of making something new. I'm grateful to Chris. I really am. But sometimes I wonder if she actually believes in me and wants me to have the career *I* want, or just the one that has the most guaranteed money attached to it.

"And then we can talk about recording a single, right?" I say softly, looking out at the blue sky and the semis that crowd the highway. Damien slides his warm hand into mine.

"That's why we're doing this," Chris says, not looking up from her phone. "No one is *really* an overnight success. It's barely been a year. You have to put in the hours. This is strategy. We make your platform as huge as possible and then, at the right time, you make your move. This is how you grow your audience."

"But, Chris, fifty million *is* huge. How much bigger can it get? I want my shot. I want to sing something and let people relate to my words. I can do so much more than—"

"You're hungry, babe. Have a bar . . ." She opens her purse with an efficient zip and pulls out a MacroBar. Maple.

I want it badly but I push it away and ask the question I'm afraid to know the answer to. "Do you not think I can do it?"

"Of course I do! But you don't understand just how short attention spans are in this business. I will get you the single," Chris says. "That's a promise. But first, you have to make absolutely sure everyone will listen." She looks over at me and finally softens as the car turns into the mall lot. "Let's get this done, go home, and then we'll talk about making some moves, okay?"

I nod as if she hasn't said this before.

Many times.

This conversation is on replay more than the song we're about to dance to.

Damien pulls me against his chest in a hug, but doesn't back me up even though I know he's feeling stuck and frustrated too. He probably knows when to quit more than I do right now. But

I know how much he wants to get into the studio, to write new songs, feel inspired again.

I try not to be annoyed as we follow Chris out of the Lincoln. The parking lot is packed with cars but not many people, so Damien takes the moment to adjust his Raiders hat and pull out his vape to take a quick double hit. The air around us is laced for a second with the smell of cherry-vanilla cream and weed. He always needs something to take the edge off before a show.

"Hoodie up, Love. Sunglasses on until we get in the mall. They couldn't let us in on the loading side because of lawsuits, so keep it low-key until we can get you to our security." I do what she says, and Chris brushes some lint off my chest, then gives me a look, up and down, in a way she never does with Damien. "Well, there it is."

"What?"

"That star quality everyone is always searching for. The whole world wants to be you, Love. All we need now is for *you* to want to be you."

We start walking to the doors and shame creeps up my spine. My mom sacrificed so much and Chris has worked so hard to get me here. I don't know why I can't just be satisfied with what I have.

I grab Chris by the elbow. She looks up from her phone and stops walking. "I *do* want to be me," I say. "I've got this, promise."

With the fresh air, I feel a little bounce come back. Chris is right. We really are done with this tour today, and after that, anything is possible. I'm going to get my single and make my real dream come true. I just have to be patient a little longer.

"All right, baby," she says, cupping my cheek with a smile. "Then let's go dance."

CHAPTER NINE

Austin

"Austin, hurry *up*," Zoe says, speeding through the crowd.

Once, I saw black-and-white footage of a bunch of girls freaking out at a Beatles concert, passing out and screaming. I'm an inch away from that right now. Hysteria is rising on all sides and tweens are practically melting into the floor.

"Zoe, you tricked me," I say as a girl with blond hair in a sequined purple scrunchie pushes past me. The girl's mother and I exchange a dim, apologetic glance. We're in this together now.

"I did not trick you," Zoe says. "You *do* have to purchase a shirt for graduation because you are not wearing the one you wore to Dad's burial. And *I* have the chance to meet the literal coolest human in existence. That's called a win-win."

"Yeah, except I don't think there's any way to actually purchase said shirt with this hubbub going on." She talks about Dad so easily, mentions his death all the time. I can barely stand to utter his name, which is weird considering he's always dispensing advice in my head.

She stops and turns around. The crowd streams around us. "I'm sorry. Did you just say 'hubbub'?" She doesn't wait for me to answer, just rolls her eyes and says, "I have no idea why my friends think you're hot."

A slew of choice words runs through my head, but there's no point in arguing with her now. She's too amped on fandom to spar.

I don't know why I agreed to this.

Well, I do know why I agreed to this.

Because I had no choice.

Mom insisted I needed to get out of the diner for once, even though this is the worst time for me to do it. Me being out means we have to close until dinner. And nothing is worse for business than unreliable hours.

Zoe glares at me again as she tries to pull me through the crowd.

"I'm going as fast as I can," I tell her. "There are rules about traffic flow. We will get there, okay?"

We pass under a banner that reads Feel the Love 11:11, with a picture of that Love girl and the pop guy, Lil' D, who I recognize from all the times Zoe has shoved their videos into my face. The amount of squirmy tweens in this mall right now is making me feel like I'm trying to steer through a school of jellyfish. Glitter is everywhere and the whole place is filled with girls in sunglasses and hoodies. It smells a lot like vanilla body spray and strawberry lip gloss, instead of the usual burrito/pretzel/pizza smell wafting from the food court.

As we walk toward the bench by the fountain, I catch sight of Chad and Emma, snuggling up like they always are when I have the misfortune of seeing them, which is much more often than I'd like. Emma usually un-Velcroes herself from him when she sees I'm in the vicinity, while Chad attempts to shove extra tongue down her throat, but they're too involved in each other to notice me now, and I can't help but watch them like a scene come to life straight from a John Hughes movie.

Emma's holding a blue soda, silky hair up in a high ponytail, and is leaned into Chad's chest. I list away from them, willing them not to look my way as we get stuck in the crowd, but we're close enough to hear the conversation, and Emma's words reach me.

". . . don't need you to buy me anything. Being with you for a whole year is enough of a present," she says with a little giggle.

My stomach drops.

"Yeah," Chad says, "but wouldn't it be even better with some new earrings?"

"Earrings?"

"Aw." He brushes an adorable errant tendril of hair behind her ear. "No, that's lame, far too basic for my girl."

My head begins to throb.

"How about . . ." He puts a finger on his chin, then says, "Two weeks in France, half Paris, half Mediterranean?" He nods. "Yup. That sounds much better."

Emma is speechless.

I am speechless.

"So how about we go shopping after you see this chick perform?" he goes on, smiling. "You're going to need some new clothes."

Make him stop. Make it all stop.

Emma squeals and bounces up and down on the bench. I've never seen her this happy. Not once.

What kind of cruel God would put me here, right now, and let me witness this?

Chad leans in to give Emma a deep kiss, and I quickly move past them and weave through the crowd, reeling and infinitely grateful that Zoe didn't see them.

My brain swirls with confusion. Again. In addition to the nightmare come true that is my life, the math of it all isn't working out. It's been eleven months since Emma and Chad started seeing each other, or at least since they made it public. But she just said a year. It's their *anniversary*. That would mean they were seeing each other for the last month of my dad's life. Which means I'm a total idiot.

My entire senior year was spent grieving two things: my father and my girlfriend. I loved them both and they both left me. And yes, I went to therapy. (Granted, only five times before our insurance wouldn't cover it anymore due to a lack of diagnosis and I had to quit.) Yes, I know Dad would never have left if he'd had a choice. But knowing it hasn't made it any easier. This new revelation doesn't either.

"You know, there are two types of people in the world," Zoe says now, oblivious to the knife in my back. She pulls out of the stream of traffic between Zara and Hot Topic.

"Oh yeah?" I say, knowing she's about to deliver one of her theories. She has many and is generous about sharing all of them.

"Yup," she says. "There are people who make way and people who *make* the way."

She's in a mood I recognize, wherein she is not going to give up until her point is made. Zoe is now the kid who is happiest in boiling water, like she's daring the world to deliver her one more blow.

Fists up, always.

Yeah, she can talk about Dad, but I don't know which one of us is worse off.

"You're a big guy, right?" she continues.

I don't know where she could be going with this next, but I guess I am taller than most people. "Sure."

"No, not sure. You are. You're a big, tall guy who plays baseball—"

"*Played* baseball."

"That's not the point. You could kick anyone's ass, but every time we go anywhere, you're always the one who goes around people. Why would you do that?"

"Because I'm considerate. What's wrong with that?"

"I think you're *too* considerate. If you just walked forward, then people would go around you. They would have no choice." She waves her hand up the side of my body, as though I'm a brick wall.

"No, they wouldn't go around me. No one looks where they're going."

"Or maybe you're just scared of confrontation."

That stops me. I mean, I know it's toxic masculinity to be the kind of guy who responds to accusations of cowardice, but I can't help it.

Especially because maybe it's true.

I mean, I could have just confronted them about what I overheard, but instead I scurried away.

"All right," I say. "What is your solution to this issue?"

"Um, just walk like a person? Stay in a straight line no matter what. Don't let fear of confrontation keep you from your mission."

"Fine," I say, giving her the side-eye. We charge forth, into the screechy crowd once more.

Right away, I notice a couple is headed straight for us, walking against the stream, but I fight my instincts and I don't veer.

Collision seems imminent. They are going to trample us both because they're so invested in their boba and their discussion about the best choice of birthday gift for their kid. They're so close, I can hear the details. But just when it seems like we're about to collide, they separate and pass us by.

Shit. It worked.

Zoe is extremely pleased with herself, and a goofy smile plasters itself across her face.

"See? Didn't that feel better?" she says. "Try it again."

This time in our path it's two people around my age in hoodies and sunglasses. The guy has tattoos all over his hands and isn't that much smaller than me, but the real issue is they're both staring at their phones. I start scooting to the side, but Zoe pushes me back into their path.

"Stay strong. Don't slow down. They *will* move," Zoe says, picking up the pace and pulling me confidently along with her.

They remain oblivious though. And . . .

Iceberg, meet *Titanic*.

Yup.

Reality goes slow-motion as the girl and I run straight into each other. Her hood and sunglasses fall off her head as she and her phone tumble to the floor.

I shoot Zoe the dirtiest look I can muster, then quickly turn back. "I'm sorry, so sorry." I bend down to help her up because the guy she's with is focused on his phone and barely notices her or the sea of people parting around him.

"Hey, man," she says, from the floor. "You couldn't see me?"

Not as well as I can now that her hood is off. She has shoulder-length, wavy brown hair and light blue eyes, but mostly her whole vibe is just . . . sleek.

She's pretty.

Like, really pretty.

And . . . also really mad, judging by her flushed cheeks.

"It's my sister," I babble. "She was trying to prove a point." I give Zoe another glare and she, in turn, gives me the finger. "A really stupid point."

"Don't blame me because you don't know how to use your judgment," Zoe snaps.

I pull the girl to her feet, and now I am the one with the flushed cheeks because the look in her eyes is . . . well . . . piercing. For just a second, I think she sees me, assesses me as much as I did her. But then a woman manifests out of nowhere, breaking our stare. Her hair is pulled into a bun so tight, she's getting a facelift (not that she needs one), and she's glaring at me like I assaulted the queen.

"Watch where you're going, moron!" she says, then smacks my hand. "And don't touch her."

I immediately step away from the girl and turn back to my sister.

When I do though, Zoe has the strangest look on her face. Her mouth is dropped open (and this is a girl who hates mouth-breathing unless it's absolutely necessary) and she's staring. Too much is happening at once, and before I can even ask her what's going on, the woman ushers the girl and the guy away from us, steering them by the smalls of their backs until they disappear into the crowd.

"OH MY GOD!" Zoe squeaks, when they're out of earshot. "What is wrong with you?"

"Do you know who that *was*? Do you have any idea?"

"She looked familiar . . ."

Zoe points up to the banner. "That was *Love Thompson*! You know, Grad Girl?" Zoe looks at her phone. "It's 11:09! Come on. She always performs at 11:11!"

"Oh," I say, still dazed. It *was* that girl. I just couldn't tell because this place is a giant look-alike contest right now.

"Well, *move*! We must have been going in the wrong direction! Quick. Follow her!"

Zoe has pivoted to follow the girl and is zooming forward like she's on Heelys. I have no choice but to follow.

CHAPTER TEN

Love

My ass is still throbbing where it hit the floor, and I'm almost definitely going to have a bruise, but everything else seems okay. That guy was thin and tall, but as solid as a grizzly bear. The look on his face though . . . like he wanted to plummet into the center of the earth forever? It was kind of sweet.

Damien glances over at me. "We got one minute. You sure you're good?" He pats my ass lightly.

"I'm good," I say. "Swear." At least the adrenaline has completely knocked out the last of my exhaustion.

"That's my girl!" Damien grins through bloodshot eyes.

"Sure am. Let's go!" I always perk up when there's an audience.

The guards lead us past the huge meet-and-greet table, past hundreds of camped-out teenagers, and into an elevator. They spot us and the now-familiar chanting rises up. "Lil' D! Lil' D! Lil' D!" And the answering chant, "Love! Love! Love!"

"I know we both want to do more, but they really do love us," Damien says, taking my hand. "Well . . . mostly you."

As Damien looks out over the crowd and the many signs with my name on them, guilt seeps into my chest. I wish this was the

Feel the Love *and* Lil' D Tour, but Chris said it didn't have the same ring to it. Plus she pointed out that D's numbers have sort of stagnated while mine are on the rise. He was already in the millions though, and sometimes I wonder what Chris expects from him when she hasn't let him try any new material.

"They mostly love *you*," I lie.

"Maybe," he says, voice faraway. "But for what?"

Me being the focus of this tour, even though it's his song, has been wearing on him because of the stuff we talked about that very first day we met. He's worried it's just another sign he's a nepo baby, heir to a rock-star throne he didn't earn, not a "real" talent like me. It seems like he's losing some of his swagger. It doesn't help that day by day, he's spending more and more time getting high, and I know exactly what can happen when substances take over, how they can eat away at a person until there's nothing but zombie garbage left. I'm not going to let that happen to him.

But right now we're here together, and all these people are yelling for us. I still remember being that Trailerina girl in my room, thinking of him, dreaming of this, when all I wanted to do was escape.

My dreams have come true.

And if we keep grinding, there's no reason we can't make more come true too.

The elevator doors open and Damien and I take our place at the top of the nearby escalators that have been blocked off by mall security. When Chris lifts up her phone to record and nods to someone with a walkie-talkie in hand, "Replay" blasts through the mall speakers. Damien swerves and I move automatically.

I weave around him and he shines his smile at me as we grind against each other, but his eyes are glazed over and I'm not feeling anything. I'm not feeling my fire.

We strip off our hoodies. The cheers ripple through the crowd and I get a little jolt, a spark of something. Damien reaches for me, dips me, and lip-syncs at me, and the crowd practically swoons as one. But it just feels . . . stale.

So many phones are trained on us and I think of what they're capturing. Practically the same videos that are all over the internet, just from a different day, a different mall. In a few seconds we'll get on the escalator going down and dance at the bottom, and then Damien will carry me back up, singing to me until we get to the top. For the finale I'll wind around him like I did to my principal at graduation, which always delivers, and we'll end in a near kiss, just like the one from Damien's video. Boom. Post.

If I follow the plan, we'll finish the tour successfully, professionally, and predictably.

No.

Nope.

I suddenly feel an urgency to shake things up. To feel alive, dangerous.

Whatever feral bitch lives inside me has made an unexpected reappearance and she wants to be free, like at graduation. I want this to be the last show before my pivot to serious music. So I need something more to make sure Chris doesn't back out of getting me a single again. Something that will go viral.

The first verse ends, and I lock eyes with Damien. I hope he's sober enough to read my slight shake of the head. Even when he's high, I trust him when it comes to this. This is where he shines.

At the top of the landing, the usual mall safety railing winds around the floor. It's white with bars and a banister that's about four inches thick.

I climb onto it.

The song is still going, Damien has taken my cue and not stepped onto the escalator, and he's still mouthing the words, but his eyes are terrified.

His expression says, *What the hell are you doing?* though you would have to know him to see how thrown he is.

I start dancing again, on top of the railing, and this time the crowd goes totally bonkers. All the fake plants and bobbing heads and fluorescent lights spin into a whirring halo, and I am outside myself but also more myself than I have been in weeks. Months, maybe.

I'm so caught up in what I'm doing, I get even more daring. I try to spin, but my ankle buckles halfway through, twisting painfully. I try to correct but it's too late.

The crowd of hoodie-covered heads gazing upward gasps as I lose my balance.

My knee grazes the banister and I grab on to it as hard as I can to steady myself.

But it's too late. My body swings over the side and I am hanging from the railing.

I look down at the steep drop, but instead of a distant floor I see the boy who banged into me standing below, completely focused on me, jaw set, arms outstretched. I see him nod, and I don't have time or strength enough to hold on and think about whether or not I can trust him.

I let go.

CHAPTER ELEVEN

Austin

I can't believe the same girl I knocked down is the one all over Zoe's "For You" page. This is so me. And now I'm watching her dance, live. I hate to admit it but I'm almost as caught up as these terrifying children jiggling on every side of me. There's humor and energy to the whole thing, and it reminds me of how she made me and Zoe laugh the day of the funeral.

But when she climbs onto the railing, I tense. Zoe is still shaking her hips and jumping all over the place, but I can't take my eyes off Love Thompson, and not just because she's hot. I watch each step, each swivel.

Instinct tells me this isn't going to go well. It's like being on the field. I assess everything at once. The guards, who are distracted, facing outward, trying to control the crowd. Lil' D's body, which is tense in a way it wasn't before, telling me this wasn't part of the plan. The way she is letting herself loose, eyes closed, when she should be paying attention to her feet wobbling on the railing.

It's been a while since I was in a do-or-die situation, but I know I'm in one right now.

She is going to fall. I know it as sure as I know in a game whether or not the guy at bat is anticipating a curveball or a cutter.

Sure enough, she tries a fancy move, some kind of kick spin, and starts to lose her balance. In an instant, I clock her ankle fold and automatically I push forward toward her.

She topples over the side of the rail, but grabs it in time to keep herself from falling. She's hanging on by her fingertips though.

The dancing pauses as people around me figure out something dangerous and unplanned is happening. Lil' D stops his bad lip-syncing job but the music keeps going. The crowd is a frozen sea of phones pointing up at her, waiting to find out what will happen next and doing nothing to stop it. It's like she's not even a real person, like this is all a spectacle. But it's not a stunt. Her legs shake inside her baggy pants and her fingers strain with the effort of holding on. The whole world comes into hyperfocus, every color brighter, every second distinct.

I don't take any more time to analyze.

I just push the last few steps forward and position myself beneath her. I hold out my arms, will her to see me.

Distantly, I'm aware that this is probably going out live right now and if I fuck it up, the whole world will see. But a weird calm settles over me for the first time since the last week of my dad's life. *The best time to do anything is now,* I hear him say, and even though I followed that advice before and it was a disaster, something tells me this won't be. I control my breath and keep my focus on her. I root my feet to the floor, tighten my core, stabilize my legs, and calculate the distance between us.

This girl is *not* going to wind up human meat-sack mush.

I can do this.

Our eyes meet.

I nod.

And she lets go.

CHAPTER TWELVE

Love

It was his eyes that made me let go.

Brown, deep, and concerned.

But more than that, they were certain, like there was nothing and no one who could make him fail at this.

And he doesn't. Just like before when he crashed into me, he is a brick and I'm a feather. He catches me, bending his knees to absorb the shock of my body landing in his arms, which curl and tense around me.

The crowd goes *wild.* Everyone is clapping, filming, screaming all around us. I put my arms around his neck to steady myself. The pressure where his hands touch me is just right, not too hard, not too soft. The only sign of any exertion at all is the little bit of sweat on his brow. Meanwhile my limbs are overcooked noodles.

"It's . . . you," I say, still kind of in shock.

"Austin," he says, then clears his throat.

"Austin? That's where I'm from." That was a stupid thing to say, but I keep going. "I'm Love."

"Oh. Hi, Love."

Our noses are practically pressed together and he's still not putting me down. The crowd is slowly inching in, and I'm suddenly aware of all the eyes, all the cameras still on us. I should get down, but somehow, even though we've never met, I know he's not going to let my feet hit the ground until I'm safe. This is . . . a new feeling.

"Hold on," he says, "I'll get you out of here."

The mall guards are still trying to get to us, but it's clear Austin isn't about to wait. "Let us out," he says. When no one moves, he shouts, "NOW!"

A path forms and he carries me over to the meet-and-greet table, just as Damien and Chris shoot out of the elevator.

"Love!" Chris yells, rushing toward us.

Austin ignores her, and Damien, too.

"I'm going to put you down now, okay?" he asks.

"Okay."

He places me on the white plastic chair and I let go of his neck.

"Your foot," he says, crouching down beside me. "I mean your ankle. Is it all right?"

"Oh yeah. I roll it all the time. It'll be fine in a few minutes."

"Okay, then," he says, and gets to his feet.

"You all right, honey?" Chris asks, but she's looking at all the cameras, not at me. I know Chris is assessing how this is all going to shake out, how our audience is going to respond to what I did once it gets online.

"You good?" Damien asks.

"I'm fine." My voice comes out snappish. I don't know if there's anything he could have done from where he was, but . . . he froze. Maybe it was the weed slowing his reactions or something, but that makes me all the more frustrated.

The paramedics, who are always on scene in case of emergency, push through the crowd. They listen to my heart, checking me for lacerations and broken bones. They even give me one of those aluminum blankets.

Austin is still standing there, like he wants the paramedics to confirm I am indeed fine before he goes anywhere. When Damien notices him, he reaches out to dap him up. "Thank you for taking care of my girl," he says.

"No problem at all." Austin seems to finally take in all the phones still trained on him. "Well, I'll, uh . . . leave you to it."

"WAIT!" A girl in a side ponytail and a black hoodie that matches mine is pushing through the crowd. "Get. Out. Of. My. Way!"

"Sorry in advance," Austin mumbles.

"Sorry? Sorry for what?"

"For what's about to happen," he says, giving me a lopsided half smile.

The girl slams up against the table. "Hi!" she says. "I'm his sister. I mean . . . he's my brother! Austin, I mean."

"Oh . . . hi," I say. She's cute, shiny, and has a wild, determined look about her, like she's running things.

"Can I?" the girl says, motioning to the guards now standing in front of the table.

"This is your sister?" I ask Austin.

"Yep. Zoe," he confirms. "Like I said before . . ."

We smile at each other. "Okay, let her back."

The girl grins at the guards as they let her pass.

"Hi, Zoe! Super nice to meet you!" I say as she rushes over.

"I am such a huge fan," she gushes, in the way of all Lovelings. "I, like, . . . I love you. You're just so . . . like, you're self-made and you can dance and . . . can I *please* get a picture?" She holds her phone toward me. I can see how much I mean to her, and I feel the adrenaline whoosh out of me. What came over me up there? She's starstruck and excited . . . because of me. Just like the rest of the crowd. And all morning I've just been selfish, ungrateful for all of it. Taking a risk because I was, what? Bored? Annoyed I'm not where I want to be yet? I could have ruined everything. What would Mom say?

"Of course!" I say. Then I look to the rest of the crowd. "I'll be right with you all, okay?"

Chris instantly gives Zoe a megawatt smile, and takes her phone to snap the photo. "Okay, here we go!"

Zoe leans over the chair and I shoot up peace fingers.

Once Chris has taken a few, Zoe starts talking extra fast again. "Thank you thank you thank you. And just so you know . . . you're inspiring. You're everything I want to be."

"Oh, that's so sweet," I say, thinking she would take it all back if she could have seen me just a half hour ago in the car.

Damien leans into me. "Hey, I'm starving and we still got all these people to meet." It's about munchie o'clock. "Can we get started?"

Zoe lowers her voice. "Actually, we own a diner. It's called Nathan's. You should come see it. The food is super good. Our dad made the whole menu—"

"I'm sure they're busy," Austin says quickly.

But Chris gives me a knowing look. "No, that sounds like a great idea," she says. "Lunch with the hero." She gives Austin a little poke. "That's you. The hero."

"Oh, well . . . ," Austin says.

Again, I look at Chris. I can see it on her face. She's thinking it would be a good move. Save me from any blowback from this stupid stunt.

"We'd love to," I say. "Give us an hour."

Chris holds up two fingers.

"Two hours," I correct. "We'll see you there." And actually, it's the least we can do. I really would like to properly thank him without starting a riot.

"Seriously?" Damien says so only I can hear. "Diner food? Jamie's going to lose it."

"We can make it work this one time."

He nods, but I can tell he's annoyed. Well, that's both of us, then.

"Guards," Chris says, "maybe take these guys out the back door?"

As they guide Austin and Zoe away from us, I smile as brightly as I can and face the crowd, hobbling a little on my swollen ankle.

"Let the meeting and greeting begin," Damien says, taking his place beside me.

Two hours later, Damien gazes into the empty diner, where Zoe currently has her nose pressed against the window. The place has a quiet, inviting vibe. It's got a mid-century awning and that soft-edged Bauhaus font on the sign. I still haven't totally convinced Damien to go inside.

"That little girl is mad intense," he complains. "You don't want to get some sushi?"

"What's wrong with intensity?" I nudge him. "That's the fan base, babe. It's a good thing she's intense, you know? It means she's intense about us."

"Someday maybe we'll have adult fans," he grumps.

"Why would you want that? The kids have all the power." Chris glances at her phone, checks the time. "You can have sushi when you land back in LA. Our flight's in three hours. Let's do this."

We clamber out of the cool car into the humidity, and Zoe disappears from the window, then reappears at the door, which she swings open.

"We're closed until dinner," she announces. "But not for you!"

"Aw, thanks for letting us in!" I say.

"Yeah," D says.

"Like . . . of *course*," she says, huffing dramatically.

When we follow her inside, I get the chance to have a good look around.

Nathan's Diner on the inside has the same feel as outside. Warm. Even though it's a different style than anything back in Texas, it has a kind of down-to-earth quality about it that makes me totally comfortable. It's all olive and mustard yellow, long and wide enough for booths on either side, with a lot of chrome all over. A large framed portrait of a good-looking salt-and-pepper-haired guy hangs behind the host stand and it catches my eye. Someone important. A quick scan of the room reveals more framed photos of the same man. Him on a beach, holding a surfboard. Him holding a dollar bill with an apron on. There are awards, also framed, all for community leadership.

Zoe follows my gaze. "That's Nathan."

"Cool," I say. I'd like to ask more questions but Chris and Damien are agitated and it's clear they want to move things along. Damien looks weird in here, like he stepped off a magazine cover, and Chris screams LA in every way, from her pantsuit to her jewelry to her nervous, ambitious energy.

Before I can tell them both to chill out, a pretty older lady comes through the double doors that lead to the kitchen. She has Austin's eyes and brown flyaway hair flecked with gray, and when she's standing next to Zoe, it's obvious she's the mom in this sitcom. "Welcome to Nathan's!" she says, inviting us to sit down. We settle into a booth and she slaps down a few plastic menus. "We don't get too many celebrities in here." She eyes Chris and Damien warily before turning her attention to me. "I'm Melanie. Glad to have you. And I'm glad my kiddo was there today. I haven't gotten all the details yet, but it sounds like an adventure."

"It was," I say. "I'm glad Austin was there too. He saved me."

She lifts her chin and I can see she's trying to stifle big feelings. I don't know if it's her chipped nails or her creased forehead, but her realness makes me miss my own mom so much, I could cry. But I push that down and keep it professional. "Hi, Melanie, I'm Love."

"Oh?" she says, recovering quickly, one hand on her hip. "That's your real name?"

"Yes, Mother," Zoe says, coloring. "Her entertainment name is 'Grad Girl.' Her parents wanted her to always know she had come from love, so that's what they named her. God!"

"Wow, you know a lot about me," I say, thinking if she knew the real story, how much my parents do *not* love each other and how much my dad actually does not love my brothers and me, she wouldn't be romanticizing my life. But like Chris said when she was writing the book proposal, that's not exactly a story people want to read. It's better for people to see me through this filter, and I'm not going to blow the illusion.

"That's my dad," Zoe says when she sees me lean in for a better look at the picture over the table.

"Cool," I say.

"Yeah, Nathan's was his dream come true."

"I know what that feels like," I say, smiling at her. "Everyone should have a dream. Do I get to meet him?"

Zoe searches her mom for a second, like she's waiting for Melanie to answer. When she keeps silent, Zoe says, "He passed away last year." She lifts her chin proudly, just like her mom did.

"Oh," I say, at a loss.

I know what it's like to have a dad who doesn't want you. I have no idea how to react to death. It's so permanent.

"So what can I get for you?" Melanie asks, bursting through the awkward silence.

"Coffee for me," Chris says, sliding the menu back across the table without opening it.

"Could I get four burger patties with some mustard and pickles? No buns," Damien says, placing his menu on top of hers.

Melanie raises her eyebrows. "Stack of meat. Okay. Love?"

"Hmm . . . can you recommend something vegan, organic, and gluten free?" I say automatically.

Melanie surveys us like we're creatures from another planet. And I guess we are. Without taking her eyes off us, she shouts—"Austin!"

He emerges from the kitchen in an apron, sleeves rolled up.

He really is very good-looking, and kindness radiates off him like sunshine. He wouldn't make it a day in LA and I bet he wouldn't want to either.

"Oh, hey, Love," he says, meeting my eyes, then looking over at Damien. "Hi . . . Lil' D."

"Damien," D says, trying to be friendly and failing. He's bored, bored, bored.

"Chris," Chris says vaguely. She was the one who suggested this, wanting me to get some more footage with Austin, but now that she's here, she seems to be second-guessing that.

"Yeah, hi," Austin says. "Thanks for coming by." Then, "You called, Mom?"

"Your friend here doesn't eat food." Melanie looks me up and down.

Austin gives his mom a knowing look before turning his attention back to me. "You vegetarian?"

"I was. I'm vegan now," I say.

"She doesn't believe in that." He motions for me to follow him. "Come on. Why don't you see what we have in the kitchen? I can whip up whatever you want."

I follow him in there, leaving Damien and Chris to be grouchy all by themselves, and the doors swish closed behind us. The grills are empty, the kitchen clean and quiet just like the dining room.

"Can I sit here?" I motion to the counter.

"Yeah, of course," he says, disappearing into the walk-in. A few seconds later he pops out. "I've got avocado and sprouts and some gluten-free bread. What do you think?"

"That's literally perfect."

"Okay." He comes back with an armload of food and deposits

it on the counter. He presses four burger patties on the sizzling griddle, then cuts the avocado like a pro, mashing and scooping out the green. "Your boyfriend eats a lot of meat and you eat none?"

"Yeah, funny, huh? He's trying paleo."

"Right . . ."

Everyone in LA is on some kind of diet and D wasn't going vegetarian. The look Austin gives me tells me things are a little simpler in Chicago.

"How about a tomato salad to go with the sandwich?"

"Are they organic?"

He taps the tomato, grinning. "Doesn't sound like plastic to me."

"Okay, then." I laugh and Austin flips D's burgers. "You got grill game," I tell him. And he seriously does, even if he seems a little more timid here than the self-assured knight in shining armor he was at the mall. He's still totally sexy adjacent. Wait until my followers see him behind the scenes—they'll forget about my fall and focus on their newest crush. I pull out my phone. "Do you mind if I make a video?"

He pauses, knits his brows together in seeming hesitation, but then he says, "Go for it."

I can see the hashtags before we even finish filming. #yeschef.

CHAPTER THIRTEEN

Austin

As if today wasn't surreal enough, Love/Grad Girl is now in my diner, filming me make burgers.

Love rests casually on top of the chrome countertop, her hair brushing her shoulders, heart-shaped face focused on the screen like she's a movie director. And that makes me, what, exactly?

"Okay, now flip!" she says.

I oblige.

Love smiles and the world lights up. There are some girls you know right away you'd do something monumentally stupid for, like flip burgers on command on Instagram, and she's one of them. Then again, of course she is. That's probably why she's famous.

"Where'd you get those moves?" she asks, leaning in to show me the video on her phone. I watch myself flip a burger and then the camera homes in on my bicep.

"My dad," I say, before flipping the patties again, one more time to finish.

"Oh . . . Nathan, right? I'm sorry about what happened . . ."

I nod, a little uncomfortable that she already has this information. "So am I going to go viral?" I say, eager not to pick at old scabs. Or festering wounds.

She assesses me for a couple of seconds, before peeling her eyes away from me, down to her phone. "See for yourself," she says, and she shows me the likes on the post, which are already popping up by the hundreds. I glance over at her and she grins. It's not the smile she gives when I've seen her on Zoe's Instagram. It's . . . genuine or something, goes all the way to her eyes. "I'll tag your diner," she says. "Hopefully some of my followers in Highland Park will come visit!"

"You can post, but we aren't on social media. I mean . . . I am . . . Zoe is . . . but not the diner itself." I'm fumbling. It's too hard to explain that Dad hated the socials, thought the diner should be about what he called the old ways: family, community, keeping it simple. He wasn't one of those hipster guys who wanted everyone to make their own pickles and cheese, but he did want people to come together in person, not online. He would never even do to-gos unless people called on the phone. Said we were lacking in human contact.

"Really? Socials make the world go around," she says, shrugging.

"Thanks anyway." I plate the burgers in a stack, then get all the condiments together, trying not to think about how much I like her in my kitchen, on all that chrome . . .

"It's the least I can do after you rescued me from my epic fail," she says, her phone now resting in her lap. I think again about her dropping off that railing and the gawkers in the mall who were just going to let her fall so they could be the ones to post it.

"Sometimes screwing up makes you more relatable," I offer.

I don't know if it's true or not, but it should be. In a world where people gave a shit about each other it would be.

She lets out a pained laugh. I mean, I don't know for sure if it's pained, but it sounds like it. Hollow. Haunted, almost. "People don't follow me because I'm relatable," she says eventually. "They follow me because I'm—"

"Perfect?" I say, and instantly want to shove the word back down my throat. I feel myself flush. I'm about to reach for the burgers to take to her boyfriend, who I need to remember exists and is extremely famous, when she grazes her hand across my arm, grabbing the inside of my elbow. She's leaning in and I put down the mustard as smoothly as I can because I think despite that . . . yes . . . yep, she is going to kiss me. And then she does.

On the cheek.

"You're sweet," she says. "Like, all the way through, you know?"

She says it like it's a good thing, like it might be something that would make a person want to hang out with me. But it just reminds me of Emma taking pity on me for all those months.

Chad and Emma and my miserable senior year come back to me in flashes. Emma climbing into Chad's Audi Q5. Wrapping her legs around him when he picked her up to kiss her in the hall at school. Posting picture after picture together at the holidays with both their families. And of course, before that, they were prom-court royalty.

Now I find out they're going to France.

France.

Eiffel Tower–level storybook romance. No wonder she went for Chad, the ultimate rich alpha, a guy who can surprise her with trips abroad, who makes out in public, who beats his chest whenever he gets the chance.

Meanwhile the first girl I've been attracted to since Emma is *famous*, just passing through, and there's no way I'm her type. Hence, the cheek-kiss. Love is with a Chad too. Lil' D . . . Damien . . . is a freaking star who probably also shows her the world, buys her presents, and dominates whatever situation he's in. I'm never going to care about flexing. I know that much for sure.

Why am I always attracted to girls who clearly aren't interested in guys like me?

I back away from Love to finish plating. Forget the condiments. I need to get us out of here. I add the sliced tomatoes and a couple of pickles to her sandwich, then hand it to her.

"Thanks," Love says, and I'm not sure whether she's talking about the sandwich or the extra pickles or if she's referencing me catching her. It's been an odd day.

She extends her hands. "I'll take that out too." She heads for the door but then looks back. "No one else is here. You should come sit with us."

The thought of sitting down at a table with Damien and that Chris woman makes me want to run away from my own diner. So awkward. "That's okay, I'm good. Lots to do in here."

She glances around the clean and empty kitchen.

"Okay, then," she says softly. "It was nice to meet you, Austin." With one last backward look, she says again, "Thank you. For everything. That was really . . . amazing."

When she's gone, I do some organizing in the walk-in, mostly to cool myself down. Once I've stalled awhile, I sneak a peek at the dining room and Love is still there, but she's leaned into Damien, who has completely devoured all four patties. The manager is on the phone, and the black Lincoln is parked out front, engine running.

I drift back into the kitchen, unsettled and not sure why.

Finally, Mom brings in their empty dishes and drops them in the sink. "They're leaving, if you want to say goodbye," she says.

"Yeah," I say, stalling, "maybe."

"And after that, I'm going to get a cup of coffee and you're going to tell me exactly what happened today," she whispers, steering me by my shoulders into the dining room. "*All* the details!"

But I'm too late. I watch through the window as they get in the car. Damien first, then Love, and finally her manager. I watch Zoe waving at the car until it's out of sight, knowing I'll probably never see Love again.

But then I remember, she *is* everywhere on the internet. What would be wrong with following her?

Maybe if I do that . . . I don't know . . . maybe one day, she'll remember me.

Comments

@minx666:

@austingreyhp that looked like a legit spark. You guys hookin' up?

@lilloser:

@minx666 not buyin it. BS FR. I call stunt for clout.

May 1, 2:26 PM

Paige

Hey, you're almost famous.
60 million views on you catching Grad Girl!

Austin

Yeah. Crazy right?

That vid of you flipping burgers is
kinda hot. You think she likes you?

Paige.

I'm just saying, you should get back out there.

You're always "just saying" that.
And even if I did . . . Love?

Why not? You're the best guy around.

Come by later. I'll show you a map.

Ugh. You're the worst.

May 1, 2:45 PM

Ty

Hey. Sorry about my girl dude. She really likes Grad Girl.

Austin

Yeah. I can relate.

May 7, 6:22 PM

Love
Guess what?

Mom
What's up, baby girl?

Christine finally did it.
Interscope wants to make a single!

The one you wrote?!

No. They said they needed something faster
and catchier for my launch, for mass appeal.
I should be recording a demo of it soon.
But Chris says it's going to be great!

Okay then.

That's it? I'm gonna be an actual recording artist!

I'm excited for you sweetie. I just want you
to remember you've got your own songs
inside you too. Don't forget those.

These guys know what they're doing. They did it for Damien.
I just have to get people to listen and then I can start
doing my own songs. Anyway, you guys alright?

We're fine. We miss you. Gotta find a time to get out there.
Or . . . you could come home?

Sometime soon for sure!

Okay, baby girl.

Two weeks later . . .

CHAPTER FOURTEEN

Austin

It's the day after graduation, two weeks since Love came into the diner. I've accidentally been measuring time that way.

I know, I know. *Stop it, Austin.*

The numbers on the viral videos of me catching her have already stabilized. It's fading into the past, unlike Emma and Chad, who can't stop declaring their love on social media all the time. Now that school is over and graduation is done, there's a whole wide summer waiting for me . . . filled with nothing but work.

That's not totally true. I sometimes make it to the beach at night with Tyler and Paige, where we build a fire and make s'mores. And when I can't, they don't hold it against me. They know the clock is ticking on the diner. We're saving to hire a chef while I'm in college, and hopefully forever, because Mom is great at many things, but cooking is not one of them. Last summer when I worked full-time, we almost got out of the hole, but this last school year we had to close for breakfast and lunch during the week. I quit baseball so I could at least work dinner and keep us open late, but it wasn't enough, and now we're right back in the shit.

This summer is when we either make it, or we have to shut the whole thing down.

Something has to change. We need more customers, and not

just the temporary bump we got from Love mentioning us in her socials. When Love was here, she said social media makes the world go around. But it seems like it's a monster that's always hungry, like I would have to keep feeding it and feeding it to make a difference, and who is going to care what I have to say anyway?

Plus every time I start making Nathan's a profile, I think of Dad and how much he'd hate it. So I go back to watching Love make the world go around instead, thankful Ty and Paige aren't here to see me.

I did admit to them that it felt like there was something there in that moment when she landed in my arms, and when we were back in the kitchen, just the two of us. So now Paige is convinced we could date, like Love's Insta isn't canvassed with pics of her and Damien. And even Ty feeds the flame of my ridiculous hopes, sending over constant updates on what Love's doing or posting that I could DM her about, which I won't, but even if I did, honestly, I wouldn't even need the updates because I can't help but look.

As not helpful as this is, I don't know what my senior year would have been without those two. Tyler and I didn't used to be so close, but instead of being a dick like Chad when I quit the team, he showed up for me. And Paige? Once Emma and Chad went public, she texted all the time and made sure I knew her and Ty were both thinking about me, that I was important to them and didn't just get booted out of our friendships because of Chad and Emma.

I don't want to think about that whole thing either though, so I force myself to refocus. It's sweltering outside, humid, too, and the diner is just me and Mom and a single burger, which I am attempting to pour my entire soul into.

I remember Dad back here, his brown hair a little shaggy and tucked behind his ears. How he would hold Zoe in his arms and say, *Flip!* and we would all cheer as he landed the burger right into the middle of the bun. We all have our little piece of genius, I think, and my dad's was making everything, even the most mundane moments, feel like magic. He knew how to listen, to pay attention, to make people feel totally at ease and important, even if they were sad and having their lowest day. That was his superpower.

I don't know what mine is yet, but judging by how things are going, I don't think it's that.

I less-expertly flip the patty onto the bun and add the lettuce, onion, and tomato to the top side. I slide the fries onto the plate, then ding the bell as I deposit the burger onto the counter. When Mom comes in to get it, I try not to look at the basically empty dining room behind her.

She's got some color from working outside in the garden and I'm happy to see she washed her hair, so I guess things aren't as bad as they were. I only hear her crying through the wall sometimes now, instead of all the time. She's still mostly wearing Dad's T-shirts though. Today is the Pearl Jam one from the 1993 *Vs.* tour when he was in college. They played at Wrigley Field, and before he got sick he would tell me the same thing over and over, how that show was the pinnacle of his glory days, that he had to take me one day.

"Hey, kiddo," she says. "You need something?"

I tell myself not to let the worry flood me, not to look for signs in the T-shirt choice or frequency of her crying that something is wrong with her, too . . . well, other than being broke, which we are.

"Burger's ready. What's next?" I look at her hands, hoping I missed a patron come in or maybe a call for a to-go order.

"Nothing right now," Mom says, like it's her fault there aren't any more orders to fill. She grabs the plate and heads out. When I peer after her through the swinging door, sure enough, there's just one guy sitting out here. One solitary guy.

I don't know how long we can keep on like this. That day at the mall when I caught Love, I believed again. In my own ability, you know? My own strength in the clutch. But now, with the entire fate of the diner bearing down on me, I'm not so sure.

I let go of the door and head back over to the table and chairs in the corner of the kitchen, tucked under the shelf of canned goods and a bunch of pictures of my family, where I like to hang out when it's this slow. I pull out the sketch pad Aunt Meryl gave me and flip it open. She came over with it a couple of weeks after the funeral, when everyone aside from us had gone back to their regularly scheduled existences, and it felt like someone had thrown me a life raft.

I rifle through everything I've worked on since then, examining the pages I've filled while avoiding the people I once considered friends, spending time back here at the diner instead of on the baseball diamond. At first they were just scribbles. None of them made any sense. But after a while, images started to grow out of the haze.

Buildings.

No.

Skyscrapers.

I must be up to about fifty by now, but I like the one I've been working on lately best. It's sleek and beautiful, with interesting curves and angles. It feels clean and brave and sturdy—exactly how life isn't. I let myself sink back into it and add floor after floor. As the charcoal moves across the textured page, I feel myself let go, just for the moment. Let go of missing my dad. Let go of worrying about bills and our house, Zoe and Mom and the diner. I even let go of the lingering hope that maybe Love will remember me and reach out.

When I'm in the pages of my sketchbook, it all fades as I rise up so high, none of it can reach me. Not the doubt, not the worry, not the heartbreaking suspicion that I'll never get to build one of these in real life like I've always dreamed. That real life is now just survival. Nothing more.

A few hours later, it's gotten a little bit better at the diner, meaning we've had more than five tables. One family came in with an obnoxious baby who left a pile of nachos under his high chair, and then a couple around my age, but who I didn't recognize from my school, got milkshakes and fries and stared at each other so much, they didn't even notice they knocked one of the shakes over.

But at least that meant there were things to keep me busy. Messes to clean up. Dishes to do. Which I have now done.

While Mom is taking care of the rest of the dining room, I grab the trash, which has to be removed from the premises at the end of the day no matter how little garbage there is, or we instantly get ants on every surface.

I toss it in the very fragrant dumpster that's next to the fat trap and wave at Mrs. Renaldi, who's watering the geraniums in her window.

With that last task done I'm officially out of distractions, so I lie to myself and say I'm not about to do the thing I'm about to do, even as I'm already opening up Instagram. I scroll past all the people from school posting their summer adventures. Pretty much everyone from my class is away for the summer or doing an internship or something. I think my friends and I are the only ones staying in town all summer.

Not that I didn't have the opportunity. Back in January Mrs. Schlossel called me into her office. She had bright pink fake nails, and she'd lost a few of her false eyelashes, which was an offputting combination. *You could apply for this architecture internship in Rome,* she said, spinning her laptop to show me the screen. *I know that's what you're hoping to study, so you can get a jump start. And you'd learn Italian, too, as part of the program.*

Me? I stammered as another eyelash hung at a precarious angle.

Why not? You have the grades. If you get in, there's a scholarship that pays airfare, lodging. She bent across the table, every centimeter of her makeup-caked face suddenly contorted into pity.

Ah, so this was because of my dad. She thought I needed time away from all my worries.

But I don't run away. That's not who I am.

You're so talented, Austin, she said, as if that was the real reason she was doing this, and I thought I detected the scent of tuna sandwich on her breath. *Don't sell yourself short. Just try.*

But I didn't try. I knew if I wanted to go to college I couldn't go anywhere until Mom and Zoe were taken care of, not stressing constantly, so I didn't even want the option of knowing if I could've gotten in.

Do I think about Rome and the summer I could be having? Sure, sometimes. I want to see the Colosseum, the Trevi Fountain, all those statues of gods slaying dragons and women battling swans. I would spend days . . . no, weeks . . . walking around the city, looking up, studying it all.

It's the kind of summer that might have caught Love's attention.

Hers has been epic, of course. New dance videos almost every other day, each in different streets, or museums, or old movie theaters. She never stands on a banister again, which I'm glad about, but I could swear something else about her is changing. Maybe I'm imagining things or projecting or whatever, but it's like the smiles are strained. She never looks lost in what she's doing like she did that day. Every now and then she does something dorky like pose with an orange slice in her mouth, and I see a flash of the girl I hung out with in the kitchen. But then it's gone again just as fast.

There's a thing where if you save someone's life, it feels like they're always your responsibility. I feel that, even though it makes no sense. Her life is objectively perfect, unlike mine. Though I can't help thinking of what she said in the kitchen, how people only follow her because of that. Not the things that make her relatable.

I let her new reel play. She's at a party somewhere, and she and Damien zoom across the water before emerging. She's laughing, and Damien presses her against the side of a luxurious infinity pool. His smile is white and all his teeth are straight. He's tanned and so is she. He kisses her . . . deeply, the sun setting behind them like a movie.

I lock my phone before I can see the ending. Then that's not enough so I shut it down entirely and go see if there's another bag of trash to dump. She's absolutely fine. She doesn't need me, and once again I'm reminded to stop hoping for things that clearly aren't meant to be.

May 22, 4:13 PM

Mom

Hi Love. How's the song going?

Love

Waiting to hear how it comes out!

You writing one in the meantime?

I have so much going on. I will though!

I do have some news for you.

Sorry, gotta run, call you tomorrow?

Okay. Love you, Love.

Love you too.

May 22, 5:23 PM

River

I need you to call me.

Love

So you do actually have my phone number.

You're so annoying. I'm serious.

What's wrong?

Just call me. Everyone's okay.

On my way to a party with D. I'll call you before Mom.

You're gonna want to do that. Oh, and Forest says thanks for the gold sneakers. He never takes them off.

CHAPTER FIFTEEN

Love

This is actually happening. Twelve months of lip-sync dancing and content creation have all paid off, because my time is here. The single is mostly done. There's still some engineering stuff they want to add, but I have a whole song in the can! Mom seemed skeptical just because they didn't want to pick one of the songs I wrote, which was pretty annoying, but Damien says that's how it all works. You have to pay your dues.

Damien is supportive even though he's going through a lot.

The Highland Park video got a lot of attention and didn't really make him look great (lots of close-ups of him just standing there) and then his third single didn't do as well as "Me Without You" or "Replay." That was a bummer because neither of us ever wants to hear that song again. So he's been sulking and high a lot. But I keep reminding him we're a team, a package deal. That my success is his success and he gave me my start, not the guy who caught me. This makes him feel better about himself, most of the time. I try not to think about how hot it was when Austin caught me and the way it felt to kiss his cheek later that day, most of the time. That's not real life.

Instead, I focus on the single, which D and I have listened to, like, four times in a row:

You thinkin' 'bout me every day, oh
I got that sweet taste, I know so
Head's buzzin', yeah, I'm that lush
That's me, your sugar rush

There's a lot of Auto-Tune happening and it's definitely not the measure of what I can do vocally, but it's a start, good enough and catchy enough to get my career back on track.

When we get to the party and I take off my dress, Damien tells me I look straight-up fire in my pink bikini. So maybe things are getting back to normal.

Now we're in a pool at this Kardashian-adjacent soiree. There's some connection with Justin Bieber, too. But honestly, it doesn't matter. It just matters that we're invited. Damien is always invited to A-list parties even though we're not quite there yet. He'd never want to, but he can thank his dad for that. Travis Hunter is one of the biggest rock star–turned–producers around, and everyone needs a producer. But does every producer need a family? About as much as my dad does, apparently. Seven kids, three wives . . . Travis Hunter's the kind of guy who only wants his kids around when it suits him. It's such a bummer for D. Everyone thinks he has what he has because of his dad, and I haven't even met him in the year we've been dating.

"Check this out," I tell him now as he swims up behind me and cocoons me in his arms. We're at the edge of the infinity pool and for a second, when he holds me like this, it feels like we're in our own little world for the first time in a long time, even though we're surrounded by people filming themselves or laughing or making out.

I show Damien the numbers on the reel of us I posted ten minutes ago. It already has fifty thousand views. "Sweet," he whispers straight into my ear, which sends goose bumps spiraling all across my body. "Not surprised though. Look at you. So smokin', you can't be real."

"Thanks," I say, but something about it comes out sour and sticky. Because I *am* real and sometimes I'm not sure he or anyone else really knows that anymore.

"So smokin', you need to cool off," he says. I wonder for a second if I'm getting sunburned, but then he grabs me. I drop my phone on the side of the pool just before he dunks me. When we resurface, I laugh, even though my heart is beating super hard.

"Oh my God, you're SUCH a jerk!" I say.

"Sorry, babe," he says. "Just playin'."

I love when he calls me "babe." When he's playful like this and actually here with me, not faded. I thought he would calm down when we got back from the tour, but he's been having his own hot-girl summer, I guess. I was actually excited when he said he wanted to drive tonight because then I knew he couldn't completely go off.

He kisses me right there with the music going loud, and I melt into him, our wet skin pressing. We kiss and kiss and kiss. We are young and in love, and everything is perfect.

Or will be.

We make out until Damien's friend Tanner, a guy with spiky blond hair and a long torso, interrupts us. He taps Damien on the shoulder and offers him a shot.

"Thanks, homie—" D says, and reaches for the glass.

"We brought the car," I say quickly, reminding him that he didn't want a driver tonight. "Unless you want to let *me* drive your baby home?"

Damien arches an eyebrow at me in a *girl, you're so crazy* look. We both know that will never happen. Damien's G-Wagon is only ever driven by him. He's almost superstitious about it. But we also both know I am not a person who gets into cars with drunk people. Ask my dad why.

"Tshhh," Damien says, shaking his head. He gives Tanner a commiserating grin and they dap. "The ball and chain, keeping me on point."

Hilarious.

"It's not just me. Chris told us not to drink in public," I say. "Remember what happened to Justin Timberlake—"

Tanner cuts me off. "It's all love, Love!" He has mushface, like he's been drinking all day, or all week, probably. "You just hit me up when you change your mind."

"Thanks, I'm good," I say, smiling so the guy won't think I'm judgy. I'm not a narc or anything; I get why people like it. Makes you lighter and more uninhibited, but in the position I'm in I can't afford that. Not when I'm this close, and I've seen enough of what else it can do. Besides, it's kind of fun to watch everyone else's faces melt from buzzed to drunk.

Tanner rests his eyes back on me, and as they climb my body, I can feel him like a bug on my skin. "If my ball and chain looked like yours, D, I would let her keep my balls in her purse too."

Damien tries to keep his face neutral, but I feel him flinch.

Tanner picks up the shot glasses and hands them off to a couple I don't know who are flopped on a lounge chair.

"C'mon," I say, touching Damien's chin. If I can get his mind back on me and off the alcohol and the diss, I might be able to stop this night from going south. "I'll race you to the other side."

I splash his face and he yells, *"Hey!"* and then we speed across the pool, weaving through all the bodies. I reach the deep end just before him. It's emptier than the steps on the shallow side where people are talking and drinking in a pile, and I look up. Palm trees dot the perimeter of the pool, and flowering bushes are all around us. I look at Damien and he looks at me. He grips the poolside on either side of me, boxing me into his arms, and then he cups my chin for a long beat before he kisses me. This time it is gentle and loving, like that first kiss on Rodeo Drive. Even with this feeling I've been waiting to get back though, I can't turn off the thought that it would make such a hot picture. And it would.

The sun is setting behind us.

We are glistening with beadlets of water.

We are young and beautiful. Famous and getting more so.

But right now, I just want to be us.

It's only later, after I get dragged off to film videos with a few of the girls, that I realize something is off. When I finally find Damien to tell him I'm ready to go, he's in the pool house where joints are getting passed around and people are disappearing into the bathroom, probably to do the harder drugs. He leans in and kisses me, but it's the complete opposite of the ones in the pool and his mouth is steeped in the tang of tequila. I *know* if I were to say anything to D about it in front of everyone, it'd be a fight and draw too much attention. So I sit on his lap and try to wait for him to sober up. I don't know how much he's had or how long it will take to get out of his system, but I do know the longer the better. I just need to keep him from getting any more.

We'll be fine.

He'll sober up and we'll just drive over the hill.

No problem.

No problem at all.

"You sure you're good to drive?" I say as he opens the door for me two hours later.

"I'm good, baby," he says confidently, and I consider him one more time. Except for a quick change out of my bathing suit, I've been with him the whole time and he hasn't had a thing. His eyes are a little dull, but more in a tired way, and he's steady on his feet. His hands don't shake like they do when he's wasted. But still something holds me back.

"Because we could call a Lyft?" I say. I am paused, one foot in the car and one foot planted on the gravel driveway. "Come back for the car tomorrow? I'm sure she'll be safe here."

He scoffs. "I'm not leaving her. Besides, I only did one shot and that was right after it got dark." Sunset was hours ago now, which does make me feel better. "Don't stress."

I hesitate one more second, then slide in.

He climbs in, throws an arm over my seat to reverse, and pulls smoothly onto the road.

He's fine. I'm just being extra.

When we're on Mulholland, heading back to Studio City, Damien blasts the music and I feel free. Or at least I want to. I'm still a little tense, I guess. It was a long day and my skin is tight from the sun.

I try singing along to Miley to loosen up and Damien joins in on my "Party in the USA" a little loud and he mumbles his way through some of the lyrics in a way that makes me laugh.

But then when the second verse starts, suddenly his words are coming out slurred, not mumbled. I tense back up as I do the math again. If he only did one shot, he *should* be sober by now, like he said. Except what if he was downplaying it?

He's still singing but I can barely hear the music anymore. Alarm bells are going apeshit in my head and my heart is slamming against my rib cage.

Damien swerves around nothing and the bells intensify. Because one shot alone . . . it definitely doesn't do this.

He swerves again and the realization hits me clearly and in a way I can't deny.

He's shit-faced. This is it. I'm going to be one of the human crepes who die on Dead Man's Curve.

"Damien, pull over."

He ignores me and the car lurches again. "Damien!" I shout, more insistent this time. "You're on the wrong side of the road!" A car is coming toward us, rounding the curve, headlights blinding us both. I cover my eyes. "Damien!" I scream.

"Oh shit!" He jerks the wheel, and the G-Wagon weaves back into the right lane. Its tires barely grip onto the asphalt . . .

Then—

We start to skid.

"Watch out!" I yell.

He slams the brakes. The car screeches—

But it's too late.

CHAPTER SIXTEEN

Love

We don't go over the cliff, but we do crash into a ditch. An airbag whacks me in the face the second we make impact. My arms flail, trying to brace but finding nothing but air.

Smoke billows around us as we finally come to a stop in the dirt.

It's over. The airbag deflates and I reach out my arm for Damien. "Are you okay?" I ask, panicked. I bit my tongue. I taste blood.

"I think so," he says. "You?"

I try to nod but my head thumps like bad music and I can't bring myself to open my eyes yet. Vaguely I register that Miley keeps on singing, which means the whole crash was only a few seconds. But it seemed like forever.

"Babe, you're bleeding," Damien says.

I open my eyes.

Damien's bloody fingers are in my face and he's hovering over me. "You . . . you're okay, right?" He looks confused, lost in a way I've never seen him. Like a little boy who doesn't know where he is.

"Yeah," I say, even though my brain is on fire. I wiggle my toes, touch my face. My fingers come away bloody too, but I think it's just my nose from when I hit the airbag. I hurt everywhere but I don't think anything is broken. "Yeah, I'm fine."

He takes my hand and shakes his head. Every movement is messy, disconnected. "I'm not."

"You're hurt?"

"No, I . . . I took some Molly before we left. Tanner—he said it would be at least half an hour before it hit." He slaps the wheel, hard, inhaling and exhaling deeply like people do on ecstasy, grinding his jaw. "But it started kicking in and I got confused from the lights. Fuck. I fucked up so bad."

Sure enough, I can hear police sirens in the distance, already weaving toward us on these curvy roads. If they're as close as they sound, they'll be here in less than a minute.

"Damien," I say, and there's so much in the word.

"And now I'm going to be on *TMZ*. *Fuck!*" he says miserably.

I go silent. I still remember being seven, sitting in the back of the cop car with Dad while they took him in for a DUI. The world is just the same shit on repeat no matter how much I try to get away from it. And all he can think about is *TMZ*.

"I'm so screwed," he says, and then real, actual tears fall down his cheeks. "And I could have hurt you."

I soften just a little.

"You'll post bail, right?" he says, screwing his mouth into a half smile, like he's trying to be brave. He strokes my cheek. "You're so beautiful." He takes a long, deep breath in.

That's the ecstasy. The crash has sobered him some, but he's never going to pass a sobriety test. He might go to jail, to court. His dad might be able to get him out of it. But Damien will never ask him for anything . . .

And then I think of what Chris always says, about how we're tied to each other.

And how I'm sober.

The sirens are getting closer. I make a decision in an instant. There's no time to think it through. "Switch places with me," I say, grabbing a tissue out of the package I keep in my purse. I swipe at my nose and quickly try to clean myself up. I have to save Damien. Save us.

"What?"

"Get out of the car . . . now!"

"Oh my God, you would do that for me? You're the best. The total best." He stumbles out as I slide across and adjust the seat. The cop car pulls around the bend, just as Damien folds himself into the passenger seat. It looks like an alien ship when it stops on the road above us, all sleek and dangerous. A male officer steps out of the car. He's short, stocky, with thick brown hair and hooded eyes. He's kind of young, like he's new on the force. That's good. Maybe he knows who I am. I wave at him and smile like I'm an innocent flower.

"Hi, there!" I say as he approaches the car, but it comes out wrong. My stomach hurts and my heart is pounding so hard. I suddenly realize I haven't eaten since before the party. Shit.

"Is anyone hurt?" he asks.

"No. Nope, we're good, just shaken up," I say. "We'll call for a tow."

"License and registration."

Shit again. He is most definitely not charmed by me. He's looking at me as indifferently as if he was in the imperial guard or something. "Sure thing."

Damien opens the glove box and gets the registration. He hands it to me and I lean over him, fumbling to reach my purse. I keep my eyes on the cop as I get my license out and hand it to him.

"I bet you see this kind of thing all the time, right? Famous people making silly mistakes?" I say as he looks everything over. I can hear my own desperation, my own plea for him to just let us go. We could be home in five minutes, sleeping in Damien's apartment, safe. This will absolutely *never* happen again.

"Not really," he says.

He seems to mull a moment, then stares at the smoking, smashed-up front of the car. "So what happened here, miss?"

"I think I was going too fast on the curve. I guess I lost control." I'm stammering. I sound out of my mind. I feel like I'm coming out of my skin. "I was nervous, you know, because I just heard about all the people who die on this road and I . . . I don't know . . . all of a sudden . . . boom. I lost control."

"And this is Damien Hunter? This car belongs to you?" he asks, shining his flashlight at Damien, who is once again smiling stupidly.

"Yeah, man," D says. "You know what they say about women drivers."

The cop's eyes narrow, suspicious again. He shines his flashlight straight into my face. "Have you two had anything to drink tonight?"

I can imagine what he's seeing. A girl in a fast car, in a short sequined dress, with a wasted boyfriend, who just drove into a ditch. I can't get control of my breath. I'm a good performer, but I'm not a good liar. I only have one thing on my side: I really *haven't* had any alcohol.

I just wasn't the one driving.

"I don't drink," I say simply.

"What about you, LA Ink? Anything to drink tonight?"

"Naw, man."

I chance a look at him. Damien has pulled it together more, like he did when we first got in the car. He seems calm and cool, a superstar, like someone you would want to know.

The cop hands me my license.

"Ma'am, I'm going to need you to do a field sobriety test. If that's fine, we'll see if we can get the car towed and get you home."

"Of course." When we were little, River and I recited the alphabet backward, walked in a straight line, just like we saw Dad do. At least it's coming in handy now.

I follow the cop up the hill but a ways off the road so we don't get hit by cars. My heels are four inches of stiletto though and my legs are shaking from the adrenaline, plus I'm dizzy from the crash.

"Here's good," he says finally, as his partner steps out of the car, arms folded across his chest. "Okay, miss," he says. "I want you to take nine steps, heel to toe, along a straight line. Then, turn on one foot and take nine steps back, same way. Is that clear?"

I look down at the uneven ground. "Can I take off my shoes?"

"No. There's glass on the road."

"My shoes are—"

"Either you're sober or you're not."

"Right. Well, I am, so . . ."

My knees bump together. There's no way I'm going to be able to do this. Why couldn't I have gotten a female officer? A woman would understand about the shoes and I don't want to tell him how awful I feel because it will just draw more attention to the crash, to us.

"Easy peasy," I finish instead.

The cop adjusts his bodycam so it's looking right at me. Then he just stands there, waiting. I take one step, then another. My feet are already wobbling, my heels getting caught in the asphalt as cars whip by us, then slow down to get a look at me. My ankle almost gives on the rocks, the same one that's been bothering me since the day in the mall in Highland Park.

Austin flashes through my thoughts. The way he caught me, how he was completely steady. I wish he were here now.

My nerves spill over and I stop. I've lost count of the steps.

I'm not counting.

Is this cop counting?

"Can I start over?" I ask. "It really is just the shoes."

"No," he says.

I ignore him and start over anyway, counting this time. Pretend I'm on a high wire. Patty and I always used to say we wanted to be in the circus. We haven't talked in so long, that feels like another life.

My thoughts are not right, scattered, whipping through time.

"One," I say. "Two. Three—" I can't see the cop's face but I can feel what he's thinking. "Really," I say, "I'm not drunk. I—"

I hit the ground, face-first. My head immediately starts up its angry pounding again. I feel like I'm going to throw up.

The police officer helps me to my feet. "Let's go, young lady. Time for a Breathalyzer."

As I limp toward his car I say, "You couldn't have started with that?"

CHAPTER SEVENTEEN

Love

Once I pass the Breathalyzer test the cops realize I might actually be injured, not drunk, and they drag us to the hospital. They put us behind separate curtains in the ER and through them I hear D tell everyone he meets how gorgeous they are, so the doctors get the picture pretty quickly. They keep me longer for a blood test, CT scan, and who knows what else. It's dawn by the time the hospital clears me and they let Chris and D back. She and Damien both hover around me, helicoptering and fussing.

"You okay?" Chris says, reaching for my forehead. I duck.

"I have a mild concussion and a bad headache, but the doctor says it'll pass."

Damien slumps into one of those beige hospital chairs. "This is all my fault, boo."

I look at Chris. Damien and I didn't talk about telling anyone else what happened. Not even her. "I was the one driving, D."

"Love," Chris says, "he told me everything. No need for the act." She gets my phone off the tray next to the hospital bed and hands it to me. "We have a lot to talk about but you need to call your mom. Let her know you're all right. She's been . . . she's been trying to reach you."

“How do you know? Did you already tell her?”

“No.” Chris is being too subdued, too quiet. Nothing megawatt here. Something else is going on. “*TMZ* broke the story as you getting a DUI.” She reaches for my arm but stops short of touching me. “They have the bodycam footage of your sobriety test.”

“DUI?” This is ridiculous. I am, like, the only person I know who doesn’t drink, but everyone’s going to think I got a DUI? How is that possible? “But I wasn’t drunk or high or anything! Can’t you tell *TMZ* I have a concussion? That my shoes fucked me up and they shouldn’t have even given me a field test in that condition?”

“It’s true,” Damien says miserably. “This is so unfair.”

“I believe you were sober,” Chris says. “But unfortunately, that’s not what the story says and the story is what matters . . . at least for now.”

“You—you need to talk to them!” Nobody moves. “Like, right now!”

Christine takes a deep breath. “We’ll deal with the fallout tomorrow, Love . . .” She gently nudges the hand that’s holding the phone. “Mom.”

My stomach twists. Mom is going to freak out. It’s hard enough convincing her not to worry, that I’m fine even if I can’t always return her calls or texts right away. And now she’s going to have a reason for it.

“Not here,” I say, listening to the shuffle of feet and the wheeling of carts outside the curtain.

Apparently, nowhere public is safe.

• • •

Once we're in Chris's car, I sigh and FaceTime my mom. Her image pops up on the screen instantly, like she's been staring at her phone, waiting to swipe Accept.

"Hey, Mom," I say, trying to keep myself together, voice light. I can't though. Just the sight of her—hair in a messy bun on top of her head, tan and toned, like she has been since she quit working so much—makes me want to get on the first plane out of here and fall into her lap. She's in the living room on the couch, and the house seems peaceful behind her. Everything's clean, and I can see a wide doorway leading into the kitchen where the lights are still dimmed. The boys are asleep, I'm sure, but I'd kinda give anything to see River and Forest's faces too.

"Love," she says, holding the phone up close, like she can see me better that way. "Are you all right? I was so worried." Every word is laced with hysteria and the pressure of her trying to keep her voice calm.

"It was just a fender bender, Mom. No big deal, I swear. Didn't even hit another car. It was just late." I look at Damien reflexively. He stares at the car floor and I can tell he's flaming himself now that he's finally completely come down. "I just couldn't see the road right. Maybe I need glasses or something?"

Mom's whole demeanor changes. She sits back and it's obvious, now that she knows I'm not dead or anything, that her temper is ratcheting up.

"That's not what it says online. It says you were driving drunk, and you crashed a G-Wagon in Beverly Hills."

She is pissed.

"That's not true," I say. "Mom, you know I don't drink."

"I honestly don't know *what* you do over there. Looks like a lot of partying to me."

"I didn't even have a drop."

"Don't you lie to me, Love Brooke Thompson."

Next to me, Damien cringes and Chris pushes into the shot. "Uh, hello, Ms. Thompson."

Mom continues to glare.

"She's telling the truth," Chris says. "She passed the Breathalyzer. I can have my team send you a copy . . ." She looks outside where the sun is just now beginning to come up. "Uh . . . as soon as they get to the office."

"That's not necessary," Mom says. "Now, I would like to speak to my daughter . . . *alone*."

Once Chris and Damien have exited, I say, "See, Mom, I told you. Nothing to worry about."

Mom blows her bangs off her face, softening, but just a little. "You still crashed a car, Love. From what I could see, that road is really windy. Anything could have happened."

"It was an accident," I say.

"No, it's a pattern."

"What does *that* mean?"

"Come on, Love. I can see it on your feed, just like the rest of the world. You'd think that stunt you pulled in Illinois would give you some sense, but nope. Ever since then, you've been out every night, alcohol is everywhere, and there you are, half naked." She takes a sip from her Lone Star mug of what I know is hot, strong, black coffee. "You've changed."

I don't know what to say to that. My head is still pounding, my body hurts, and although I knew my mom would be worried, I didn't expect her to be so judgmental. The parties, those posts, it's all part of the job. She's in a house I paid for, on a couch I bought. How does she think I got her those things?

I can't say any of that out loud though.

Mom looks to the side. "Your father and I think you should come home."

It takes a second for that to register, but it doesn't compute. She must have misspoken.

"Hey, honey!" My father comes into view. Brown hair, blue eyes, broken capillaries, probably handsome for an old guy, if you can stand the sight of him. Which I can't.

He has the balls to sling an arm around Mom's shoulders as I try to comprehend that I have not been talking to my mother alone at all. That my dad has been there, in person, the whole time. Why didn't I notice she was hugging one side of the couch?

"Wow," I snap finally, "I get Mom a house and suddenly you're back in the picture."

"Love!" Mom looks shocked, like I slapped her in the face. But my head's the one throbbing, violently.

"Oh, come on, now, honey," he says, like he talks to me every day, like he hasn't been out of our lives for almost six years. "We just think this Little Joe is no good for ya."

My vision collapses into a single pinprick of rage. I am only fury. I may be pissed at Damien too, but he has been here for me this whole year. No way this loser gets to talk about D like that, or actually talk to me any way about anything. My voice lowers. "Clearly I got my shitty taste in men from Mom."

Again, Mom reels like she cannot conceive of this level of

disrespect. "Don't talk to your father like that," she snarls.

"I didn't want to talk to him at all!" I shout.

Outside, Damien and Chris startle from where they're leaning against a Toyota Highlander. I need to end this call. I look back to my mother and my lousy father. A thousand snipes come to mind, and I can't stop the one that will hurt Mom the most from sliding out of my mouth. "Did you forget he's the one with the actual DUIs? The ones he got on the way home from the strip clubs, Mom?"

Dad puts up his hands like he's not going to fight me or deny anything. "I found God, Love," he says, in a voice so serene I almost throw my phone out the window.

"Jesus Christ," I say instead.

Mom pulls the phone back her way. She looks pale, upset, but she isn't yelling anymore. "This isn't about your father. This is about you and me. It's my fault this happened. I've barely talked to you for weeks. I haven't seen you for months. I should've come out there."

She always blames herself for everything. That makes it all so much worse. "I'm an adult, Mom."

"Clearly not," she says. "You almost killed yourself and someone else. You have a problem."

It's like my dad has his fingers in her ears or something. But I want her to hear this. "I am not the one with the problem! Everybody *loves* who I am except for you!" I end the call before she can say anything else.

I pull my hood up, lean my head against the seat, close my eyes, and wish as hard as I can to sleep this all away.

CHAPTER EIGHTEEN

Austin

Zoe's the first to tell me the news about Love. I've been trying as hard as I can to quit my Love habit and mostly succeeding. But when Zoe told me she drove drunk and wrecked her car, I started tracking all the stories.

They . . . aren't kind.

Over the last twelve hours, I've watched the comments rise like a wave as the tide changes for Love. The hate oozes off my screen. Her fans feel betrayed. The presiding recommendation is to unfollow her. Damien, too, for good measure. Because following her is supporting drunk driving or the toxic lifestyle that got Love there.

But even though we spent, like, fifteen minutes together total, something keeps telling me that's not Love. I watch the bodycam footage for the zillionth time, stuck on how she pleads with the officer about her shoes, the shaking in her ankles but nowhere else. What if she was just scared? Or hurt? Has anyone even thought to ask what happened next?

In my bed, showered and tired after such a long night, I wonder where she is, how she's feeling, whether Damien is taking care of her. Even though she's a powerhouse, I think maybe she needs that right now.

Crickets chirp outside my window, Zoe listens to Spotify, and Mom bangs pots and pans downstairs as she unloads the dishwasher. Here in Highland Park, I couldn't feel farther from LA.

But somehow in this moment, it feels like I'm with her. And I let myself pretend for just one night, that I'm the one taking care of her.

CHAPTER NINETEEN

Love

In the elevator on the way up to Chris's later that night, Damien says, "I'm telling you this'll all blow over. Chris has handled these things a million times."

We're both in sweats, showered and napped, but this still feels like the longest day ever. My body is stiffening, getting more and more sore, and the fact that Chris has still called us both over to Impression Partners to meet "right away" is doing nothing to help the edginess that hasn't abated since my fight with Mom. Fiona meets us at the elevator as usual, and she looks extra business-y today: cropped black jacket, black high-water pants, a blouse. Damien clocks her pinched expression too and we exchange *WTF* looks. It feels like we're taking a gallows walk and are super underdressed for the occasion.

When we get to Chris's office, six people are crowded around her desk. Three of them—two women and a man—are in suits. Vida from PR and Ella from HR are there too. And, of course, Chris. When she sees us in the doorway, she says, "That's enough for now."

One by one the team files out. A few of them nod at us, while the rest skedaddle without any acknowledgment.

I'm going to puke.

But . . . Chris is smiling. "Take a seat," she says.

We slump onto the couch.

"So where we at?" Damien says.

Chris leans forward. "In a word? You're both canceled."

"Canceled?" I say.

The worst word.

The word everyone fears.

I'm only *nineteen*. I can't be canceled yet.

Damien pales and rests his elbows on his knees. It's a position he's been in a lot in the last day.

Chris nods. "I'm afraid so. That *TMZ* story has twenty million views already."

She hands me an iPad. On it, there's a YouTube clip from the released bodycam footage called "Drunk #gradgirl crashes Mercedes G-Wagon."

"There's no easy way to say this . . . ," Chris begins.

Isn't that what the cops say before they tell you someone died?

"Your sponsors have dropped you," she goes on, clipped. "And Interscope pulled your single, Love."

"This can't be happening," I say faintly.

"Yo," Damien says, pulling the iPad out of my hands and putting it on the table. "Fuck that *TMZ* shit! Release the police report. All the facts are there!"

Chris purses her lips so thinly, they almost disappear. "Like the fact that *you* were on ecstasy *and* over the legal limit?"

Realization paralyzes Damien and he clams up. My headache starts up again.

"So . . . ," Chris says, "it's a good thing no one cares about the facts. People want stories. They liked seeing you rise, now they *love* watching you fall. And that's a problem for us."

"So what can we do?" I ask, though I'm sure the answer is nothing. We're doomed. It's all over. I got way more than fifteen minutes, but it's been taken away so fast, it doesn't feel like it.

Chris stands up and comes around her desk. She seems to be brightening. "We move the narrative forward."

"Okay . . . ," I say.

"Everyone loves a good redemption arc. For Damien, that's easy." She points at him. "You're going to rehab. A two-week program somewhere on the beach—" He starts to protest but she waves at him in a way that communicates that it's already done and is no longer even interesting to her.

Instead, she turns her full focus to me. "For you, it's harder. People don't love a bad girl as much as a bad boy. You need to get back to your roots." Chris goes behind her desk again and flips her monitor around so we can see it. "And this is how you do it."

On her monitor is a side-by-side of Theo March and Leon Hayes, two of the most wholesome actors around. I've even seen memes that say the world continuing to spin depends on whether they're actually nice in real life.

"What's with those guys?" Damien asks.

"While you're drying out, Love is going to pick one and have a calm, brief, much seen but unverified romance with one of them. Image rehab one-oh-one. Then when you're back to being a good guy in the eyes of the masses, Damien, you and Love can *carefully* reunite."

"I don't even know those guys," I say. "That would be so embarrassing. Who would even ask them?"

"Come on, Love. You think I would suggest this out of nowhere?" Chris says. "Please! Their manager owes me a favor. They'll do it, trust me. A week of holding hands and eating ice cream, hanging out with the internet's favorites, and you'll be back in play."

I don't want to fake-date a celebrity. I don't want to fake-date anyone. I'm with Damien and that's the story I'm committed to.

But when I look over at Chris, the steel in her eyes tells me I'm going to do this. And if that's the case, it should at least be someone I already have some sort of plausible connection with.

"I'm not going to do that," I say, getting to my feet. Chris objects, but I grab her keyboard and type fast.

Then her screen fills with a goofy smile, a grill, and a very nice bicep.

Austin Grey.

I turn the screen so they can see it. "If I'm going to fake-date someone, it's going to be someone real. Someone I actually know. Someone the internet already kind of loves."

Damien squints at the screen. "Burger King? How does *he* help?"

"She's a small-town girl and she needs a small-town boy," Chris says, nodding, "Very good, Love. Even better since you don't have to tell him what you're doing so it won't feel staged."

"This dude ain't even from Texas," Damien mutters. I roll my eyes, but her words make me hesitate. Maybe this isn't a better idea.

"Isn't there something else we can do? Just ride it out and let it blow over?"

Chris looks firmly between us. "You need to tell a story, and a short-term sacrifice is going to be required."

"Emphasis on 'short,'" I say. "Because, Chris, I didn't do anything wrong and I'm tired of pretending. I want to make music. You promised I would."

"Do this, show people some of that glam girl next door they fell in love with," she says, "and I can make you the new Beyoncé and Jay-Z."

"What's wrong with Love and Lil' D?"

"Right now? The fact they're canceled. Which makes them nobody," Chris says sharply.

Damien takes my hand and gives me a look. "She might be right, and if you'd rather hang with that dude than an A-list actor, I'm down. I'm down for whatever is going to fix this fuckshit."

I look back over at Austin on the screen. He's sexy. That's for sure. My followers loved him, and when I was in the kitchen with him, we maybe sort of had a spark. But more than anything, I felt safety in his arms that I haven't felt since. No matter what, I know he won't hurt me. He's . . . stable. That's what I need to make this work.

One more fake thing to get myself back on track, and then I'm never doing anything like this again.

I nod. "Austin Grey."

"Good." Chris flips the screen so it faces the back of her desk again. "I'll have Fiona draft an itinerary and you'll make the call."

I redden at the thought. What if he has a girlfriend? What

if he is disgusted by the footage of me falling down? "Okay, I just . . . I need a couple of days to get my head straight."

"Yeah," Chris says, giving me a pointed look. "Just don't wait too long. This isn't going to get any better on its own."

Damien squeezes my hand. "It's going to be all right, boo. You got this."

Yeah, I got this. This is just something I have to do to save us both. Again.

May 23, 6:42 PM

Love

Hey, Patty. I'm sorry it's been so long.
Things have been kind of crazy.
But I could really use one of our talks right now.

Patty

I saw the crash footage.

It wasn't what it looked like.
It was all a mistake.

That's convenient.

Can I FT you?

Patty!

Can't, I'm working. At a bookstore
in case you were wondering.
Since you never asked.

I really am sorry. It's just, you don't understand
what it's like out here. How about later?

I don't think so, Love.
I'm not a receptacle, someone you
can ignore for a year and then pop back
in when you need a real friend to dump
your shit on. Take real good care of yourself.

. . .

. . .

. . .

CHAPTER TWENTY

Austin

Zoe and I are with Mom in her room. It's exactly the way it was before we lost Dad: his stack of snapbacks on his bedside table, his watch sitting next to the empty charger. His favorite Pearl Jam poster is still framed over his side of the bed, and on the small shelf sit five small pictures of the two of them over the years.

We've lived here my whole life, so I can remember so many moments in here. Jumping on their bed, seeing Zoe for the first time, watching cartoons, running in after a nightmare, and even some of those heart-to-hearts Dad loved so much.

Be brave.

The best time to do anything is now.

And of course:

Life is short, man. Shorter than you think.

It's like he's in here with us.

"Come on, people. We gotta do this," Zoe says, breaking the silence.

Mom hasn't been able to clean out Dad's things and I thought I could help her before I go to school, but now that we're in here, it just all seems sad and tragic and I don't know if I can do it either. It's like packing up every single one of those memories, too.

Zoe flings open the closet and crosses her arms, eyeing us both.

The clothes are neatly hung, but worn and comfy like he was. Dad liked a worn sweater, a lived-in bowling shirt, and a really colorful pair of shoes. His sneakers and chef's clogs are all lined up on a shelf underneath. His prescription skin cream rests on top, along with his cuff links, and his only two ties. Each item is proof he was here, that he meant everything to us.

Mom's clothes take up the other half of the closet and are much less organized. She loves pastels, pink and blue and green. Denim, too, plus cardigans and hoodies. But it's all mixed in together. Despite their different styles though, you can see they both leaned into comfort and ease. It's probably why their marriage worked so well. So different, but the same where it counted.

"Maybe we should call Aunt Meryl," Zoe says when neither of us moves.

"We're not calling Aunt Meryl," I say quickly. I know what happens if we do. She'll take over, and something about it will make Mom cry and we'll have to listen to it for weeks. I don't think I can take that right now. "We'll handle this. The three of us."

Mom runs her fingers over the hangers still holding his clothes, like we didn't say anything. "Did you know everyone told us we were never going to make it work, that when you fall in love in high school, you're doomed?"

"But you did, because it was true love," Zoe says, patting Mom on the back.

"Yeah, it was. We were lucky. We still *are* lucky. We got you and we got twenty-three years together. Twenty-three *good* years. More than most."

Seems like the way of the universe. You don't get a perfect love, or if you do, you don't get it for long.

Mom worries her hands as all three of us continue to stare into the closet. Then finally, just as I'm about to force myself forward, she says, "No."

"No?" Zoe says.

"I'm not ready for this. I thought I was, but it's too much all at once. I don't know what we're doing with the diner or where we'll be six months from now. All I do know is that your father's toothbrush is sitting next to mine, where it's supposed to go, and that his shoes are right where he kept them and that his watch is still on his nightstand where it belongs. I am not ready to let that go. I'm just not." Her voice cracks a bit at the end.

"I'm not going to let anything happen to the diner," I say, even though I have no idea how if our plan doesn't work. "We will fix it this summer. We'll be able to hire a chef by the time I leave for school." I put a hand on Mom's very tense shoulder. "I will make sure you and Zoe are okay before I go anywhere. I will make sure things are . . . stable."

I don't even know how I get the word out of my mouth.

Zoe snorts and rolls her eyes.

Mom gives me a look like she thinks I'm a good person but also like there's no way.

All three of us know there's no such thing as stable. All three of us know life loves to knock you off-balance without any warning. But I'm not taking it back. I'm going to try.

I slide the closet door closed. "We'll do this another day," I say firmly. "Come on . . . I'll make us some lunch."

• • •

Two days after the closet incident, I'm walking the neighbor's dog Fluffers in exchange for using her shower because our boiler went out last night. Fluffers is cute, but waiting for her to have mercy on me and finally poop is not. She's prancing about like I have all day and don't need to go home, then get to work while Mom waits for her friend. Jo is going to come over and hopefully fix the boiler. Of course, Dad wouldn't need Jo. He would know what to do. About the boiler. About the diner. About Mom and Zoe. And maybe most of all, about the rest of my life.

Deep, powerful anxiety rolls through me, like my whole life is passing me by right now and I'm just standing here, waiting for excrement.

My phone buzzes in my pocket and my first thought is that the boiler blew up, but when I look down and see the new text, I'm frozen to the spot. Fluffers tries to yank me forward, but she is small and fluffy and I am tall and my legs aren't working, so we stay put.

310-555-0119: hey Austin. remember me? It's Love, from the railing?

My stomach immediately clenches and a weird pulsing starts up in my neck. Love. Like, as in secretly-living-in-my-head-rent-free Love?

What do I say? Something witty, friendly, thoughtful, cool?

Thankfully, now that I've stopped following her lead, Fluffers is finally circling a tree to do her business.

No, definitely not cool.

"Good girl, Fluffers! You can do it."

I fire off a response before I can overthink it.

Me: Hi Love

Yeah. That was brilliant.

She responds right away. Hey do you want to FaceTime?

Fluffers seems to have completed her task. But FaceTime? With Love?

Now? I ask.

Her Yeah pops up just as instantly.

I scroll through the possibilities of why she wants to talk to me and a stupid voice deep inside my head thinks maybe she's calling to tell me she can't stop thinking about me, either.

No, Austin, you selfish asshole. Her whole life has just disintegrated. She is not just sitting there thinking about you.

I type Sure.

But just as Love chimes in with a FaceTime request, Fluffers squats again.

The universe has a very consistent sense of humor.

I hit Accept and as her face populates my screen, I make matters worse by brushing up against the camera-flipping icon. Suddenly, she is watching Fluffers take her second poop of the morning.

"Sorry. So sorry," I mutter, quickly flipping it back while also bagging the shit. "When they've got to go, they've got to go, right?" I add weakly and tuck the bag out of view. Fluffers doubles back for home and this time I let her pull me along.

That's when I finally see her.

Love.

She shouldn't look any better now than she does on her IG, but she does. Haloes of light beam out in all directions behind her head. Wait . . . maybe that's actually the glare hitting a pane of glass behind her, but whatever. The point is she looks angelic, beautiful. Perfect.

And I am blowing it.

"Ugh, let me try again. I didn't expect to hear—"

"From me? Why not?" she says, and it almost seems like she's . . . nervous? I search for signs of Damien in her vicinity but I don't see anyone. Then again, I can't see much, other than the wall behind her, and some beige blinds. I glance around reflexively at the oaks and cherry trees.

"I barely even thought you'd remember me," I say.

"What?" she says, tucking her hair behind her ear. "You're the only guy who's ever saved my life in a mall."

We both laugh. It's awkward, but I'm still happy just hearing her voice. I steer Fluffers to a park bench where I can sit down and appreciate this. Even if it makes me late, I want to take in every second before she's gone again. Also, I'm genuinely curious about how she's handling everything.

"So . . . how are you doing?" I ask.

She raises her eyebrows like she's surprised at the question. "I'm okay. It's been a rough week." She chews her bottom lip adorably and then looks up from under heavy lids.

"I bet," I say. Then, "I'm sorry, Love, that all this is happening to you."

For a second her eyes fill and I'm sure she's going to cry, but she sniffs and beats back the tears.

"No, it's fine," she says, when she's calmed down. "It's just . . . not what it looked like. I wasn't drinking. But anyway, I know this is going to sound crazy, like super ultra weird . . . but you know, this whole cluster has made me think a lot. About the last time I felt safe and like myself, like the person I really am . . . and, well . . . it was when I was with you." She looks soft, lost . . . real.

I wasn't imagining the spark. I can't even believe it. "So I thought I would call you," she goes on. "I wanted to thank you. It was one of those moments in life, you know. A moment that matters."

"Oh," I say. The day I caught her at the mall was the first time in months I felt like I had done something worthwhile. Something brave. And it mattered to me, too. "I can understand that, sort of. I've thought about that day a lot too."

"Sometimes I wonder, if we lived in the same town or something, if maybe we would have hung out. Maybe you would have even taken me out, showed me your life. Honestly, even though we don't, I still kind of wish you had. But you never reached out."

Reached out? Paige and Ty told me to but it never occurred to me that it would be a good idea. She has a boyfriend, and after Emma, I'm allergic to rejection. Alarm bells are ringing in my head, but I ignore them and ask the question. "Aren't you with Damien?" I ask.

"Damien? . . . No. Not anymore," she says, that quaver coming back. "We broke up after the crash."

"I'm sorry."

"You should stop saying that so much."

"I'll try." I hardly register the people walking by. I'm totally locked in to her. This is really happening. "Even if I knew that though," I say, "I never thought you might actually be interested in a guy who just grills hot dogs and flips burgers. Never even crossed my mind."

Well, that's not *entirely* true.

She smiles so big, her eyes twinkle. "You know, you're hot, but you'd be even hotter with confidence."

"Yeah. I guess Zoe's version of a confident me is what made us collide at the mall."

"Ah! Zoe! How is that girl? How's your mom?"

"They're both good." Well, Mom has now gotten one single box in place and has dropped in two of Dad's files, which made her weep. And Zoe? Well, she's crawled inside her phone and I don't know if she's ever coming out. "Everything's good. How's LA?"

"LA is just so . . . LA, you know? I need a . . . change," she says. "I wish I had somewhere to escape to, somewhere simple where I could . . . I don't know . . . get back in touch with myself, I guess. I have to figure out how to fix things, and I think the best way might be just to leave for a while."

Flashes of the LA I've seen on TV or Instagram whip through my mind. The chaos caused by her presence at our tiny mall was epic. It has to be worse there.

"Can I be honest with you? Like, really straight-up?" she says, and her tiny fingers clutch at her throat before dancing out of sight again.

"Sure, always," I say.

She flushes. "Honestly, with everything that's been going on lately, I feel like I'm falling, and I need someone to catch me again."

This is a do-or-die moment for her—I can tell. I handled the first one, why not the second? I know my plate is already overstuffed but if I'm giving up my entire summer, can't I just have this one thing that isn't the diner or taking care of Mom and Zoe?

I make a decision. A brave one, I think. I open the door to my life a little tiny bit. She needs it. Maybe she even needs me. And she said she always wished I'd showed her around. Not much is happening in HP, but I could take her into Chicago, show her all my favorite buildings, give her some downtime. I mean, maybe I could make a difference for her.

"I know this might sound strange," I say, "but do you want to come here?"

"There?" she says. "To . . ."

"Highland Park."

"Highland Park," she says, seemingly tasting the words, trying them on.

"We have an extra room . . . well, it's my dad's old office. It's nothing fancy, but if you wanted you could come here and get away for a bit?"

My eyes scan the park. I wave to Mrs. Alexander, who's walking Frank, her German shepherd. A couple of pigeons coo from a tree. The most exciting thing happening is a couple of kids playing with a Frisbee, their parents off to the side snapping pics with their phones.

"There's not a celebrity in sight—except for the occasional guest performance at the mall," I add.

"Ha—good! Just like home. I'm from a town so small, you've never heard of it, right on the outskirts of Austin, Texas." She folds in on herself and her sweatshirt falls off her shoulder, exposing skin freckled from the sun.

"Right. I remember you telling me . . . when we introduced ourselves." That takes me right back to holding her, which sends something rushing through me. "I have to give you fair warning though. My sister is insane. My house is pretty small. And the boiler is out." All I want is for her to come here, but I also want her to know what she's getting into. Life here is fine, but it's not sushi and limos.

"That's perfect," she says. "Really. A week there would give me a break, and also . . . a chance to see if there's something . . . between us."

"Are you sure?" I ask. I can't believe this is happening. Love Thompson is coming here.

"I'm sure. Are *you* sure?" she asks, laughing.

"Totally," I lie.

"Okay, then I'll work on a ticket and I'll send you details as soon as I have them. Send me your addy." She waves. "You're the best. It's going to be fun, Austin. I promise. Even if I am a mess."

Without waiting for a response, she disappears, and the wallpaper of me and Dad and Mom and Zoe at the water park two summers ago pops up again.

"All right, Fluffers," I say, wondering what the hell just happened. "You better hold yourself together. I'm out of bags and we've got things to do."

CHAPTER TWENTY-ONE

Austin

The next morning, my family and I wait on the curb.

Mom has almost forgiven me for asking Love to come without checking with her first. When she saw what happened to Love online, she got that *mom* look, like she has seen many horrors and knows just what needs to happen next. She lost that look when Dad got sick, so it was nice to see it back. She even hired someone for the next week so I won't have to work while Love is here. Took a chunk out of our meager pot, but she insisted it's a good trial run for when I head off to school.

It's dawn and our quiet street is still asleep, but I am tense. It only gets worse when a scary-looking black SUV pulls up in front of my house. A million what-ifs run through my head. *What if it's awkward? What if we have nothing to talk about? What if she gets bored of me like Emma did?*

"Don't embarrass me," Zoe says unhelpfully through clenched teeth as she watches the car door open and waves frantically. "Love is an actually cool person, so keep it together, okay?"

The nerve of this kid.

As Love gets out of the car, I can't tell if she's actually moving in slow motion or if my brain is just refusing to compute her presence. She is wearing head-to-toe black. Black boots, black leggings, and a black hoodie. The sun isn't even all the way up, but she's wearing a full face of makeup, her hair's wavy, and I smell a whole lot of perfume. My heart thumps and flops as she comes closer.

"Hey, you!" I say, and stick out my hand.

Clearly, as usual, this is the wrong move. Her mouth drops in surprise and she looks back to the car briefly, like maybe she wants to run away. Real fast. A lot.

But then she lifts her sunglasses up onto her head; ignores my hand, still hanging in midair; and leans in for a hug. She rests her head against my chest, and her smell—delicious, like burnt sugar—brings back that moment in the diner when she kissed my cheek. She squeezes me just long enough to give me half a hard-on.

Jesus.

I pull away.

"Hey . . . ," I say again. I can feel Mom and Zoe studying us.

"Smile!" Love gets her phone and snaps a selfie of us, her head leaned into mine.

I step away after, confused. The warning bells in my head clang distantly again. I thought she said she needed to get away? I watch her *tap tap tap* out a caption on her phone. "#myhero #findingmyself . . ."

Odd. But I guess maybe not for LA, where everything is on display all the time, and—I remind myself—this is Love Thompson. Social media is probably a reflex for her at this point.

Zoe is approaching from behind Love like she's about to tackle her, so I quickly steer us back to the car. "Can I grab your bags?" I ask.

"Oh yeah. Thanks!" A hint of surprise laces her voice. "That's so nice of you."

The driver sees us nearing and pops the trunk to reveal *six* matching Louis Vuitton suitcases. I can see Zoe *dying*. She lives for this stuff and is always telling me one day she's going to own bags just like these. I wonder how much they cost. Probably more than our house. I help get two of them, the driver grabs two, and Love gets the two smallest.

As we all shuffle up the path to the house, I wonder exactly what I've gotten all of us into.

I mean, six suitcases? Is she moving in?

But I also feel some of the tension ease out of my shoulders. Because for at least the next week or so, I have a purpose again, not just problems.

CHAPTER TWENTY-TWO

Love

I follow Austin, Mrs. Grey, and Zoe into the cutest little lovebug of a house. It may be outdated or whatever, but it smells like popcorn and family movie night, minus Forest's base notes of apple juice and string cheese. The cross breeze flows from the back door to the front as I note the adorable kitchen and its baby's breath wallpaper, the vintage record player, and an old Wurlitzer piano with a Beatles songbook leaned against the front. It looks like the diner, except make it homey. It's clean and cozy and soft, just like the houses Patty and I used to dream of having. I wanted something bigger and more comfortable than our trailer, and she wanted something smaller and more personal than her McMansion.

She won't even talk to me now, and it hurts like a hard pinch every time I think about her.

She would have really liked this house. I can imagine her, hooking her arm into mine and saying, *Check this out, Love. These are real people.*

I think of my own loft, with the big windows, high ceilings, modern furniture. I thought it was what I wanted, but now I wonder if I would feel like more of a real person there if my house actually felt like a home the way this one does.

Like Austin. Adorable. Corn-fed, bright-eyed, gym shredded, tall . . . but mostly he's nice and trustworthy, and those two things are what I need most right now.

"Hang on," Austin says. He looks at Zoe. "You. Come with me. I need your help with something."

The two of them leave, and suddenly it's just me and Melanie in the hallway.

She rubs at her eyes. I think of my mom, of how tired she was, how ground down by things going wrong before I started making money. It was so fun when I got to take her to her first overnight spa and saw how her skin brightened and the wrinkles around her eyes softened.

Melanie is still in the before picture.

"If you ever come to LA," I say, thinking out loud, "I know the perfect esthetician to work on you."

She flinches for a second, like I was trying to insult her.

"No really," I say quickly, trying to explain what I mean. "The balm she uses smells like strawberries, not the artificial ones . . . real farmer's market ones! And it's super relaxing, so I just meant I promise I'll take you . . . if you decide to visit. Especially since you're being so kind and everything . . . letting me crash your home."

"Thank you, Love. And welcome." She smiles at me. "Austin told me what happened to you online. I don't know how your generation deals with social media. Gen X got up to all kinds of shenanigans and it was never public record."

"Yeah? Did a rock star sign your boobs?"

She lets out a big, unexpected laugh. "Something like that. The point is, now with AI and everything," she says, "how is anyone supposed to know what's real?" She looks me right in the eye and under her softness I see that she's sturdy, too, firmly planted. "I just want you to know I believe you when you say you weren't drinking that night. And even if you had been, that wouldn't mean you're an irredeemably bad person who should be exiled or canceled or whatever. That would mean you needed help." She pauses. "And frankly, stilettos are a menace."

It's my turn to laugh. "Facts," I say.

"And one more thing?"

"Sure."

She checks down the hall, then folds her arms across her chest. "Austin is a good boy. Do you get what I'm saying? I don't know much about you or the boyfriend who came into the diner, but I want you to understand Austin will always do the right thing as he knows it to be, and he doesn't pretend anything. He can't." She lets out a light snort. "Like his dad. True to a fault. You understand me? There are not many people as good or as true as Austin Grey. Don't take advantage of that."

"Yeah . . . yes, of course." She wants me to know Austin has been hurt before and she's communicating with me like only women can, saying it without saying it.

"I got you," I say to her. "For real. I understand."

Satisfied, she gives me a half smile and says, "And good luck with Zoe. She thinks you walk on water."

I laugh, but I feel off. I don't know what I thought . . . that I would text randomly after a month, enter this woman's house, and no one would be suspicious about it? I should call a car, get back on a plane, and leave these nice people alone.

But then . . .

Mom would suffer.

The boys would suffer.

Damien would suffer.

And so would I. No single, ever, back to Trailerina, nothing but a blip of a year where I was someone before I was cast out of existence.

No. I can't.

But if Austin can't pretend like his mom says, that means Chris is right and I can't let him in on this scheme like I was going to. I can imagine how I would feel if someone said, *Hey, you're super ethical and pure of heart, so can I pretend-date you for the whole world to see to help me repair my fucked-up reputation, then go back to my life?*

Yeah, no.

I *am* using him. There's no way around that. But that doesn't mean I have to hurt him, right? I will find a way not to. I'll try to be entertaining and fun like Zoe thinks I am. I'll keep it light and casual, flirty but nothing that could constitute a heartbreak when I leave again.

I need to come out of this able to live with myself.

Now that Melanie has released me from her attention, I'm drawn to the framed pictures on the wall, kind of like the ones we had back in the trailer. Ours were never that happy, but if I can pull this off, I might be able to turn that around for Forest and River, give them childhoods like Austin and Zoe's—at least the ones I can imagine, looking at these pictures of them.

All four of them are together in every frame, looking literally picture-perfect.

Them outside a Broadway play.

Them at the beach.

Them at football games.

As Austin comes back, Zoe following close behind, I point to the most recent ones and say, "I love these."

I glance at him, but when he follows my finger, he looks down at his Converse.

Huh. He doesn't see the happiness I see. He doesn't want to look at these photos at all. Whatever joy Austin felt in these memories has turned into pain. Come to think of it, Zoe was the only one who would talk about their dad at the diner . . .

"I can show you the albums if—" Melanie calls from the living room, distracting me.

"It's okay, Mom!" Austin says quickly, motioning for me to follow him down the hall. "She doesn't need to see Aunt Meryl's bat mitzvah from 1974!"

"I totally want to see Aunt Meryl's bat mitzvah from 1974," I say, nudging him with my elbow. "Seventies fashion never gets old."

"Fine. Another time. But I'm holding you to it!" Melanie calls.

"Come on—we'll show you where you're staying," Austin says, continuing to a room on the right.

He throws the door all the way open so I can see a bedroom with a bookshelf that takes up most of a wall, a window looking out onto a big tree in the backyard, a daybed covered in a quilt, and a desk in the corner. A basket sits in the center of the desk with a journal, some pens, glitter glue, and a range of snacks . . . pickles, olives, Goldfish, but also protein bars and bottles of water.

Welcome, Love, a handmade card reads right in the middle.

"I made the card," Zoe adds unnecessarily. "And the glitter was my idea. Like a glitter of Lovelings!"

"We thought you might want somewhere to write things down, while you're figuring things out. Somewhere *not* online," Austin says. "Or maybe not. But if you want it . . . or need it or whatever . . . it's there."

The journal is blue and has a single flower embossed on the cover. So pretty. It's such a small thing, but it's also everything. Again, I fight the urge to run away, out of here, save these people from me and all my baggage.

"Thank you," I say, barely holding it together.

The apples of Austin's cheeks go bright red. "Sorry it's not a lot of space," he says, swiping some dust off a vintage picture of the Chrysler Building. He's so anxious and I don't understand it. He should have so much swagger, but it's like he doesn't even know he's attractive.

"It's perfect." I mean it too. Yeah, it's small AF, but it has this feeling to it that almost knocks me over, like oatmeal with honey or something. Pure comfort. And the second I think it, it's like my legs are made of sand, disappearing under me, and I just want to lie down and let that comfort wrap around me.

Chris wants me to start posting all this "down-to-earth" stuff ASAP, and I know she's going to start spam-texting me soon, but I'm the most tired I have ever been. Worse than when we were on tour. Maybe she'll be satisfied with the pic I took outside for a few hours.

"If you don't like it in here, you can stay in my room," Zoe pipes up. "Or in Austin's room . . ."

"Umm . . . Zoe? Please behave yourself," Melanie says,

appearing behind her. "Love, do you want some breakfast? You must be hungry after your flight."

I really do, but also, that bed looks so good right now. "Thanks, but I think I need a nap first, if that's okay. I couldn't sleep on the plane."

"Oh, that's awful. Red-eyes are the worst." Mrs. Grey squinches her eyebrows together sympathetically and seems like she's about to comfort me further when Austin gives her a look. She stops, her hand hanging in midair, and then corrals Zoe like the expert she obviously is. "Come on. Fan club time is over. Let's let Love get some sleep."

The two of them leave Austin behind. "I'm really glad you're here," he says.

"Yeah, me too," I say. "Thanks again for having me." Inside my bag, my phone starts buzzing with notifications again. I guess the West Coast haters are getting their lazy asses out of bed and back into my mentions because what else is there to do?

Last night on my way to the airport, I posted a pic of me in the back of my Uber, with a caption that read:

> **@LoveThompson** Everything that's happened in the past few weeks has changed my life, FR. Lil' D and I aren't good for each other right now so we've decided to take a break. We'll always be in each other's lives though, no matter what. I'm heading to the Midwest for some chill time and to see a new friend. Getting back to my roots. More soon! #takingabreak #timeforsomeselfcare #heartachegirlie #friendsforever #consciousuncoupling

Damien posted something similar on his socials so people wouldn't think I dumped him or vice versa. The comments are all over the place. Anxiety starts rolling through me. Austin watches me as he putters around the room.

"Don't even look at that right now. Just get some rest," he says as he lowers the blinds, shutting out the garden and the tree.

"Thank you, Austin." I squeeze his hand. "Really. I appreciate this."

"Don't sweat it." He raps his knuckles on the desk. "I have to go to the diner today, sorry— I have a few things to deal with on the business side that I can't put off, but I have backup for the next few days so we can hang."

"Oh, it's totally fine."

Damn. Is he *running* the diner? I assumed it was just a part-time thing.

"Okay," he says. "My mom will be here until this afternoon if you need anything."

"Bye, Austin."

"Bye, Love." He leaves me alone in the stillness of this small room. I lie down and let the soft sounds of his family moving around the house become a music that relaxes me. I run my fingers over the journal, then open it and flip through its thick, empty pages.

The notes of a song that doesn't exist yet play where I can't quite hear them.

For the first time since the night of the crash, I feel like I can breathe. And for some reason, that makes me cry.

Hard.

• • •

Later, there's a knock at the door and I twitch awake.

"Come in," I say automatically. Then I realize I probably have mascara all over my face, and my hair has got to be a mess. I try to flatten it and look around frantically for my sunglasses, but it's too late. Austin is already walking in.

"Hey," he says, scanning me with concern, eyes shooting to the tissues on the bedside table and the general mess that I am. I'm not a person who can hide when I've been crying, which is why I try not to let it happen very often.

That hasn't been working lately.

"Did I wake you up?" he asks.

"No. Well, yes, but I'm glad. I shouldn't have slept so long." The light that slips through the blinds in the guest room is the blue-gray color that follows sunset and my heart sinks. I must have slept all day. I need water and a shower and to brush my teeth. My stomach grumbles. I never ate. Chris must be going crazy. I was supposed to start building trust and content, but now I'm going to be a day behind. I need to stow my chaos away and try to remember what I'm here for.

"I just got home so don't worry. I'm sure you needed it." He pauses. "The thing is, I planned a little surprise for your first night here, but I can totally cancel if you don't feel up to it."

He's wearing a hoodie and jeans and his hair is wet, probably from a shower. He looks delicious and it sounds like maybe the day is not totally lost. I perk up.

"No! I'm totally up for it." I get to my feet, zip up my hoodie. "When do we have to go?"

"Fifteen minutes ago. I'm late too." He rubs the back of his neck. "I got caught up at work. But I think we can still make it if we leave in the next half hour."

"Give me twenty?" I say. "I *love* surprises!"

"Oh good." He grins. "I'll let them know." He makes to leave the room, then turns back. "Make sure you bring something warm, but also wear something not. And I know you're probably starving so I packed you some food . . . all vegan."

"Thanks," I say. He remembered?

This is why I picked him, and also why I shouldn't have. If I had gone with one of the celebrity options, it would all have been planned, no chance of hurting anyone. But every chance for someone to hurt me for their own agenda. *Selfish*, a little voice pipes up.

But I'm here now and I can't risk turning back.

"I'll be right out and ready to hang," I say, psyching myself up like I'm about to perform. "Trust me."

CHAPTER TWENTY-THREE

Love

Austin's got a beat-up army-green Jeep with old controls and dials, nothing computerized. It's not a Mercedes, but there's something I like about bouncing around in this thing. Zoe's in the back, clutching her beach bag, which clunks around every time Austin makes a move or hits a bump.

"Austin, remind me that we need to discuss your driving," Zoe says as he rolls into the parking lot. "I almost vommed."

"Yeah, or we could just leave you at home next time," Austin says.

"So cranky," she mutters, which makes me laugh. I like her.

I tug on the hem of my miniskirt, feeling self-conscious in it and my shiny silver crop top. I don't know what I was thinking when I packed but I brought some clothes that now seem completely over-the-top. I'm not sure what we're doing tonight but I'm pretty sure it's not a video shoot like this outfit suggests.

"Welcome to Lake Michigan," he says as we come to a stop. "This is our beach."

Even in the dark I can tell this beach is not one where you have to watch your feet so you don't get impaled on a needle or trip over a used condom. More Malibu than Venice, it sits in front of a big-ass house and trees on the cliffs. A fire crackles in the distance.

"I thought maybe you could use a night out. Feet in the sand . . ." Austin trails off like he might be having second thoughts.

I take his hand in mine and squeeze it reassuringly, then leave it there. It's time to get the plan rolling, no matter how awkward I feel about it. But honestly, it feels so natural and reassuring, I barely have to pretend. The thought makes me feel guilty once again though, like I'm betraying Damien, even though he knows about it all. But I can't worry about him if this is going to work. At least he's in rehab and doesn't have his phone, so hopefully he won't have to actually see any of my posts.

"This is exactly what I need," I say. I mean it too. I never get over to the beach anymore, like I did when I first got to LA. Even if I wasn't so busy, it would be impossible without getting mobbed. Everyone I know out there has a pool anyway, but there's always been something about the beach for me that's different . . . a natural wonder.

"I prepped some corn on the cob, street cart–style," Austin says, smiling a little more easily, "fruit salad, grilled veggies, and my friends brought the s'mores, so . . . What do you think?"

"I think . . . thanks. I mean, thank you. It's everything I didn't know I needed . . ." I don't know why my throat feels so big, like it's taking over my body. He's trying so hard, it hurts. But why? He can't have actual feelings for me, can he?

"C'mon," he says.

I let go of his hand and we jump out of the old Jeep, heading for the sand. Zoe is behind us in a pink sweatshirt over her bathing suit, and two good-looking people about our age are already sitting by the fire we're walking toward. Other bonfires dot the beach and as we get closer, a bunch of casual conversations echo our way.

Austin pauses just short of his friends, staring at the next fire over, then he looks back at them. "You serious right now? I thought they were in France."

The guy pulls out a Coke and hands it to Zoe. "They're leaving next week," he says. "I know, dude. I'm sorry. Just ignore them."

"Who?" I ask.

"No one," Austin says in a way that tells me to leave it alone.

I check them out anyway and see it's three guys and two girls, all looking like they belong at a frat house and sorority mixer. The girls are pretty. One has her black hair in pigtails, and the other has a short blond bob. The guys are lining up cans and using a baseball bat to launch them into the night.

"This is Tyler," Austin says, steering my attention back to the fire.

Tyler, tan and shirtless, comes over to me and shakes my hand. "Welcome to Highland Park."

"And this is Paige," Austin says. "Guys, this is Love."

"You're introducing me to her, Austin?" Paige says. "I'm insulted. Not only did I watch you catch her at the mall, like, a hundred times, I am a big fan of all things Grad Girl."

"Thanks so much, Paige. Nice to meet you."

We spread out a comfy striped beach blanket to sit on and Austin starts dealing with the food, pulling containers out of his picnic basket.

"Hot dog?" Tyler asks, lifting up a skewer with a bubbling meat stick impaled on its end.

"She doesn't eat meat," Zoe and Paige say in unison.

"It's true," I say. "Don't eat the homies."

"Sorry." He slides the hot dog into a bun and hands it off to Paige. "I'm a little unprepared. When Austin told me Love Thompson was coming to visit, I assumed you were a catfish and you'd be some old lady from . . ."

"Kentucky," Paige finishes for him.

"Oddly specific," I say.

"It could happen," Tyler says, sliding a new hot dog onto his stick and smirking at Austin. "Don't pretend you're not the perfect target."

"All right, guys, we get it," Austin says. "I'm a lonely guy who uses a BlackBerry and still calls first instead of texting."

"Wait. For real, a BlackBerry?" I say. I don't think I've seen him use his phone yet. What if he actually has a BlackBerry? That would be amazing.

"No," he says, and everyone laughs. Paige hands out sodas and bubbly waters while Austin cooks over the fire. There's no alcohol here and I wonder if that's because of me. He really has thought of everything. I watch him move as the flames crackle and cast shadows on his cheeks until he presents me with corn on the cob, nice and hot.

"Here's to Love," Tyler says, holding up his Dr Pepper once we all have food. "Both the emotion and the person. May they always be real—"

"And not an old lady from Kentucky!" Paige finishes, and I almost choke on my coconut LaCroix.

"Cheers!" I offer, sputtering and laughing. But I can't erase the thought that while I may not be a catfish from Kentucky, I'm not exactly who Austin thinks I am either.

• • •

After dinner, marshmallows melt over the fire until they're perfectly browned, and Austin reaches into the basket again.

"A little something extra," he says.

"Yay, I love s'mores Austin's way!" Paige says.

He pulls some kind of cookie from a container, placing each disc between the marshmallow and the chocolate, before squeezing it all between the graham crackers. "Churro-round s'mores," he says as he flips one over onto a paper plate like he did with Damien's burgers when we first met.

I pause, even though it looks incredible. I've never had one and I haven't eaten sugar in a year. Not one bite of it. I have eaten exactly what my trainer instructed in exactly the prescribed amounts.

I lift the s'more to my lips, and after a second of hesitation, I bite down. Immediately, the truth I have been repressing crystallizes.

I have wasted my life.

Everything, all the goodness in the world, is this: milk chocolate, crisp graham crackers, melted marshmallow, cinnamon sugar.

"You all right over there?" Austin asks.

I get his concern. My eyes are practically rolling back in my head. "Amazing" is all I can say as I finish my last bite.

"This guy," Tyler says. "He's a food wizard."

"Yeah." I lie back to rest my head on the blanket. "He really is."

The moon sits like a fat pancake overhead and the water swishes and sways behind us. Everything inside me settles. Until I check my phone. The IG comments are scrolling at a steady pace, but the only thing I pay attention to is a text from Chris.

WHAT'S WITH THE RADIO SILENCE? it says. YOU NEED TO BE POSTING OFTEN. I'M WAITING.

I feel the tug of a leash around my neck and try not to go all Texas at Chris's tone. Instead, I remind myself that I am a professional, dutifully snap some sweet, wholesome fireside pics to post later, and put the phone away in my bag, so it doesn't get sand in it. I even put it on silent for once. My small, probably insignificant act of rebellion.

"So is it a little weird to have random people know everything about you?" Tyler asks, after a minute.

I scoot up onto my elbows. Immediately I clock that this is an opportunity to build trust like Chris told me to, so my attempts to make myself more approachable online feel authentic, but I don't have to play a part for this.

"They don't," I say. "Just like I don't know my followers beyond their profiles, they don't know me. But it's my job to make it feel like they do. I mean, I try to show my followers a good time, entertain them or whatever, but that's not the reality . . . or it's not the *full* reality of me anyway."

"I thought your whole deal was sharing your life twenty-four seven," he says, confused.

"Yeah, it's not that simple though. My *actual* deal is that I'm a singer and a dancer. The part you see on socials is mostly to keep people thinking about me, I guess." I search for the right words to describe something I didn't understand myself a year ago, that sometimes is still so elusive, I'm not sure I can explain. I do post all the time. And I do share a lot that other people wouldn't. My calloused, disgusting toes after a wicked rehearsal. My messy notebook with cringe ideas for song lyrics. Makeup tips after a whole night out where I look like a zombie. But that's only a small fraction of who I am and there are still things I hide or filter. "I think it's like I only share the parts I want people to see. Even if it's something that seems messy or cringe or whatever, it's in a way I'm in control of, that tells the story of me I want to tell."

Like how Damien and I went out to Joshua Tree the day before the accident. We dressed athleisure cute, like we were going on a hike, snapped selfies and faux-candid shots by the trees so we could caption about getting in touch with nature with these all-natural granola bars that were newly sponsoring us. Then we immediately got back in the car and went home, so D could play video games.

We didn't film that part though, or take selfies of me sitting next to him on the couch, munching on a salad, trying to find my songwriting mojo again while he disemboweled his enemy on the screen. It might sound fake or dishonest, but this is a job for us, and that's the thing about me and Damien: We both understand that. We know when we need to be on and when to let each other be ourselves, too.

Maybe when I'm back and this is all behind us we can sneak away for a beach trip and cheat on our diets with these magical s'mores. Find new ways to be ourselves around each other.

"Guys," Austin says, probably misreading my moment of silence for discomfort. "I think she came here to get away from all the—"

Paige slaps her hand over Austin's mouth. "Tell us more," she says. "And you stay out of it, Austin."

"I'm okay," I tell him. "I'm . . . glad you guys are asking

questions. It's way better than all the people out there who are making assumptions and getting it totally wrong." I get my phone out of my bag, ignoring any and all notifications, and whip through IG until I find a good picture so I can explain a little more. "Take this picture of me in Palm Springs." I'm in a bikini and sunglasses. Tan, thin, muscular, happy. I'm in the pool and there's what looks like that pink, purple, orange sherbet-y sunset—the kind that makes you want to cry—behind me.

"Jealous," Paige says drily, then coughs out, "Sorry, go on."

"Well, don't be jealous," I say. "Because none of that is real."

"You faked the background?" Tyler asks.

"No. But that's not sunset. It's dawn. And it was freezing. I'd been up all night for a commercial shoot. I was completely exhausted, but I needed a post for the day and none of the reality of my day was sexy or interesting in the right way. So when I saw an opportunity for a shot that would make people think my life is aspirational, I had to take it. I just retouched my makeup, climbed into that freezing pool, and had Damien take my photo over and over until I got that shot that would make my followers continue thinking I was worthy of following."

"No way," Tyler says, after taking a closer look at the pic.

"Yep. And that's why I always bring a pair of sunglasses anywhere I go now. They turn any situation into sexy mystery."

"Okay, but hot selfies aren't what made you popular," Paige says. "It was the Grad Girl video. That was totally you, right?"

"Grad Girl . . ." This one hurts, but the moon is so big, I feel small enough to tell the truth one more time. "You watch me rescue my best friend Patty from social destruction, dancing like

I don't care what anyone thinks. That was all me. But what you don't see is that once I became Grad Girl, Patty and I stopped being friends." I don't add that it's my fault, that I blew her off in Boston and now she won't talk to me at all. It made sense at the time. Things were running behind and I was sure they would calm down enough for me to visit soon, but they didn't. They never do. I should have told Chris and D seeing her was a non-negotiable. But I thought Patty would understand. I force myself back to the conversation. "And you don't see what everyone from my hometown called me before that either."

"Which is what?" Zoe asks. She starts in on her second s'more, but she never takes her eyes off me. That little brain of hers is very busy and at first I hesitate. My memories of high school are like the pictures of Austin's dad above the staircase. The pain is so raw, I don't ever want to look at them again.

"Trailerina," I finally say. "It's kind of genius actually, as far as bullying goes. People who live in trailers don't become ballerinas, right? I think they came up with it as a reminder of that, and they made sure I couldn't forget all day, every day, that my dreams were doomed. Even when I first started gaining traction online, they tried to make it some big hashtag for my haters to use, but the more successful I became, the less successful *they* were at getting it to catch on. At least . . . until now."

The night stretches out around us and still no one says anything. Maybe I spilled too much. Maybe I just proved my own point. Maybe I'm just going to keep canceling myself over and over again until I disappear into oblivion.

I look at Austin and he's watching me. They're all watching

me. Part of me wants to break into a dance or something to shatter the heavy energy. But Austin says something first. "Well, I wish you were at my middle school graduation. I walked across the stage with my fly open."

We all burst out laughing and I feel, weirdly, like I belong.

CHAPTER TWENTY-FOUR

Austin

Just as we're all cracking up at my dumb joke, something hits me on the back of my head and bounces off onto the sand. I pick it up. An empty beer can.

And I know exactly who threw it.

"Yo! Sorry, Grey," Chad yells. "It was an accident!"

I can hear in his voice that he's drunk. But I can't look. I don't want to deal with him or worse, Emma, who is right behind him. Not here. Not tonight when everything is going so well.

"It's okay!" I shout back, still not looking, hoping they will just leave me alone.

Zoe gives me a pointed look and purses her lips.

"At least it was an empty can," I tell Zoe.

"Yeah but we all know *you* should be the one throwing things at *him*," Zoe says. "I can't believe you were ever friends with that dick."

"Wait, you know that guy?" Love asks.

"Yeah. That's Chad. He was the captain of the baseball team I was on before I quit for . . . a lot of reasons." I sigh. "Actually, we were also best friends."

"Until he showed who he really is," Paige spits.

"There was a little bit of a rift because of . . . a thing," Tyler adds, finishing vaguely when he sees the look on my face.

Love squints in Chad's direction, so I force myself to follow her gaze. He's still swinging his bat at cans, whipping them all over the beach. Chad may be kind of a tool, but he's got great aim.

In other words, even without the laughter I would have known that can hitting me wasn't an accident.

Emma's in a green one-piece, hair up, pearl earrings in, and when she meets my eyes, she shrugs apologetically.

I look away.

"Real captain material," Love says, rolling her eyes.

"Just ignore him," I say. I don't want this to be the thing Love remembers about tonight.

To my relief, everyone but Love turns back to the fire and watches the flames flicker. I add another log. "More s'mores?"

Everyone shakes their heads. We're all well-fed, it's a beautiful night, and other than the last few minutes, it's been nice, really nice. Love held my hand on the drive down here, Ty and Paige seem to like her, and maybe she's just acting, but she doesn't seem totally bored by our humble beach hang either. Exactly what I was hoping for, that here she could see a little of what makes this place special.

"Love," Ty says, "please don't take this the wrong way, but you're not what I expected."

"Superficial, you mean?" To my relief, Love finally wrenches her eyes away from Chad and looks at Ty, her mouth turning up in a wry smile.

"Yeah. You're actually sort of cool."

Love laughs just as I feel another thwap on the back of my head. This time there's the sting of metal against my skin as the can hits me with extra velocity. "Ow!" I say before I can stop myself.

"That's it." Love bounces up and is on her feet before I can stop her. She tears across the sand and I rush to catch up, Zoe close behind me.

"Hey! Where are you going?" I call to her, trying to get her to slow down, but she's picking up speed.

"I hate a fucking bully. Chad needs to learn some manners," she calls back.

"Yusss," Zoe says.

"Zoe!" I snap.

"Well, he does."

I lengthen my strides until I'm right on Love's tail. "This is technically his beach. That's his house up there."

"Like I give two shits. Privilege doesn't mean you can just go around assaulting people. That's not okay."

Chad sees us coming and I try to picture what it must look like in his head. This tiny girl stomping over to him, looking like she's about to kick his ass. Emma's still sitting by their fire, eyes shooting back and forth between them, while Tom and Simon laugh obliviously as if they all weren't once my friends.

"What's your problem?" Love says, wasting no time getting in Chad's face.

He looks confused by the question, dulled by the beer.

"C'mon, let's—" I say.

"What's your problem?" Chad sways, face contorted as he adds, "Bitch."

"Whoa, dude," I say, but Love throws out an arm, letting me know she can handle this. She doesn't need rescuing this time.

"My problem," she says, "is that you think it's okay to hit beer cans at people on the beach who are minding their own business, trying to enjoy the night. What the fuck?"

Chad chuckles and looks from side to side at Tom and Simon, like, *Can you believe this?* "It's my beach. I do what I want."

"Yeah, funny, that's what Austin said. Thing is, I'm pretty sure it's your dad's beach," Love says. "Or your mom's. Am I right?"

"Huh?" Chad says stupidly.

"It's definitely not *yours*," Love presses. "You have not *earned* your own beach, right?"

Chad finally looks over at me. "Austin, who's this mouthy cunt?"

Love's eyes widen and for just a second, I can see the down-home Texas girl in her, ready to scrap.

"Whoa, dude," I say, "get your shit under control. You need to apologize to her."

"No, no, no, Austin." Love never takes her eyes off Chad. "Please, go ahead. What was that, now? What did you say?" She leans in until there's no space between them. "Say it again so I can fucking—"

"Oh my God, you're Love Thompson!" Emma squeals. Somewhere in the last two minutes she has stood up, and now she's pulling Chad away from Love. "I'm sorry about him. I . . . I love you."

"Huh?" Chad says, looking around dully again.

"Grad Girl . . . ," Emma says through gritted teeth as she pokes Chad in the kidney. It brings him to life and recognition falls over him.

"Holy shit." Chad's mouth drops open, making him look even more like a buffoon.

"Doesn't matter who I am," Love says. "You shouldn't treat anyone like that." She glares at Emma. "And you could do a lot better, sis." She pauses. "A *lot*."

Emma's gaze automatically reaches for mine and holds it. My stomach thumps and turns. My heartbeat picks up. I try to pull my eyes away but I can't.

Finally, Emma breaks the stare, turning to Chad, face flushed.

"Apologize to her," she says to him in a low voice.

Chad bobbles, looking from me to Emma to Love. He seems to be considering the consequences of his next move.

"Uh . . . look, I'm sorry," Chad says finally. "And you're right. It is my mother's beach." He clears his throat.

Love waves her hand in his face and he zips it. This is amazing. I find myself leaning back on my heels like I'm watching a show.

"Okay, so you're a bully *and* a liar," Love says. She is totally unaffected by the change in his tone. He did just call her a cunt, so . . .

"No, I'm not. I'm a nice person," Chad argues.

I grin, because he sounds like a three-year-old who just dropped his ice cream on the floor and is stomping his foot to demand another.

"Then tell me why you would hit your old teammate in the head with a beer can?" Love puts her hands on her hips. "That's not a *nice* thing to do, is it?"

He reddens. "Uh . . . it was an accident."

Love shakes her head, clearly not satisfied with his explanation.

"Love, it's okay. Let's—" I start.

"So why did you do that?" she insists.

Chad mumbles something at the ground.

"What was that?" Love cups her ear.

"Austin got his feelings hurt and quit the team to fuck us over, just because his ex dumped him for me," Chad says. He turns on me. "I know you were pissed, Grey, but you killed all our chances of getting scouted when the team tanked without you. We *needed* you."

I don't even know how to respond to that. That's why he's been such a dick? He didn't get recruited because he's not D1 good. Neither am I. That's just how it goes. But he's such a self-centered asshole he thinks me quitting was about him and Emma, not about saving the diner or, you know, my dad *dying*.

Love registers shock, then understanding as she turns her focus to Emma. "You?"

Emma looks away.

"Oh man," Love says, "you fucked up real bad."

"So did he," Chad says to me stubbornly.

Love makes like she's going to lunge at him and he stumbles backward into Emma, who immediately pushes him off. It looks like she's suddenly taking Love's assertion very seriously.

Love isn't done. "Maybe," she says, "Austin had to quit the team because he doesn't *own* the beach." She gives him a disgusted glare. "Did you ever think about that, narcissistic dirtbag?"

Chad clutches himself like she just delivered a death blow.

Love loops her arm through mine, done with him now. "C'mon," she says, leaning her head on my shoulder. "Let's go."

When we turn around, back in our crew's direction, my euphoria is short-lived because I see Zoe has her phone pointed straight at us.

"How long have you been recording?" I ask. The look of triumph and the way her eyes glint and glimmer give me my answer. She filmed this whole thing.

"Don't post that." This is supposed to be a romantic night, not getting Love into another online scandal. This is not the vibe we're going for.

"It's live," Zoe says, shrugging. "Sorry, Chad!"

"Oh."

Poor Love. She can't even get a second of privacy, of just living, even out here. I don't know what I would do if that were me. I'd probably be certifiable.

"Hey," Love says, shaking my attention from death-glaring at Zoe. "Will you make me another s'more?"

Love hasn't stopped touching me since we left Chad across the beach, which is kind of surprising. She doesn't know all the details of my breakup with Emma, but I would have expected her to think I'm weak or pathetic. She doesn't seem to think that at all.

First, she rested a hand over my thigh while she was reaching for something. Then she played with my fingers, and even squeezed my bicep when she made a joke about me having to catch her at the mall. Now she's walking just ahead of me on our way back to the car and if I didn't have my picnic basket in my arms, I get the feeling we'd be holding hands again. All things that would have seemed impossible three days ago.

Tyler, Paige, and Zoe are carrying their bags back to the cars in front of us and it's silent except for the sound of the occasional car. I feel silent too, calm for the first time in a while. I breathe Love in, sip her presence. She's only supposed to be here for a week and then she goes back to LA, to her life. But one day in,

I already don't want her to go. It's like I've stumbled into a glass atrium filled with sun. Love shivers, which gives me the perfect moment to shift the basket under one arm and put the other around her. She leans into me again easily.

"You're wrong, you know," I say.

"About what?"

"About hiding who you really are. I just saw her back there. The OG Grad Girl, sticking up for the little guy. Although in this case, the little guy is six foot one."

She stops and pulls away from me. "You watched the original video? Oh God."

"Yeah, I watched it. Actually, it helped get me through a really hard day. Zoe, too."

"Oh. Well, I'm glad about that," she says, sounding surprised. "What was the hard day?"

We walk in silence for a second. "Nothing. No big deal, really." I can never talk about Dad to anyone except Zoe and Mom, and barely even then. Besides, it's not exactly a romantic subject.

"Okay . . . well, then, what did you like about it? That first video, I mean."

I remember back to her grinding on that lady, all the teachers trying to corral her while she danced her heart out. "How you made a special day going south into something legendary." *That's what she does with everything,* I think. "You're awesome. I could never do what you do."

"Not a dancer, eh?"

"No." I don't tell her I can be, when the need arises. I'll keep that in my pocket. "But I meant being a public figure . . . I would never want to do that." I got thousands of followers on my dinky personal IG and started getting some wild DMs, too, after the mall and diner videos, but I set everything to private pretty quick after that. "There's a lot that goes along with it that I couldn't deal with. You have to be special to handle it like you do."

"Yeah, okay, but life outside of the socials has problems too. I mean, people judge you IRL, too, right? Is your life always fun?" she asks.

I flinch.

"I didn't think so." She sighs. "No matter what, there are good days and bad. Fans and haters."

There's so much I want to say, but maybe not here, not now, with Zoe and Paige and Ty nearby. So I nod and we continue walking. This time she threads her arm through mine. "Speaking of haters, it seems like I got in the middle of some history there."

"Yeah," I say reluctantly, but I do owe her an explanation after what she did. "Emma . . . she broke up with me at a really bad time, at the end of junior year. Then I wound up quitting the baseball team and they were down their clutch spot hitter, which I guess he thinks was all about him, which it wasn't. And yeah, if that wasn't bad enough, I recently realized that it had been going on between them for a while before she broke up with me and I didn't see it because I was preoccupied, dealing with other things. And, well, I haven't really dated anyone else since."

"Really?" she asks, eyebrows raised. "That's hard to believe."

"It's just complicated. But . . . well, thanks for saying what you did."

"It was only the truth," she says. "Chad is an eleven on the douche scale and now I know Emma is right around there too. You, on the other hand, are definitely not."

I still don't know how to reconcile the Emma I thought I knew, who was by my side at the worst, with the one who lied and did all this. But it feels kind of good to have someone drag her in my defense. "And you?" I ask, turning to the subject I've been curious about since our FaceTime. "What about Damien?"

"That's complicated too. We've been through a lot together. I don't think I would be where I am if it wasn't for him. But . . . we're not in the same place we were when we met, you know? It got toxic, so it's over."

Over.

The alarm bells in my head switch off for once. For the first time in almost a year, my heart is light with hope.

CHAPTER TWENTY-FIVE

Love

Paige and Zoe and Tyler are skipping toward the pier ahead of us, laughing and carefree.

I hesitate, because this is going to be awkward, and I don't want to ruin everything, but I'm going to have to ask this at some point, so it might as well be now while he thinks I'm a good person.

"Austin," I say.

"Mmm?"

"You know how my reputation is destroyed and everything?"

"Yeah?"

"Uh . . . well, I know you're not a socials guy but if I want to salvage my career, I can't go totally dark. I . . . I still want to take a step back, but I was thinking about what we talked about at the fire, and this week I think it would be really good . . . helpful, I mean . . . if I could show my followers more of the real me."

"Okaaay . . . ," he says, casting a confused look my way.

"What I mean is, there's some stuff I've always wanted to do, like visiting some Chicago landmarks and stuff, and I think it would be cool if we did it together. When I was little and trapped in Texas, I always wanted to see the rest of the country, and even being on tour I've basically seen the inside of my hotel room, the gym, and whatever venue we were going to. It would be a total dream come true to see Chicago . . . with you." I watch his face for a reaction but I can't tell what he's thinking. "So . . . since you're off work and everything, could we maybe pick a few places to visit, and would you mind me taking some pictures, making some reels of us doing it?"

"Well—"

"You don't have to do anything. I'll take care of it."

He watches me for a long minute and then, finally, he nods.

"It's just part of my job," I say, letting my body bump against his. "My life, and unfortunately anyone who's in it, kind of has to be open to it." I wait and he doesn't say anything, so I add, "Are you? Open to it?"

"Yes," he says. "Um . . . I mean, I'll get used to it."

"People are going to recognize you. They're going to know you're the guy who caught me and it might be more intense than last time." I don't know what possesses me to say this when I really can't afford for him to say no here.

"Yeah . . . that's okay, I think," he says when we reach the top of the pier, surprising me. "I told you to come here for whatever you need, Love, so really. I can handle it."

"That's really great of you," I say, feeling like complete trash even though I should be thrilled. "Just tell me if you change your mind. I'm a big girl. I can show myself around Chicago."

"Not a chance!" Austin says. "You need a native to show you the real best spots."

I grin, but I'm starting to understand now what allowed that dummy girl to think she could break up with him and date his friend. What made his friend think he was allowed to hit him with beer cans. And it's what allowed me to manipulate him into inviting me here, to think I could get him to go along with this wild plan. Austin is too nice for his own good. At the expense of his own good actually.

Thankfully, Tyler interrupts my shame spiral by putting the box he's been carrying down and opening it.

"What are these?" I ask, peering into the box.

"A highly illegal Illinois tradition . . . ," Tyler says, handing me a cylinder. "Fireworks from Indiana."

"Don't worry—we still have all our fingers," Austin says. "Come on. I'll show you how."

Austin leads me down to the water, then puts his arms around me, Roman candle in hand. My body warms against his and I let my weight sink backward. He traces my arm, then eases it upward until I'm gripping the firework too. Pleasant, unexpected chills run up and down my skin.

"Now point it out to the water," he whispers, lips nearly brushing my ear in a way that does things to me. "And don't drop it."

"Okay," I say, breathy. *It doesn't mean anything,* I tell myself.

I grip it tight in both hands as Austin lets go to get the lighter out of his pocket. Once lit, the wick burns so much quicker than I expect, like a stick of TNT, then—

WHAM! A bright red ball of flame shoots into the sky and I gasp.

We fire one after another until the entire night is alive with magic. I keep myself wrapped against him the whole time, like it's a real fireworks show just for us. Damien and I had everything, could do anything. Why did we never just hang out like this and watch the sky light up?

Austin's arms are strong and calming and I'm surprised by how my body is responding to his, how I'm thinking about what it would have been like if I had done what I wanted when we were in the diner, and kissed him on the mouth, not his cheek. Just like then, my pull to him is achy, stronger than makes sense. Maybe that's why I wanted to come here. Maybe subconsciously I wanted to know more.

As soon as I have the thought, I'm filled with guilt. Damien helped me from day one. We're meant to be. I knew it before I was Grad Girl. So why does this feel so good?

"This never happens," Austin says.

"What's that?"

"Oh . . . things going the way I want them to . . . so thank you for that."

A new wave of guilt slaps into me. I know firsthand that things going the way you want them to isn't always what you think it's going to be. But I want Austin to feel this way right now. Just a little, just for now.

What I wasn't expecting is that I would be feeling this way too.

Later that night, when I'm back at Austin's, I pick up the journal he gave me and turn to a fresh, clean page. The paper quality is good, thick, and I curl up under the blankets with it and a pen. I close my eyes, let the night play out again. That tune that's been slipping in and out of my head since I arrived starts up again. I could almost hum it. Lyrics trickle in and out of my thoughts, getting louder, clearer, as I replay each firework bursting through the night.

After a moment, a phrase comes through clear, the song

beginning to reveal itself in the way that tells me I'm onto something. I write it down.

I go to sleep

Drowning in the ocean

Then I follow where it takes me.

CHAPTER TWENTY-SIX

Love

My phone buzzes me awake with an email notification.

From: FionaJackson@impressionpartners.com
To: gradgirl@lalaland.com
Subject: SUPER AMAZING DATE WEEK

Hey Love,

Here's what the team came up with to hit all the beats of a romantic week. Exciting, frothy, and will give all your followers some Chicago flavor.

I got your SOS about the clothes sitch, so I did a little shopping and a package will be expressed to you this afternoon. Think denim, athleisure, sneakers, flats, a couple of pastel florals (so in this year). You, but natural. Light gloss and mascara only and a little highlighter if you need it. An "I'm sweet and innocent and fun" vibe.

I've attached details, with maps and inspo pics, so you

know exactly what Chris is looking for. Make sure you use the hashtag #myhero, okay?

Here are the broad strokes of the plan:

MONDAY: Mount the Lions at the Art Institute of Chicago, Chicago-style pizza to follow, of course. (We'll preorder for the photo op but you can get something else to actually eat when you're there)
TUESDAY: Stay close to home. Lean in to the cozy suburb of it all.
WEDNESDAY: Snaps at the Bean. Super touristy and kitschy is relatable.
THURSDAY: Ride the Wheel (at sunset for max golden hour shots that tease the romance unfolding)
FRIDAY: Seal the Deal (Chris says a kiss by end of the week is a MUST)

Further details to come!

Let me know if you have any questions and Chris wants me to remind you as soon as we hit 50M again, we can pull the plug. (Oh and that she'll be watching every step of the way.) She was a little crabby about your minimalist approach to the socials yesterday so . . . crank it up!

Best,
Fi

PS The #myhero guy is super hot!

The journal is still open on the pillow next to my head, and the pen rolls off when I sit up. I shut it gently, trying to remember when the flow of writing led to the deep, satisfying sleep I've just awoken from.

The phone buzzes. It's a call. Before I check the screen, my first thought is that it's Damien, that maybe he somehow got his phone back, saw the live stream from the beach, and is feeling jealous. Or maybe he just wants to check up on me. That would be sweet.

But it's not D.

It's Chris. Her new user photo appears, her in a maxi dress smiling broadly, holding a glass of champagne, standing under a tree.

Chris at rest?

Improbable.

"Who died?" I ask, before Chris can say anything. "Just get it over with quick and put me down like the dog I am."

"No one's dead," she says, and I hear the whir of the treadmill going in the background. I can much more easily see her there in her Yasss Queen T-shirt, snapback on—with her cell, iPad, laptop, and desktop all cranking at full speed—than on vacation. "Have you looked at your socials today?"

"No." It's almost eleven, so that makes it nine in LA, meaning I was her first call. That doesn't seem good. I slap the phone back against my ear. "I'm not exactly adjusted to the time here yet, and Austin and his family don't seem to want to disturb me."

"Good, good, you need the rest. Take it while you can."

My anxiety beast squeezes at me even more intensely because Chris *never* suggests rest. I don't even want to ask the next question, but I have to. I shut my eyes, try to visualize happiness, ease, joy. Unbidden, I feel Austin's arms wrapped around me last night. All the softness and sweetness comes back in flashes, but then I force my lids open again because that is nuts.

Austin and I are not a real thing.

"What happened?"

"I'll wait while you look," she says. My stomach is already flipping all around like a dying fish. I can't read her tone. Maybe there's a fresh crop of trolls demanding blood, for me to discover.

I throw her on speaker and open TikTok. Video clips flash across the screen. Me with my finger in Chad's face, pointing at him. I barely recognize myself. I look very short because I am, but also kind of fierce, and for the first time in weeks I sit up straighter. Off to the side, Austin is watching and he looks . . . proud. *Really* proud. I lean up against one of the gray linen pillows on the bed and search the stats on the original.

"2.5M likes"

"20K comments"

"100K shares"

It's captioned, "#myhero @lovethompson."

Zoe.

That diabolical little genius.

"Does this mean I can get my single back?" I ask hopefully.

Maybe everything Chris wanted has been accomplished on day one.

Maybe this can all be over before Austin gets hurt.

"Not quite," Chris says. "Your failed sobriety test is still trending across all platforms. But the social-mob tide might be turning."

"Great . . . ," I say.

There's a knock at the door that startles me back into this room.

"Come in," I call, and straighten my pink camisole set, pulling my strap back over my shoulder.

It's Austin. He's in a T-shirt and shorts, definitely coming straight from a workout. But his sweaty face is still adorable: friendly, generous. He scans me, pausing at my neck, my collarbone, my exposed midriff, all the way down my bare legs, before forcing himself back to my eyes, gluing his attention to a safe spot.

"How'd you sleep?" he starts.

Before I can answer, Chris chirps from the phone, still on speaker. "Oooh, is that him?"

"Yes . . . ," I say.

"God, even his voice is sexy," Chris purrs.

"You're on speaker!" I cut her off. Then, I usher Austin into the hallway before Chris can say anything else.

He drops his mouth open like he's going to say something but I close the door, take Chris off speaker, and start rooting through my stuff for anything that feels not too overblown until Fiona's package arrives. "We're alone again," I tell her.

"Sorry," she says. "You got Fi's itinerary?"

"I did."

"And you saw the plan? Most important part is at the end of it, you're going to bring it all home with a kiss photo." I hear the treadmill pad come to a stop. "That ought to do it."

"Are you sure we should rush things?" I whisper, afraid Austin might hear me. "A kiss on camera in a week? He's not really into that stuff."

"Hmm . . . well, frame it a different way. Tell him you're making up for lost time, as in those wasted weeks after he saved you in front of the world." She squeals. "It's so ideal. I mean, thanks to Jeremy Allen White, blue collar and Chicago are trending. I'm a genius."

"Okaaay . . . ," I say, fighting the urge to remind her choosing Austin was my idea.

"And it will be so romantic, it'll feel organic. Your first real kiss as a couple is going to be above the city lights, with fireworks . . . real ones, not whatever Podunk firecrackers he showed you last night. It'd be criminal *not* to kiss."

It's like she doesn't even see Austin as a real person. What if he doesn't *want* to kiss me? What if he catches on to this whole thing? I can just see him, the disappointed expression he'd get, those gorgeous lips of his frowning. "*If* it happens . . ."

Chris sighs. "Right, right, if it happens, when it happens, same thing. Just stay light and fun, but do every single thing on the list and post."

I whisper, "Got it. Keep it spontaneous and stick to the script."

The irony is lost on Chris. "Exactly. Then you can come home; act like he broke up with you; explain you're heartbroken, which will elicit even *more* sympathy; and finally, you and Damien can stage a reunion, after how much you've both grown. The people will eat. It. Up. And you, my dear, will be in the perfect position to release your redemption song that will take us right to the top of the charts. Okay, my nine thirty is here. I have to bounce. *Mwah!*"

I open the door again. Austin's still waiting right outside.

"Sorry," I say. "Chris can be . . . a lot."

"It's okay," he says. "Just so you know, I wasn't listening or anything."

I don't know what to say and the pause gets awkward.

"New topic." He flashes me a big smile. "Where are we going first on your list?"

CHAPTER TWENTY-SEVEN

Love

First up on Fiona's list is the Art Institute in the city on Michigan Avenue, and thank goodness for her clothes delivery. I've got some shorts and a cute white tee on, plus some lily earrings and a simple necklace to match. As ordered, I have toned down the makeup and thrown on some Converse.

I know I should feel like I'm wearing a costume, but I don't. I actually feel kind of . . . free, more like I used to back home, before I started dressing to be seen every day.

We take the train and then walk twenty-five minutes to get to our destination. Chicago is supposed to be the Windy City or whatever, but it seems ideal to me, nice and cool with just enough sun. I wasn't lying about how much I've wanted to actually see the places we've been passing through. A quick lion photo seems like a small price to pay for getting to actually explore it.

When we get there though, I see they are enormous. Like, so much bigger than I was expecting, and green with time like the Statue of Liberty. They are also looking a little judgy, if I'm being real. Fiona's itinerary said to get some shots of us snuggling up on top of the lions, but I have no idea how we're going to do that.

Austin must not either. "You sure about this?" he says.

"Yep," I say, though I'm not at all.

"I guess what's more classic Grad Girl than climbing them just to get a pic?"

"Exactly."

Austin looks around for a minute, then jumps on the lion pedestal and climbs onto its back. He makes it look easy. Once he's saddled up, he leans down to give me a hand. I grab his outstretched arm and he hoists me behind him in one sweeping move.

Even though Austin is probably hating this, he says, "How do you want me?"

"Just smile like you're having fun."

He leans back a little and I wrap my arms around his waist. "I am having fun," he says. "I'm with you."

Butterflies fly through my insides. I catch my breath and for a second, forget how to exhale. We smile, snap a selfie, then Austin jumps back down. "Give me your phone and I'll take another picture," he says. "No one's going to want to look at me."

Apparently, he has not visited the internet if he doesn't know he's trending.

"Okay," I say, suddenly feeling shy up here alone. "That would be nice."

I note that people have stopped to stare and a couple of them are pointing at me.

"But we better hurry!" I add. My reputation may be in rehab but as Chris said, I'm not out of the woods yet, and I'm not exactly inconspicuous up here.

That point is proven further when a cop approaches behind Austin. He does *not* look happy. My smile holds but my stomach goes liquid as I flash back to the night of the wreck.

Austin snaps the picture, then offers me his hand again.

"Miss—" the cop says.

"She's getting down." Austin cuts him off, already deftly escorting me back to solid ground.

"All right," the cop says. "Stay off there, would ya? The last thing we need is another trend. Public safety and all."

"Yes sir," Austin says, with not a trace of sarcasm. His voice is calm but his hands shake slightly.

Once the cop is gone, we both breathe a sigh of relief.

"What should we do next?" Austin says. "Climb the Hancock?"

"Um, no," I say. "I think I need to keep my feet on the ground for a while. I was thinking something more along the lines of . . . pizza?"

Uno's Pizzeria, the sign reads.

It's supposed to be legendary, and Austin tells me it's been here since 1943. I get a confirmation from OpenTable right on time and they seat us at the window looking out onto the busy street. We settle in, and the waiter, who has a giant mustache, immediately drops off a Diet Coke with a lime for me and a Coke for Austin.

"We got your preorder," he says. "I'll be back with your food soon."

"Whoa," Austin says, looking from the glasses to the long line of people waiting to get in. "You really do get special treatment."

I shrug, feeling self-conscious about it, and my face. I'm basically "au naturel" right now and Austin keeps staring at me, so I wonder if I grew a blemish I didn't see or if maybe without makeup I'm more terrible to look at than I thought.

Waiter with Epic Mustache circles back with a pizza in hand. And it's . . . a calorie bomb. When I first started with Jamie, my trainer, he taught me how to quickly add up the calories of anything I ate. And the deep-dish pizza in front of me is a two-inch-thick slab of buttery crust, tart marinara, and melted cheese topped with a layer of vegetables probably cooked in more butter. My nutritional spidey sense says four thousand calories for the whole pie, or around what I eat over two and a half days. I don't even want to think what the dairy and gluten will do to my innocent insides . . .

But then why am I salivating?

"One Farmer's Market pizza for you to share," the waiter says, not giving me any extra attention at all, which I like. I see where it gets its name. This thing could feed an entire market.

"Is this going to work for your diet?" Austin says as if reading my mind.

I inhale, reconsidering some life choices, which allows the steam rising off the pie to hit me like a tidal wave . . . the most pungent oregano . . . the perfectly burnt crust . . . OMG. I quickly wave Austin off. "Cheat day!" I say.

The guy is about to leave when this time I stop him and hand him my phone. "Could you take a picture of us?" I ask. Chris and Fiona will come for me if I forget. And anyway, a part of me does want to remember this . . . sitting here with this sweet guy on a good day in Chicago, eating what I want and wearing what I want.

"Of course," he says.

Austin leans across the table toward me, and we both point to the pizza and grin like we're having the best time ever.

Then I take a bite. The feel of the bready crust is foreign on my tongue: crispy, salty, incredible. But the cheese . . . the *cheese*!

He watches me for a second before taking his own bite and chewing thoughtfully.

"I thought you were vegan," he says, once he's swallowed. He takes a pull of his straw.

"I've been vegetarian a long time, but I've only been vegan since I moved to LA. And this is supposed to be the best."

"And you're sure you'll be okay with that much dairy?" He looks worried, for my soul, and my stomach. "It's a lot of cheese for me and I'm a pizza connoisseur."

"Yeah," I say, still distracted by the taste on my tongue.

"Okaaay," he singsongs, and I chomp down another huge, yummy bite.

"Sometimes there are things that are more important than dietary restrictions. Like pizza." I grin at him.

"I'm getting the sense you like playing with fire," he says, grinning back as he serves himself another fat slice.

I guess maybe I do, because aren't I always? Seems like everything I do is a tightrope and I'm always about to fall off, like that escalator. It's tiring though, always trying to keep from hitting the ground.

I went from invisible, never having done anything—no high school dances, no kissing under the bleachers—to having everything I do under a microscope for fifty million people to view.

Yeah, I can't give that up, but for once I want to have a tiny moment of balance, even if it is on a knife's edge. For once, I'm not missing out.

CHAPTER TWENTY-EIGHT

Austin

"You okay in there?" I call through the bathroom door at home. I don't want to be intrusive or anything, but the noises coming out of the bathroom are . . . not good.

Like, throwing up followed by loud burping noises I didn't know could come out of that small a person.

"Jesus," Zoe says, staring at the bathroom. "Monstrous."

Uno's is legendary but if *I* had been the one to order, I would have made sure to go with the gluten-free thin crust. Another eruption of gags and groans floods the hallway. If Mom were here, she would know what to do, but she's at the diner. Seems like the cook who's subbing for the week is doing a good job since she's only texted me once to ask where I keep the extra smashburger press. So that's encouraging.

Another riot of noise bursts from the bathroom.

"Zoe, can you go make some tea?" I say. "Mint or chamomile or something?"

"Why don't *you* go make her tea and *I'll* stay here?" If she was giddy over Love before she came here this week, she's obsessed with her now.

"Because I'm asking you," I say.

She crosses her arms.

"Please."

She rolls her eyes but finally pads off to the kitchen, where I can hear water sloshing into the kettle.

I knock on the door again. "Hey, Love," I call, a little louder this time. "Is there anything I can do for you?"

"No!" she says in a strained voice. "I'm fine."

The toilet flushes and she comes out, sweaty and pale, yet somehow still totally gorgeous. Today was the first time I've ever seen her pared back to bare bones and while she is objectively stunning either way, without as much makeup it's like I can see more of her, not just the glamour. It feels rare, like I'm privileged to be one of the people to see her like this. She said she picks and chooses what to show, and it feels like I'm getting to see parts of her I've never seen on Instagram. Unfiltered.

"I really fucked up with that one, huh?" she says, a little color coming back to her cheeks.

"I did try to warn you . . ."

She pales again.

"I'm sorry." I want to touch her, to make her feel better. "I'm just glad you're okay."

"'Okay' might be an exaggeration, but I don't need to go to urgent care or anything." She takes a deep breath and smiles wanly. "I'm sorry. This is totally mortifying. If you give me a shovel, I'll go bury myself in your backyard."

An aggressive belch escapes her and she covers her mouth with her hand. "Oh no."

"You need to go again?"

She shakes her head. "No, I think I've gotten rid of everything."

We both slide down the wall, facing each other so our legs

are entwined. She's in an oversized button-down shirt and white ankle socks. Her hair is messy, and her hands worry at her shirt collar in a way that is ridiculously sexy.

"Do you want to go back to bed?" I ask, trying to pivot my thoughts away from her jawline, her collarbone, her long neck. Everything about her is so compelling, it's like I have no control over my thoughts or where my eyes linger.

"Why, Austin," she says, like an old movie star, "how forward of you."

Or apparently what I say.

"I mean . . . ," I say, "do *you* want to go to bed? Not *us* . . . ugh . . . I just meant, you don't have to feel pressured to hang out with me."

"In bed?" She raises an eyebrow and smiles.

"Yes . . . I mean, no. Stop fucking with me, would you?"

She smirks. "Fine, you know what I want?" she says. "I want to lie on a couch. Watch a movie. Not think about anything else for a minute."

I stand and pull her up to her feet. "Okay, I've got the perfect thing."

My dad's collection of John Hughes movies is sacred. He had all of them, from *Sixteen Candles* to *Uncle Buck*. John Hughes was from here and Dad always said each of those movies, even the ones that haven't aged well, capture something special about Chicagoland, from its class systems to its humor. Every DVD is in mint condition and never leaves this house.

When I open the drawer, Love standing behind me, I expect her to instantly point to a favorite but instead she says, "I haven't seen any of those."

"Not *The Breakfast Club*?"

"No."

"*Sixteen Candles*?"

"Nope."

"Not even *Ferris Bueller's Day Off*? How can that *be*?"

"I don't know. They're old?"

"Classics!"

"I'm busy!"

I crane my neck to look at her. "Do you not watch movies? TV?"

"TikTok, YouTube, reels," she says, putting up a finger for each one. "Gotta keep my eyes on the trends."

I can't even conceive of not having movies in my life, especially these.

"I work out first thing in the morning and then I have to practice routines, set up social events—all that stuff, all day. And Damien . . ." She stops, seems to want to stuff the word back in her mouth.

I cringe at the thought of him, but say, "Go on."

"He played a lot of video games. That's all."

"Sounds like a douche canoe." Zoe has come from the kitchen, where she has clearly been eavesdropping. She hands Love one of the brown coffee mugs we brought home from the diner and says, "I wasn't sure if you take honey?"

"No sugar for me, but thanks," Love says, but there's something the tiniest bit prickly about it. I think she's about to defend Damien or talk more about it, but she takes a sip instead.

Zoe plops down on the couch and stares at the TV expectantly. "I suggest we start with *Ferris Bueller's Day Off*." She shoves her hand into a box of Cheez-Its. "And then I'd go *Breakfast Club*."

"Zoe!" I'm still not over her filming us last night and now she's just sat down in the middle of the couch, where she'll be between me and Love. For someone so observant about everything I do, she seems totally oblivious now.

Before I can think of a way to get her to leave though, Love makes herself comfortable on Zoe's right, wraps up in the nearest blanket, and settles in. "Okay," she says. "*Ferris*, it is."

CHAPTER TWENTY-NINE

Austin

The Bean sits on a stone plaza and reflects the entire Chicago skyline in its mirrored surface. As I report to Love, it's the centerpiece of Millennium Park in the Loop, the downtown heart of Chicago, and people call it that because it looks like a giant silver bean, like something that landed from another planet.

I understand not everyone is as into buildings as I am, but she seems to like that I'm interested in them, so I feel okay expounding. Actually, I'm not sure Love is into the fact that I like buildings as much as she's into the fact that I love *something*. It sounds goofy, but I get the feeling it's the passion that matters.

Or I could be totally wrong.

When I finish telling her all about the Bean's architect, Anish Kapoor, Love says, "Let's not just sit here looking at it. Life is short! Let's capture the moment."

She gets a running start and jumps in front of it. I snap a photo of her at just the right time, then go to show her. She's caught in midair with a huge smile. Despite everything she's going through online, she seems to really like this . . . all the pics, the staging. I know Dad always thought people were missing out on life, trying too hard to capture it. But it's creative, too, and I can see how it's an art form, trying to catch all the beauty of life in its little moments, making mini movies about ordinary things. Showing everything in its best light.

I don't post on Instagram very much, but if I did, I would want it to be a picture of yesterday. After *Ferris Bueller* we decided on a whole John Hughes marathon . . . some dry toast and applesauce, and Love seemed back to normal. In between movies, she even made an Instagram account for the diner and told me I should post on it and see what happens. While we were watching *Ferris*, Zoe scooted over and Love rested her feet in my lap, and when Mom came home, she sat on the edge of the couch. We all watched the part where Ferris's sister finds the principal in the backyard and kicks him in the face, and we laughed so hard, it felt like we were really there. I think it would have made Dad happy too, although if he had been there he would have demanded absolute, religion-level silence, except laughter.

It was so ordinary, but magic.

Mom also told me the guy she hired for the week at the diner said he would need more money if he was going to stay on long-term. So that'll be the end of that. Two more days and it's all me again.

But I didn't even get that upset about the news because for once Love wasn't fielding texts or calls. She didn't try to take a picture or film anything and I was almost sorry it didn't get captured so I could go back and look at it whenever I wanted to. Maybe it was because she had just been sick, but it didn't feel like that was why because she barely checked her phone. For that one day it seemed like she enjoyed it just being us all together like that. I know I did.

"Want to try something else?" she asks, all bubbly. "How

’bout . . . this?” This time she sets up the phone and we pose so it looks like we’re both hugging the Bean. When the camera has snapped the picture, she falls into my arms dramatically, and I pull her in.

“You gonna catch me every time I fall?” she says.

“Anytime you need me to,” I say.

She looks up at me and I maybe could kiss her, maybe could lean down and see what she would do if I went for it. But before I can decide, her phone starts bouncing around on the wall where she’s propped it.

Even from here I can see it says, “Damien My Boo,” and his face fills the screen. He is giving the camera a pointed look, eyes lined, stubble just right, shirt open.

I’m nauseated.

“Someone’s calling you,” I say, letting her go, trying not to betray any emotion.

Love rushes over, grabs the phone, hits the red button, and says, “What? He’s not . . . I don’t think he’s supposed to have a phone.” She’s more nervous than I’ve ever seen her, stuttering and babbling. “I haven’t talked to him since I got here. I don’t know why he’s calling now.”

I hate how happy I am that she didn’t take that call, that she said they haven’t talked.

She pulls me close to snap another selfie of us, and I try not to feel like I’ve won something.

“Hey, I have an idea . . . somewhere else we should go,” I say because I don’t want to think in that direction anymore.

“Oh yeah? Where’s that?”

“Trust me?”

She holds my gaze, hesitates, then says, "Yeah. I do."

It sends sparks of desire rolling through me. I wonder what's happening for her. "Come on, then."

We drive back to Highland Park, to a place I think Love is going to . . . love. She's quiet, like she's thinking, and she murmurs every now and then about a pretty tree or a song that comes on from my playlist.

About halfway to our destination, I pull out a protein bar to hand to her. I've noticed she forgets to eat sometimes and I definitely don't want a repeat of yesterday morning. Vegan all the way from now on. Regulated blood sugar levels.

She takes it and looks at me and for a second I think she might cry. "You are so sweet, you know that?"

"'Sweet' is usually code for 'boring,' in my experience," I say, then immediately go into an awkward spiral. I didn't mean to vomit my worst fears out of my head like that. I focus on the road.

"You're not boring at all," she says. "You think about other people and you try to do the right thing for everyone in your life. You make them feel special, and there's nothing boring about that. I get that we haven't known each other long, but I've never met anyone like you, ever."

My ears are on fire, an affliction I've suffered my whole life. I wish Emma had felt that way.

But actually, no. I don't. Because if she did, I wouldn't be here with Love right now. I'd be following Emma around the mall instead. We did that a lot, now that I think about it. I love to walk and talk, to see new things and places that may feel simple to other people but that make me see everything that makes them special. Emma hated to walk without a destination, or if she indulged me, it was to get her steps in. I've spent so long thinking I wasn't interesting enough for her, that I forgot to even entertain the possibility she might not have been for me, even if I did love her.

When we get into town, I pull over and fortunately find a parking spot right away. Love lets me guide her and when we stop, she makes an "oh" sound, just like I hoped she would.

"Recognize this?" I ask. We're looking at an almost all-glass cube that floats above a ravine. We can't get any closer, but we don't need to. It's spectacular in the afternoon light from here, open and enclosed, all at once.

"Is this—"

"Cameron's house . . . in *Ferris Bueller.*"

"Oh my God!" she says. "Wow . . . it's so beautiful."

We stand there, as people do when they come to see it, letting other Highland Park residents walk by with knowing grins on their faces. Even though I'm a native, I love coming here. When I stare at the house, the wonder of it washes over me, the genius of James Speyer, how incredible it must have been to learn from a master like van der Rohe.

"So tell me about this place," she says. "I'm sure you know all about it."

I check her for sincerity and she smiles encouragingly. "On one hand, it's the amazing modernist building that a rich person like Cameron would live in."

"A rich, miserable person," Love says, staring at the house.

"Could be," I say, excited that she gets it. "People live there and for some it's probably fine, but also . . . it's a fishbowl. A prison for the wrong person, right? It's pretty much the perfect representation of how life feels sometimes."

"Totally," she says.

"I . . . I wanted to show you because it kind of reminds me of you."

"Me? Why? Should I be offended?"

"No!" I say, pulling her in closer to let her know I don't mean it to be insulting. But I also want to tell her the truth. "It reminds me of you because it seems like you're in this beautiful prison where everyone can see you. Kind of like that."

"Ah," she says. "So you're my Ferris Bueller, trying to show me that a whole life is waiting for me outside?"

"Maybe," I say, "but I'm not that different, I guess. I'm in a prison too, just a different kind. Everything seems like a 'have to,' not a 'want to.'" I pause. "Everything except hanging out with you."

I don't know why, but that seems to upset her.

The silence stretches out between us.

"Let's go," Love says.

I don't start the car when we get back in. I don't know what I did wrong. Maybe I shouldn't have said what I did about her being in a prison.

Actually, I *definitely* shouldn't have said that.

"Can I ask you a question?" Love says, after a minute.

"Shoot," I say, grateful she's talking.

"You just graduated, right?"

"Yeah."

"Are you going to college?"

I'm so stunned that for a second I can't answer her. The question of whether and how I'll be going to college in three months is what keeps me up at night.

Besides her, I mean.

"I'm supposed to," I say, not sure how much she wants to hear about this, how much I want to tell. "I got a lot of financial aid. I was thinking about studying architecture." I glance at her, then away. "What about you? Do you want to go to college?"

"I might someday," she says, surprising me. "I got into Middle Tennessee on a full ride for dance."

"Of course you did," I say.

"It wasn't Juilliard or anything, but it was a path I understood. All I ever wanted to do was perform, and all through high school I had a plan about how everything would go once I'd graduated, but it so . . . didn't. Because my high school graduation is kind of legendary, ya know? Sort of a big deal?" She flips her hair off her shoulders dramatically, making fun of herself, but when she turns toward me, her eyes are glistening. "After Grad Girl, when I saw LA and what could happen here, I decided to give up my scholarship and go straight to the endgame. I think I wanted to prove I had value so much, and I thought getting famous would do that. It turns out it's still a grind, just not the grind I thought it was going to be. There's always something more to prove because I . . . I have other things I want to do." She gnaws at her lip a second, and it's almost like she's listening to something I can't hear. "Real artist things."

I can feel how important all this is to her. She nudges my shoulder with hers. "Now, will you tell me about your plan? What do you mean, 'supposed to' go?"

I think of how to put it, how to tell her we're the same, but so different, all at once. "My plan was a lot like yours. I thought it was to go to school, get the credentials, dream job, and make a life. But my junior year was kind of a mess and senior year I was just trying to survive, you know? Breaking up with Emma, the rest of it, I couldn't really see more than one day at a time."

She nods. "I totally know. I mean, not exactly, but I get the vibe."

"Still, I was super excited when I got into everywhere I applied—"

"Uh, like where are we talking?" Love cuts in. "I mean, you're not saying no to your dream school, are you?"

I look down at the floor, embarrassed. "I didn't think for a second that I would get into Northwestern." And never in a million years did I think I would ever be so ungrateful as to turn it down. But here I am: ungrateful, ashamed, and lost at a situation that a thousand other people would kill to be in. Finally, I meet Love's gaze to face her judgment.

But she's not judging. She's impressed. Ecstatic even. "Austin! You got into Northwestern? That's huge!" she basically shouts at me.

This is a new response. I mean, Mom was definitely proud of me, but there was a huge side of unease that came along with getting accepted. Because the next word after "congratulations" was always . . . "how"? Then I got the financial aid, and it seemed possible again, if I could just bail out the diner.

"It kind of was, but for . . . reasons . . . it felt weird to celebrate."

She nods, brows furrowed in a question I'm grateful she doesn't ask.

"There's so much I need to learn, if I'm going to be an architect, that I never pictured not going," I admit. "It was just a matter of getting in. But now I don't know."

"But you're still going, right?" She pauses, searching my expression. *"Right?"*

I haven't talked about this with anyone but Mom. Not Aunt Meryl, not Zoe or Ty or Paige, even though they've tried. But something about this beautiful girl in my car makes me let go a little and admit, "The diner is really struggling."

"But how? You're a food wizard, like Ty said."

"I'm okay, but when I was in school, we could only open certain hours because we couldn't afford a staff anymore. I have to step up this summer and fix it or we'll lose it, and I can't let that happen. I have to take care of my mom and my sister. That's the most important thing. Is that stupid?"

"No, I totally get it. I have a mom and two brothers to help take care of. Makes your head fuzzy from stress when you see them struggling or think about not being able to pay the bills."

"Exactly." Tension I didn't know I was holding releases from my chest. I thought giving voice to the fears would make them worse, but it's such a relief to talk. "I just keep thinking if things turn around at the diner, we can hire a chef to replace me and I can go to school like I planned, like my mom thinks I'm going to. But things are still slow and I can't just bail on them." I think of telling her how much Dad's death changed everything for me, Mom and Zoe too. I want to tell her all about him actually—but I still just can't. I move on quickly. "I'm not totally out of the game though. My aunt—"

"The one with the fabulous seventies attire—"

"Yes, that one . . . she gave me a sketchbook and I still draw in it sometimes."

"Yeah? What do you draw?"

"Ha," I say. "Buildings. Ones I'd want to make someday. One in particular."

"Yeah, tell me about it."

"It's very . . . tall."

"Like you. I bet it's perfect."

"No, but maybe it could be . . . someday."

She watches me and I'm overwhelmed again by how she smells, salty and sweet, and that she's even in here at all. I want to stroke her arm, trace her spine, know what it feels like to have her legs wrapped around my waist.

I want to know what it feels like to have Love be mine and to be hers in return.

This, I need to smother. It's not an option. She's leaving in a couple of days and I'll probably never see her again except on Instagram. I know I'm not her real life. Why would I be?

"Hey," she says, searching my face. "I don't know a lot, okay? But Zoe said the diner was your dad's dream come true. I know you've got to do what you have to right now for your family, but . . . don't give up on your own dream just to keep his alive." She grabs my hand and pulls it onto her lap. Just a few days ago it felt like such a strange and comforting thing to have her hand in mine. Now it feels so natural, I can't believe it could ever go away. "I've never met a guy who is so into buildings and statues and landmarks. Like, you were born to be an architect. And it's a lot more practical than wanting to sing."

“I don’t know,” I say, running my thumb over her soft skin. “There are a lot more architects than buildings that get built. Anyway, I thought you considered yourself more of a dancer?”

“Yeah,” she says. “I did, but that’s more because we could afford the lessons at first and everyone kept telling me how naturally talented I was. But it was music that gave me dance, not the other way around.” She lets out a little laugh. “I used to sing all the time. Couldn’t help myself. People said I had a good voice, but they never gushed about it quite the same way as dance. Since Mom couldn’t afford voice lessons too, I had to basically put it on the back burner and hope dance would get me in the door.” She takes a deep breath and I can tell this isn’t easy for her, so I squeeze her hand and keep listening. “And that’s what happened. The video went viral, Chris signed me, and after a year of dancing and posting, I finally got offered a deal with Interscope for a single. It wasn’t going to be one of the songs I’ve written yet, but it was right there in front of me. And now it’s not.”

“Because you got canceled,” I say, wincing.

“Right.”

“God, if I were you, I would never post again. People online are so vicious. Why do you let them have any access to you at all?”

“It cuts both ways,” she says after a moment. “I had fifty million followers on Instagram alone that are the reason the deal was on the table in the first place. That’s why I *need* to fix this, get my feet back on the ground, and make a song that blows everyone’s minds.” She shrugs. “Then hopefully, like dance got me here, singing other people’s songs and doing what other people tell me will give me the chance to sing my own. Because I really want to *write*, too." She pauses. "I haven't really had the chance to lately though. Until last night." She pauses, then does a little shake, like she's banishing the thoughts. "Anyway, I didn't mean to make this about me."

She pulls her hand away and I reluctantly release my hold on her. My whole body is throbbing, wanting. Wishing I could kiss her, wishing she would kiss me.

"Dreams are all about believing in yourself, you know?" she says. "I made it happen against basically all the odds—there's no reason you can't too. Your life force will tell you when the time is right, and when it is . . . don't hesitate. You deserve a *great* life, Austin. A dream life."

From what's online, I thought that she was funny, silly, a little manic maybe sometimes . . . but she's so much more. She's not just having fun on the internet; she's building a road map to the life she wants. She's smart, insightful, passionately dedicated. It's beyond sexy.

I want to pull her onto my lap, but I also don't want her to feel like she revealed something personal and my response was to try to make out with her.

"I guess we both want to make an impact in different ways," I manage to get out finally.

"Exactly," she says, eyes lighting up. "I want to make people feel something, whether it's happy or sad or just entertained, in a way that sticks with them. And I think it's extra cool you want to build something that's forever. I wish I could do that." She hesitates. "The truth is—" she starts, then shakes her head. "Never mind."

"No, what?" I say.

"No, nothing. It was dumb." She goes back to munching on her protein bar. The green ash trees shiver around us, shushing us as the wind blows through their leaves, and Love gets a faraway stare. "Let's just sit here and dream for a minute, okay?"

So we do. We sit like we're glass cubes, hanging over a ravine, suspended in space until time doesn't matter anymore.

With Love, I would sit here forever.

June 5, 10:07 PM

Damien

You didn't answer your phone, yo.
Call me when you get the space.

Love

I can't call you.
This place is small and has cardboard walls.
I thought you weren't allowed to have your phone.

I have my ways. I'm dried out, doing good.

Good. That's great.

Yo those pics are driving me insane. A lil too cute, know what I'm sayin'. You lookin all happy and shit.

I thought we agreed to do this.

We did. But maybe we shoulda thought some more. I'm getting hella jealous. Burger King with his hands all over my boo. Maybe we should call it.

I know, baby but the numbers are back up to 45 mill.
It's working and like Chris said, we're nothing if we're canceled.
We need to make sure.

Alright but it's bullshit, right?

Right, bullshit. Totally.

Comments

@wannaberich:

@lovethompson You must be out of your gourd. @lild is a smokeshow.

@smalltowngirlie:

@lovethompson don't listen to the haters—you and @austingreyhp are amazing. Can't wait to see where this goes. #myhero #yeschef #romanceisnotdeadyet

@atrociouspelican:

@smalltowngirlie @wannaberich I don't care what happens. I just wanna watch.

@wannaberich:

@lovethompson either way, #gradgirl is back!

@rugrat23:

them by the house tho—did you see how they looked at each other #truelove #myhero #swoon

@dinerdroog:

@austingreyhp is giving dark-haired early Brad Pitt and I am here for it

@atrociouspelican:

@lovethompson @austingreyhp this better not be a trick—all our hopes for the world rest on whether you're as nice as you seem

@smalltowngirlie:

please be real please be real please be real #myhero #whattheworldneedsnow #ibelieve

CHAPTER THIRTY

Austin

The next day, Thursday, Love is different. Jittery. Quiet. Sullen. And I can't figure out why. I tear myself away to go into the diner and make sure the stock deliveries are right and we have everything we need to go into the weekend, hoping maybe I'm imagining it. But when Mom comes in for her shift, she tells me Love has been acting weird and asks me if something happened.

We had such a good day yesterday, I can't think of anything, and I tell her Love was fine when I said good night.

I, on the other hand, had trouble sleeping. It was like I got pried open and couldn't close the door again. Everything we talked about, everything I'm discovering about her, was running through my mind on a loop. I couldn't tell if I was ravenous or too nauseous to eat. I couldn't tell if I wanted to think about her until the sun came up or be asleep forever. All I knew for sure was that I wanted to be with her. I wanted to talk about everything, kiss her, hold her more, closer, tighter . . . It's like the more I discover about Love, the more I want to know because with every new thing I discover, being with her feels like exactly what I need.

And that . . .

That is terrifying.

Because the week is waning and I'm not going to be with her for much longer at all.

When I get home from work, Love and Zoe are in the living room watching *Car Masters: Rust to Riches*. Love is in black sweatpants and a hoodie, looking like she hasn't showered or moved all day.

Mom was right. Something is off.

"You okay?" I ask her.

She looks up at me, eyes red. Has she been crying?

"Yeah," she says, getting to her fuzzy-socked feet. "Let's go ride a Ferris wheel." She doesn't sound peppy or excited or any of the other things she usually is when we tackle something on her list. Given my life with Mom and Zoe, I consider myself kind of an expert on the female-mood weather system, but I can't read what's going on right now.

"We don't have to," I say. "I mean, it was your idea."

"You're right. But I only have one more day here, and I'll regret it if I don't," she says, again without any enthusiasm. "Let's go make the magic happen."

She mopes down the hall to the bathroom and Zoe and I exchange a look. Zoe shrugs.

"What did you say to her?" I ask her suspiciously.

"Nothing, rude-ass. She just sat here all day. Didn't say anything. Kept looking at her phone. I tried to snoop but she was guarding it like dragon treasure." She throws some popcorn in her mouth and some of it lands on the couch, probably to disappear inside the couch cushions forevermore. "The question is: What did *you* do?"

"She was fine last night," I mutter defensively. I run upstairs to wash the hot dog off me before Zoe can accuse me of anything else, but I start to wonder: While I was being so turned-on by Love's honesty, was she maybe being turned-off by mine?

But when I round the corner twenty minutes later, Love is smiling brightly, light jacket on, bag slung across her chest, Converse laced, and ready to go.

It leaves me wondering for the first time which version of her she's faking.

I watch her carefully on the train, but she chatters along nonstop, talking about everything and nothing as we head to Navy Pier to ride the Centennial Wheel. But to her phone, not me. She's using more slang, taking pictures and reels the whole time, so eventually I just sit back and watch the scenery roll by outside the window.

My blood runs cold when I remember the call she ignored yesterday. I wonder if she talked to Damien last night. If what has been developing between us is gone now. Maybe he wants her back. Either way, she leaves the day after tomorrow and she's going to run into him way more than we'll be able to see each other. They have the same manager and have been dating and performing together since she got to LA.

What if what we're building is just like the skyscrapers in my sketch pad? Beautiful, full of potential, but not going anywhere? For the first time in days, I feel the alarm bells going off in my head again.

"Hurry up!" Love says as we arrive. We walk over to the looming ride and climb into our carriage, a pod just for us. Lit in neon, the wheel slowly lifts us up, and it's so wondrous, all my worried thoughts and alarm bells silence. There are a lot of things I know about the city, but also lots I don't. I've never done this before, never seen the skyline from this vantage. I can barely breathe—it's so pretty. I should have done this a long time ago. I wonder if my dad ever did. It seems like something he would have liked.

Love, however, is still messing with her phone. In fact, she hasn't looked up once.

Our cabin rises farther still until we get to the very top of the wheel, high above downtown, where it stops.

"Smile!" Love says immediately.

She leans into me, snaps a picture before I have the chance to comply, and then starts editing furiously. What the hell?

A familiar confusion is starting to creep in again. I smell the secret or whatever she's not saying on her, but I don't know where it's coming from.

Or maybe I'm misreading. What if she's feeling the same way I am about her leaving soon?

Either way, we need a reset and the best time is . . .

Now. Now. Now.

I wrap an arm around her and pull her toward me. She leans in but doesn't look up.

"Love, you're missing it," I prod gently. "Check out this view. People did that. Built that. We may do a lot wrong, but buildings? Skyscrapers? We got that totally right."

"Yeah, it's so lit . . . totally serving," Love says, but she's not really looking. She's also not typing anymore, just staring at her phone.

"I'm serious, Love. This is the best view I've ever seen of downtown," I say, tilting her chin up with my finger. When our eyes finally meet, I feel her soften.

"Sorry, sorry . . ." She stashes her phone away. "I'm really sorry, Austin."

"For what?" I ask.

She doesn't answer though because she's finally looking at the uninterrupted two-mile stretch of skyscrapers on the lake, and her breath catches. "Oh wow."

There she is. With me again, finally. I relax, realizing how tightly I was holding myself, and say, "Right? And see that tall building over there? With the antennas?"

"Yeah."

"That's the Hancock. It's, like, the skyscraper that set the bar for all other skyscrapers after it."

"It's beautiful," she says, and lets her head rest on my shoulder again. I think she sees it. Not just the building, but what's special about it.

"And that one over there? The one that looks like waves are flowing over it?"

"Oh my God, yeah, it does . . ."

"That's Aqua Tower. It was built that way so everyone's balcony would have a great view. No one thought of that before."

Love's eyes glint in the dark and she's looking at me like she was that first day in the diner kitchen. Like she might want to kiss me. And not on the cheek this time. *I* definitely want to kiss her. But something's still holding me back, even after I heard her tell her manager she was into me, even after our moment at Cameron's house yesterday.

I want to kiss her.

So why do I feel like I might lose everything if I do?

Because she's a star.

Because she's leaving.

Because this is too good to be true.

The Ferris wheel starts moving again and the moment passes.

A silence settles over us that has everything to do with this week passing by so quickly, leaving the questions swirling in my head about what's going to come next.

I want to tell her I would be there to catch her, no matter what, if she let me. I want to tell her I see her for who she really is, flaws included. She's as beautiful after puking as she is in a filtered photo. Laughing with her on the couch is just as fun as this, even if it doesn't make good content. She's trying so hard to hide the real her, but she's making a mistake. Because knowing all this makes me like her even more than when I thought she was a perfect image on my screen. And whatever is making her sad . . . I want to know that, too.

There is so much I want to say.

But my lips don't move and my voice doesn't come out. I wanted to tell Emma I loved her so many times and then when I did, look what happened. What would Chad do? Maybe that's the question I should be asking myself.

But I'm not Chad and I can't jump that electrified fence. So I just watch the city, flaming silver, splayed out before us until we sink below the horizon, and there's no sound except the hum, deep inside me, of everything I didn't choose. As the sky darkens, I try not to wonder if I'm going to be brave enough to reach for what I really want before it's too late.

June 7, 10:27 AM

Chris

Tonight we pull out all the stops.
Dinner at Nobu with an incredible view
of the Chicago skyline for your small-town man,
and BONUS . . . I even hired someone to shoot
fireworks at the end. Make sure you get the kiss on film.
Pics or it didn't happen.
Good luck!

June 7, 12:55 PM

Love, did you get my message?

June 7, 3:48 PM

Love, can you let me
know you got this
and the plan is a go?

June 7, 5:51 PM

Love?

June 7, 7:01 PM

Love!

CHAPTER THIRTY-ONE

Love

I'm in the bathroom and tonight I finally have a reason to wear some of the things I brought. I'm trying on one of three possible outfits when there's a knock at the door.

"Hey, Love, you in there?" Zoe asks.

"Yes!" I call.

"Okay! Just going to grab the Scrabble out of the office on my way out."

"No problem," I say, zipping up my dress.

The clothes have to be undeniable so I can make this kiss happen.

Then as soon as I do, I'm going to tell Austin there's an emergency in LA and I have to leave. Because yesterday was . . . well . . . hard. Beautiful, but hard. I felt like I had a piano on my chest and I kept wanting to yell, *I am a liar!*

So yeah. I am going to leave Melanie, with all her salty kindness, and Zoe, who is and will always be my favorite person to watch movies with.

And I am going to leave Austin, because he needs someone who is much, much better than me.

This needs to be over.

It was an awful idea from the jump and it's even worse now.

Sure, I have fifty million followers again. The #myhero hashtag is going wild. Everyone is watching Austin and me fake–fall in love.

Everyone is falling in love with him too.

But I don't know what's fake anymore.

When Damien wanted me to leave, I used the plan as an excuse, but that wasn't what I was thinking about. I just . . . wasn't ready to say goodbye to Austin yet. Which means my plan of flirty, light, no heartbreak has been completely blown to shit.

But I realized yesterday that's exactly why I have to leave. Before I make it any worse.

So now I just have to make this a night Austin will never forget. I owe him that at least.

I decide on the navy slip dress, some gold hoops, and a necklace with a sapphire that hangs at my throat. My makeup is perfect, a step up from what I've been doing, but not totally glam. It's a look that hopefully says *KISS ME.*

Melanie is at the diner late and Zoe just left for a sleepover, so it's only Austin and me in the house. I put on my shoes, my first time back in heels since I fell, and shimmy over to the stairs. "Austin!" I call up. "You ready?"

"Yep!"

I give myself a once-over in the living room mirror next to the bookcase, pinch my cheeks, and run back to the room to grab my phone off the charger by my bed.

But it's gone.

In its place, I find a bright pink Post-it.

Enjoy some free time without your phones.—Zoe

Even though her scrawl is easy to read from here, I take the note and squint at it like I must be reading it wrong.

Austin comes in behind me and surveys the room in all its chaos. He looks good. Really good. He's in beige plaid pants, shiny rust-colored shoes, and a white button-down. His hair is even styled differently. He looks like every girl's urban-chic dream, but he smells fresh and woodsy. It would be perfect for the picture I need if I had any way to take it.

"Um," he says, "did you by any chance get a note from Zoe?"

I hold it up.

"Jesus, I'm sorry." He shows me a matching one, stuck to his index finger. "She's a demon."

I struggle to think about the last time I didn't have my phone on me and come up blank. My mom worked so many extra shifts to get me my own phone for my fourteenth birthday. It's been like a gun in my holster ever since. What am I going to do, try to snap a subtle romantic pic with my laptop?

"Where's the sleepover? We can just go get the phones."

"She's at a birthday party sleepover a half hour from here. We could go after her, but we'd miss our reservation." Austin shrugs. "She'll be back tomorrow. It'll be okay. It's just one night."

"One night?" I squawk. "Oh God, no! She *has* to come back."

Outside, the world is doing all its things. The sun is setting; dinners are being eaten. But in here, the whole thing has fallen apart.

Scientific query: If a Love doesn't have her phone and she experiences an event in her life, did it really happen? Nobody knows for sure, least of all her.

I flop onto the bed. "This is a disaster."

"Yeah?" Austin says. "I'm sorry. But we can still go get dinner. You look . . . you look amazing."

For a second I'm not sure if he's messing with me. Maybe

they're in on it together. He did seem annoyed with me for being on my phone last night at the Ferris wheel. Maybe he had Zoe take both phones away so it could just be the two of us?

Except he looks so mortified.

No. Austin wouldn't do that. Would he?

He comes and sits down next to me. "You okay, Love? I know this isn't ideal, but it's not a . . . disaster."

It is though, because I buzz a little, being so close to him now, and there's nothing to distract me from that. Which is why I stand up and cross the room to the pics of Austin and Zoe on the desk. I need some space between us. I don't know what I'm doing. I have become a horrible, evil person filled with spider eggs and I need my phone so I can do what I came to do and go back to sucking in peace.

"Why would she do this?" I ask a picture of her younger self in a softball uniform hugging her brother.

Austin hesitates, then says, "I might have said something."

I knew it! He is not so good and kind. No one is. "You told her to take our phones?"

"No, no! I just told her how tiring it seems to have to post all the time. It looks like a lot of pressure on you, like you don't ever get to just *be*."

I'm about to argue, to tell him I wouldn't do it if I didn't love it, if I didn't want to, but my limbs are so heavy. Because he's right. It *is* tiring. What I want to do is perform, create something meaningful. *That's* what I love. But I have to create a whole life, too, over and over, just to make sure people will pay attention. Any break, any misstep, and it could be gone just as fast as it came. There's no time to just enjoy anything.

Suddenly my fight is as gone as my phone. This is what's happening right now and there's nothing I can do about it. "Okay."

"I'm sorry. I shouldn't have said anything to her."

God, Austin looks like he wants to put his head in a meat grinder.

I sink back onto the bed next to him. This has been my base for the last week and I'll be sorry to leave it. I like it so much. I like *him* so much. And the truth is, I don't actually want to spend our last night together in a loud restaurant where people are going to clock our every move. Tomorrow I'll have to deal with a world of shit, but right now Chris can't reach me, neither can Fiona, or Damien, or the fifty million other people who have something to say about everything. I want to be alone with him for the time we have left.

"Listen," I say. "Screw our phones. Screw our plans. Let's spend tonight here, just you and me."

Austin watches me like he's waiting for more. Like I'm about to say, *Let's spend tonight just you and me BUT in a very public place so someone else can take our photo.* But when I don't say anything else, he grins and it lights up the whole damn room. I almost want to shield my eyes. It makes me think back to that day in the diner kitchen, the smell of burgers and fries all around us. Every unexpected thing that's happened since I fell into his arms.

"Sounds good," he says. "Really great."

A long silence follows. I can think of millions of people who might think I could never run out of things to say, but here we are. "So what should we do without our phones?"

"Wanna see Aunt Meryl's bat mitzvah?" he says.

I laugh so hard, I almost pee my pants.

• • •

It turns out he's serious. Five minutes later our shoes are off and we're in the middle of Austin's living room flipping through an honest-to-God photo album with sticky pages and crinkled plastic and pictures you could touch and hold if you wanted to. It's brown with disintegrating gold leaf and packed with old photos of Austin's family. After the infamous bat mitzvah and some truly iconic seventies hair, we get into Austin's parents' memories. In each one, his mom and dad hold each other tight. In Paris, the standard pic in front of the Eiffel Tower. In New York . . . Statue of Liberty, of course. But there are also shots of them around the kitchen table, or in front of the diner, the sign looking brand-new. And no matter where they are, his parents are kissing, kissing, kissing. Then, just like in the frames all over the house, his dad suddenly goes missing.

"Why don't you and your mom ever talk about your dad? I know he died, but were you not close? Because I get it if it's complicated—I know all about shitty dads," I say softly. I've been wondering all week, but it feels like a thing you don't just ask. Only I just did.

Austin looks up like he's surprised. Then he closes his eyes like he's deciding something, and I wait.

"No. My dad was the greatest guy. Maybe the actual greatest guy ever in the history of guys." He sighs, avoiding eye contact. "It was a little over a year ago. He got this rare, aggressive cancer. We only had a few months to get used to the idea that he was even sick, and then he was gone. We all took it pretty hard, but especially my mom."

Melanie. It's so lucky to find the man of your dreams. But

to find him and then lose him before you're even old . . . that's rough, epic, tragic. "She's handling it better than I would," I say.

"Yeah, she hides it pretty well. Says she knows they had a good thing for a long time and she's not the type to show all her feelings. But she can't let go of any of his stuff and half the T-shirts she wears are his. They were total soulmates ever since they met in high school. They're why I believe in that, why I thought maybe Emma was mine. Turns out that kind of luck isn't genetic."

"I don't know, someone who treats you like that? Seems like you dodged a bullet. You deserve a much better soulmate," I tell him firmly, reaching for his hand. "But what about you? Are you okay?"

"Yeah. I mean, sort of. I was in a bad place at first. But working at the diner is my way of staying close to him. He built it from the ground up, brick by brick, so there's a piece of him in everything."

I'm flooded with images of this happy family being shredded by circumstances they couldn't control. Looking at these pictures, I get why he and his mom would work so hard to keep the diner alive.

"It was his skyscraper," I say.

Austin looks surprised again. "I never thought of it that way," he says after a beat, "but yeah. I feel like it's our way of keeping him around." Then he sinks a little farther into me, actually lets me carry some of his weight this time. I wrap my arms around him, but it doesn't feel like enough.

"I think it's beautiful," I say, and I really, really do. I've never much thought about being older, what my life will look like in a time beyond all the hits and likes and views. Everything in my life right now is fleeting. I live at the attention span of the internet. But something about these photo albums and Austin takes me there, makes me start to envision a future where I might care about a person so much, I would keep anything connected to them sacred.

What would that be with Damien? The car he crashed? His video game console? "Replay"? The song we fell for each other during and can't stand to even hear now?

"Thing is . . . ," Austin says, pulling me back out of my thoughts, "I told you about the diner the other day and I was trying to be optimistic, but what I didn't say is the place is dying. Slowly. I've been trying to save it but nothing is working. And I'm afraid when we have to close, it's going to feel like losing him to cancer all over again. I can't do that. So I've been thinking about it all week and I've decided . . ." He takes a deep breath.

"Decided what?"

"I'm going to defer for a year, work at the diner full-time so I have longer to turn it around. I have to. It's what my dad would have wanted."

"Have you talked to your mom about this?"

"No . . . I haven't talked to anyone about it."

I don't even know what to do with that. My phone, my life, my cancellation, all the crap I think is so important all the time now feels like a big fat pile of nothing compared to this.

This, Austin sacrificing his skyscraper dream for his family—I don't want him to have to do it, but I understand now why he would. The situation is a mess, not picture-perfect like I thought when I got here, but still beautiful, because their love is so real.

I want to be real too. The desire bubbles up in me so fierce, I want to cry out. But I don't want to ruin the quiet in the room.

"Can I tell you something else?" Austin asks.

"Anything."

"The day of my dad's funeral, before we buried him, Zoe was not okay."

"I mean, how could she be?"

"Right, but . . . there was a lot going on and Mom couldn't stop crying and I had to deal with all the funeral stuff, and . . . well . . . I walked outside looking for Zoe because it was time to say goodbye, but when I found her, she wasn't crying. She was watching something on her phone." He pauses. "And she was laughing."

"Oh," I say, confused about where he's going.

"She was watching *you*, Love. The first Grad Girl video. That's how I saw it. It was the worst day and there you were, being wild and free and uninhibited, and it was hilarious enough to break through the sadness. The look on that principal's face. Well . . . I'll always be grateful for that."

I remember that night on the beach and feel the pieces click into place as we go quiet again. It's a balm for the feeling clawing its way out of my chest right now. That it hasn't all been bullshit. That something I did actually helped someone.

Both of us stare at our warped reflections on the dark TV screen for a long moment. "Man. The world before phones was intense," I say finally.

To my relief, Austin bursts out laughing and I join in.

"Okay, okay," he says. "Your turn to tell me something that you've never shared with anyone."

"Like what?" I say, suddenly nervous.

"Like . . . something that scares you so much, you don't even want to say it out loud."

"No way. I've got nothing to follow that." Truly. My worries, even being canceled by ten million people, feel so flimsy next to his. He's dealing with the impossible odds of an Oscar-winning epic, while my drama is more on par with *Love Is Blind*.

"C'mon. No judgment, I promise. Do it for the guy with the dead dad." He grins, knowing he's played his trump card.

"Fine!" I say after a minute. "But I need a computer."

Austin and I move to sit on the bed in his room, my laptop open in front of us. It's my first time in here and it's more minimalistic than I expected, sparse, hardly any color. He's got a notebook on his desk that I'm betting is the sketchbook he told me about, plus a couple of family pictures, but looking around, it's hard to detect anything I didn't already know. I wonder what it looked like before his dad died. Was there more color? A hint of childhood? Actual joy? Whatever Chris and Fiona would say, Austin is not bland or beige like this room.

I refocus and click on "LOVE.DEMO.mp3."

It's the song that Interscope wants to be my single. The beat starts, then a little guitar, some bass, and then I begin to sing:

You thinkin' 'bout me every day, oh
I got that sweet taste, I know so
Head's buzzin', yeah, I'm that lush
That's me, your sugar rush

I haven't listened to it since the night we wrecked. It sounds worse than I remember. Thin, tinny, formulaic.

Lick me like a lollipop

Spin me round, baby, don't stop
Head's buzzin', yeah, I'm that lush
That's me, your sugar rush

"What do you think?" I ask, bracing myself.

"That was you singing, right?"

How did I not notice there was that much Auto-Tune? Austin's right that you can barely tell it's me. I can't believe I'm even subjecting him to this.

"Oh my God, you hate it."

"No, no, it's great. I like it. I really do." This guy cannot lie and his face is telling me he definitely, absolutely hates it.

"It's not. I suck. That's my biggest fear that I've never told anyone."

"You don't! It's really impressive." He's trying so hard to be supportive, it makes me even more self-conscious. Why couldn't I hear how bad the song was before? Was I so caught up in making it happen, I couldn't hear how not me it was? Now that I've been writing again, I understand how far away this is from what I want it to be. Why didn't Damien tell me? Why doesn't Chris have my back? "And my second-biggest fear is that no one will be brave enough to tell me the truth."

The tops of Austin's ears redden. I can tell he's upset that he's upset me, which makes me feel even worse. "Maybe I just need to listen to it again."

"The rest is the same shit, Austin. It's verse, chorus, verse, chorus, bridge, chorus. And it all *sucks*! Admit it."

"Okay!" Austin gives me a side-eye. "It's bad. But it's not, like, climate change . . ."

I slap the laptop shut. I get that I'm not as tortured as him or whatever, but this is my life, my future, and it's a mess, but it still means something to me. "To you, it's just a bad song, but for me, that could end my career before it starts. Or if I don't do it, I might never get a chance at a singing career at all."

He pushes the laptop to the side, and his eyes soften. "I'm sorry. You're right. I think the problem is it just . . . sorta sounds like everything else."

"Like nothing," I say, agreeing.

"I guess?"

"Interscope hired the same producer as Olivia Rodrigo." It made me feel like success was guaranteed, like I would be in great hands.

"The words feel pretty generic, too."

"It's Ariana Grande's songwriter." But I'm obviously not Olivia or Ariana. Not yet. They were only probably willing to give me their castoffs to see if I could take it anywhere. I didn't think or push back or improvise. I just listened to Chris.

"Oh. Well . . ."

"Exactly, if I work with these people and my song still sucks, then I'm the problem."

"Or maybe the problem is there's not enough of you in the song."

When I met with Interscope and showed them my beat-up book of songs full of me though, they flipped through a couple of pages and told me to trust them. They didn't want my songs. They didn't want me. Not the real me anyway. Oh God, my mom was right. I totally lost myself.

"But this is all they think people will want to hear from me. I've spent my whole life chasing bigger and bigger stages, for what? To realize everyone thinks I have nothing to say? That I have no real talent and it's only a matter of time until the whole world wakes up to it too?"

"You *are* talented," Austin says.

He inches closer while I sit up. He puts an arm around me and I lean into his shoulder. I wrap my arms around my knees, rest my chin on top. I think, for the first time all night, about Damien and how he might feel if he could see me right now, cuddling with no camera in sight, no one to watch. But what's left, with no phones around and no one's opinion but my own, is a deep burning inside me, like I used to feel dancing, that drowns everything else out.

I want to climb onto Austin's lap and kiss him all the way deep, pull him against me and see what happens if neither of us worries about anything but what's happening right here for a while. His breathing is shallow all of a sudden, like he can read my mind. My breath quickens and I am about to lean toward him because fuck it, you know . . . but before I can, he says, "Let's get some fresh air."

"Okay," I say, but I don't move yet.

The buzzing from earlier gets louder, but this time I'm sure it's because his arm is draped over my shoulders, and his thigh is pressed against my bare legs, and somehow our inhales and exhales have synced up so it feels like my lungs are more open than before. I want to tell Austin he's already fresh air.

Like with him, I can finally breathe.

CHAPTER THIRTY-TWO

Austin

I am always thinking about time, about how fast it goes by and what to do with it. Time zips and careens and there's nothing you can do except be there for it while it's happening.

And now, right now, I feel alive for the first time in . . . well . . . too long, and even though I know this week with Love is going to end, I want to be here for it while it's happening.

We're in my little backyard next to the old swing set Zoe and I haven't used in years. Seeing it reminds me that I should be furious when she shows her meddling face again, but right now I can't bring myself to be pissed.

Love and I are on the red-and-white checkered picnic blanket my mom has used for every major outdoor event in my life. Okay, it's not the fancy restaurant Love planned on going to and it doesn't sound like the most romantic setting, but somehow it is? The sky is black, with a waning moon, and stars twinkle above us. The air bleats cricket song, and fireflies light up the night.

"What are you thinking about?" Love asks.

This time I don't overthink before I answer her.

"I'm thinking I've got another one for you," I say.

Austin, my inside voice says, *what are you doing, man? Abort! Abort!*

But Love's lids have been getting heavier, her blinks slower, and I don't want her to drift off. Not yet. I want more of her, every second I can get. Because tomorrow is a trap and possibly an ending.

"Another what?" she says, voice husky.

"Unspeakable fear," I say.

"Tell me," she says.

"I'm terrified of telling people I love them."

"That's pretty common," she says, still looking up, which helps me keep going.

"I'm not talking about an irrational fear. Like people who are scared of spiders for no reason. My fear is rational. Like, I was always nervous about it, but then I actually got bit by a black widow."

"Emma?" Love asks.

"Emma."

"I'm listening."

"It was right after my dad died. The funeral day. My dad . . . before he got sick, he was just about spending time with us and being as supportive as he could be. But once he got sick, it was like he thought he had to dispense as much wisdom as he could, as often as he could, until he couldn't get the words out anymore."

"What would he say?"

"'The best time to do anything is now. Be brave. Life is so short, live a courageous one.' Actually . . . he would have really liked you."

"I would have liked him back," she says. "I never got a dad like that."

I make a note to ask her more about that, but if I don't keep going, I'll chicken out again. "Yeah, he was great. We were never the kind of family that says 'I love you,' but that day at his funeral I had all his advice running through my head and I decided to take it."

"Oh," Love says.

"So I told Emma I loved her and she told me she didn't love me back."

"Cold!"

"I wish she'd been colder, way sooner. Turns out, she was only dating me because my dad was sick and she felt guilty breaking up. But hearing me say 'I love you' made her feel even more guilty, so I guess she had to tell me the truth. And then . . . you know . . ."

"Chad."

I nod.

"I bet she wakes up every day wondering why she did that."

"Ha. If she does, it's only now that she's seen me hanging out with you."

Love doesn't protest but she does seem to be thinking deeply about what I said.

"What I mean is," I say, "your presence makes me more interesting to Emma, you know? She went for Chad because he was not like me in so many ways. I have not gotten the impression she regrets her decision."

"How were you so cool around them? On the beach?"

"I don't see the point of making a scene. You can't control who you fall in love with. I can be mad about how she did it and how she told me, but I can't be mad at her about that. Love is complicated."

"Ha. Yes, she is." Love grins mischievously. "I'm sorry that happened to you. You deserve a lot better."

She is being gentle and my stomach corkscrews. "And you?" I ask. "Damien? What happened there?"

She shakes her head and there's a long pause before she speaks again. "It was everything I always wanted at first, you know? The dream? I had a crush on him before I even met him, and then when I got to LA and we met in real life, he literally swept me off my feet. We'd already been together a year when the car crash happened and everything had been going so fast, it wasn't until after it that I realized . . . that everything had become about how it looks to the outside, and when we were hanging out together, it was all we even talked about after a while. There's nothing but the parties and TikTok and singing the same song over and over. Actually, sometimes I think a relationship is like a song, one you just want to hear again and again. But if the music isn't deep, if it's just *catchy*, then eventually it loses its power over you. You hear it and you sort of roll your eyes." She pauses, looking up at the stars before she meets my eyes. She takes my wrist in her hand and rubs her thumb across its seam. "That's not the song I want. Damien and I are friends. We'll always be friends. But we don't belong together anymore."

The certainty in her voice gives me courage I've been searching for.

I lean in. So close, we're breathing each other.

I tell myself I'll just take a quick dip into her eyes, but then . . . I am in the ocean, lost in a full-blown sea, no idea how much time passes.

So I reach for her like she's a life raft. As our lips meet, she grabs the back of my head, all the fire she naturally carries flowing into me. It's a terrifying, exhilarating thing to finally get what I want, to have her clinging to me. Her mouth opens to mine like an invitation and I accept, deepening the kiss, savoring her lips. Her breath comes out raw and uneven as she breaks contact and kisses my neck, then presses herself against me.

Before our lips find each other again though, she pulls back and looks at me.

I see the worry there that I've become so familiar with. *I'm afraid there is so much I want to say to you and not enough time. That I have so many questions I'm not sure you'll ever answer. That I want you closer, want to know all of you, but I'm afraid you'll run away.*

But it's like when I went bungee jumping and was scared until the second the guy pushed me off the ledge. Once I was in the air, I decided to be okay with falling. I want her to be okay with that too. I want her closer, closer, closer.

The air around us quickens, tightens as I lean in again. Her lips are salty and sweet and even though we shouldn't be, we're a perfect fit. She arches a little as I trace her spine and then she tightens her hold on me, until it's like we're one person. One with this whole night.

The fireflies are us. We are them.

And if that's the case, maybe this doesn't have to end after all.

CHAPTER THIRTY-THREE

Love

I'm still lying against Austin's chest when I wake to a butterfly landing on my index finger, just at the base of his jaw. We're still curled up on the blanket in the backyard and the morning sun is just starting to heat up my cheeks, so it must still be early.

He holds me so securely against him, I could just go right back to sleep like this, but as the butterfly flaps its gold-and-black wings, I hear a car pull up nearby, music thumping loudly that's vaguely familiar. The butterfly takes off, up into the bright blue sky, and I nestle back into Austin's chest and close my eyes again. But then there's another sound, one I can't ignore.

"Hello?" I hear a voice call. "Yo, anyone there?"

Damien?

Damien is here.

No. No way. This can't be happening.

I clamber up and run out of the backyard, down the little alleyway between Austin's house and his neighbor's. I charge into the driveway to see Damien in a flashy rental car, the top down, standing up, sunglasses resting on his forehead. The whole neighborhood thumps with his music and I wave at him frantically to kill it. He turns off the car and somehow the silence feels even louder as I wrap my arms around myself.

"Damien. What the hell are you doing here?" I hiss, getting up close to the car like I can possibly undo the fact that he's here, and has woken up the entire neighborhood, by whispering.

He flinches, looking legitimately hurt. "That's how you greet me?"

"I just—why are you here?" I soften my tone, even as my whole body throbs with discomfort. I knew after last night I would eventually have to talk to him about Austin, but not like this, in Austin's front yard. Melanie is probably inside, watching. This is a nightmare!

Damien's in a T-shirt and red sweatpants and has a snapback on his head. His stubble is just right, his arms sinewy, but when he pulls me into an embrace, it feels all wrong. "Sorry, sorry, baby," he says, leaning down to whisper in my ear. "Don't wanna blow your cover."

"Then why did you come?" I don't know how to get him out of here before Austin wakes up.

Austin. I've never wanted to hurt him, but after everything we said last night . . . I can't. I won't.

"I came to celebrate! Babe, you're uncanceled." He shows me his phone: It's the photo of me and Austin on the Ferris wheel . . . and it has five million likes. "You're pulling mad numbers! You got your fifty mill followers back, and then some. And everyone is feeling all sorry for me because you already got a new guy, so my numbers went up again too! Plus I did so good at rehab, Chris sprung me out early *and* I got my ride back. She said to tell you it's okay that you didn't . . . kiss him." He stumbles over the last two words.

Immediately I think of Austin and me, mouths locked, bodies pressed hard against each other. It sends sparks flying through my body, heated memories too recent to shove away.

Guilt courses through me that I did in fact kiss him, and not for the cameras. But even so, I don't regret it.

That's what's standing in the space between us.

"That—that's great," I say, stalling. I should be relieved. No, I should be *elated*. Five million likes is a ticket back to LA. Back to my single. Back to my real life.

No. That doesn't sound right.

It doesn't *feel* right.

And I can't take my eyes off the picture of Austin and me on the Ferris wheel.

For once, I feel like what I experienced was so much better than how it looks, and it looks great.

Except that the guy in the photo isn't actually my boyfriend.

D is.

Damien hugs me tight, strokes the side of my cheek more tenderly than he ever has. My body responds immediately, even though my brain still hasn't caught up. He has a magnetic pull on me, a power that's instantaneous and intense.

"You can come home now. Once we're there, we can figure out how to announce we got back together. But I couldn't wait to see you." Damien brushes my hair away and sends shivers all through me, just like always. "I called you yesterday to tell you that, but I heard nothing."

"Austin's sister stole my phone . . . it's a long story."

I've had so many epiphanies in the last few days, but now I'm confused again. It was always the plan for me to leave, and up until a week ago, I was so sure Damien and I were soulmates, like

Austin's parents. And the fact that Damien came all the way here to get me in person? Well, that means something . . . doesn't it?

But all the things I said to Austin last night are still true, and they meant something too. It's only been a week, but things have changed too much for me to just go back and leave everything such a mess. Especially after what Austin told me about Emma. I can't break his heart like that. I need to understand what happened, to get clear about how I feel.

I'm not ready to just walk away from him.

"Damien," I say, taking a deep breath. "I think I want to stay here a little longer."

He follows my gaze, looking up and down the street, confused. "You want to . . . stay here? For what?"

"I . . . I need some time. It's quiet here. I can think. It's like I can hear my own soul better or something."

Damien cracks a smile like I just told a joke, and when I don't return it, he says, "You serious? What even is that?"

"I don't know. I . . . I've been writing . . . my own songs for the first time in a while, and I think there might be something there. Something better than 'Sugar Rush.' I think maybe LA is too loud for me to hear it."

Damien looks at me like I have ten heads and they're all speaking different languages. "But Chris said—"

"It's not about Chris." I don't know how to make him understand that I can't imagine going back to the way it was. Stupid parties, making content out of every single moment, and when we're not, sitting sidecar while Damien plays video games. I don't think we've ever had a conversation like the one I had with Austin last night. "It's about me and you . . ."

Damien lets go of me, takes a step back. "Are you serious right now?" He clutches his chest with one hand, like I'm really hurting him again. I am suddenly pretty sure no one has ever rejected him in his whole life. "Is it this new dude?"

I don't want to say yes, but it is. I wouldn't have realized any of this without Austin. "I think so," I say finally. "I'm so sorry. I didn't expect this."

Damien narrows his eyes, folds his arms across his chest. Then he cocks his head to the side. "And he's cool with everything? This guy." He points his chin at the front door. "With all your lying, I mean? With the way you used him? The big plan you made with Chris?"

I stay silent, and D goes berserk.

"Yo! You haven't even *told* him? Hold up. *Hold up.* You want to blow this up for a guy who doesn't even know who you *are*?"

"He knows who I am!"

"No, he doesn't." D shoots me a harsh look. "If he doesn't know what you did, he doesn't know shit about you, Love. I *know* you, Love. I've seen the pictures you've been posting all week. The sweet hometown girl, no makeup, all innocent? She's great. I love the hell out of her. But I also know the you who's the star. Hollywood didn't want you . . . shit . . . it didn't even see you coming, but you forced your way in. You made sure to shine so bright, you couldn't be ignored. And you're only at the beginning, boo. Hollywood is about to worship at your feet in ways you don't even know. Me and you, we're going to make them all kneel. So yeah, you got the down-home girl inside you, the one who likes all the quiet . . . but she's just one piece of you. And she wants the rest of you to succeed." He traces my jaw and looks lovingly at me. "This place? It's for people who aren't like you and me. They don't need what we need. They don't have what we have either." He shakes his head. "Stay here? You'll be bored as shit in a week."

Like an excerpt from my worst nightmare, that's the moment the front door swings open. Austin steps out, sleep still all over him. "Love?" He looks from me to Damien and back again. Even in this situation, just looking at him now, I get a quiet deep down inside, something I've never had on my own.

But Damien's words are slicing through it. When I look at him, I see a year of history and I wonder if maybe he knows me better than I know myself. Maybe he's right. This place is just another escape and I have to face my choices.

"What are you guys doing out here?" Austin says. Now that he's more awake, his face blooms with alarm.

"Damien just showed up here out of the blue," I say quickly. "And he's about to leave."

But Damien gives me a warning look and leans over. "Yo," he says, keeping his voice low, but not so low Austin can't hear him, "you gonna tell him everything or do I have to do it?"

Austin descends the front step and comes over to us, never breaking eye contact. "Tell me what?"

My brain is going a million miles a second and I can't get it under control. My lips buzz like I'm having an allergic reaction. If I tell Austin the truth, he'll never speak to me again. Knowing everything I know about him now, I understand it would be the worst thing for him to find out I came here with an agenda, that I tricked him into thinking this was all his idea. He'll never believe I wasn't faking everything, even though I wasn't, basically from the start.

Our night on the beach showed me I'm still capable of real joy.

Our day on the couch and watching the movie marathon with Zoe made me remember I could slow down. That I could be sick and taken care of, not always taking care of everything.

The glass house, the Bean, the Ferris wheel . . . each one validated for me that something new and beautiful can still be built to last.

And even having my phone stolen and held hostage by Zoe showed me that moments away from the cameras could be even more electric than being in front of them. Kissing Austin last night, that will only ever exist for me and him, and it's the most satisfying thing I've done with another human being, maybe ever.

That kiss, this whole week, are the only true things I've done in a long time.

But there's no way to separate them from the lie that started it all.

And if I take the risk and tell him, I'll lose both him and Damien, probably my career, too. Then where will that leave me?

I look between them, not missing the subtle warning pulsing off Damien. I have no choice. I walk over to Austin, take his hand in mine, and force myself to look into his eyes as I say, "I came here because I needed to get away, but also to try to get over my relationship with Damien. And I thought it was working—I really did, but . . . seeing him now, I realize I still have feelings for him."

"Oh . . ." Austin reddens immediately and takes a reflexive step back. I want to run to him, to pull him in. But I can't stop now. I'd rather lose him like this than let him know what we built was based on a lie.

"I'm so sorry I had to figure it out this way," I say, hoping he can hear the sincerity in it.

But you know what? I'm so messed up, this is probably the best thing to ever happen to him. People might like Austin and me together right now, but Austin is a private person. He would get sick of it. Plus even if I stayed longer, eventually something would have to give. It's not like the Greys were going to take me in forever. And what would I do once Chris dropped me like she definitely would and I had to ditch out on my platform and my single deal? How could I make a living here and support my mom and brothers?

Damien isn't wrong.

Even if he hadn't come, there's no path forward for Austin and me. It was always going to be over. This time I was just lying to myself.

"You're a really amazing guy," I say weakly.

He nods like he's not even here. "Say no more. I understand."

Damien is practically tapping his feet behind me.

"I'm sure you'll meet someone way more perfect for you," I say, though the thought turns my stomach.

"Yeah, bruh," D says, offering a dap, which Austin awkwardly accepts. "I can give you the handles of, like, ten thirsty girls who'd be all over you."

"Thanks." Austin tightens his mouth, the muscles in his neck contracting. "That's exactly what I'm looking for."

Oblivious, D nods enthusiastically. "I'll DM you."

"Great," Austin says. "I'm going to head inside now."

"Austin . . ." I want him to stop. This all feels wrong.

But he only turns around and says, "I've got to go. Busy

day ahead, you know, waiting for that DM. You can get your things, okay?"

I tell D I have to pack and rush inside. "Austin, wait."

All I want to do is stop Austin, keep him, hold him, but he puts up his hand as we stand a couple of feet into the entryway "Don't worry. I'll get over it. I've gotten over much worse."

"I—I don't want you to get over it." I'm scrambling because my brain is scrambled eggs. I can't stand the look on his face, the disappointment, the confusion. "I don't know what I want."

He pauses, and in that moment there's the slightest crack in the wall between us. An opening where I could take it back, take the small chance I can make this right.

But then Austin looks behind me, at Damien leaning against the car. "You want a rock star," he says. "That's not me."

He disappears up the stairs, and I go pack my things as quickly as I can. I leave a note for Melanie and Zoe, thanking them for everything and telling them not to worry about the phone, that I'll get a new one. Then I put on my extra-large sunglasses so D won't see me cry as I make a few trips back out to the car, my excessive number of suitcases now a personal walk of shame.

Once they're loaded in, Damien takes a long pull of a vape and blows a stream of bubblegum-smelling steam into the air as he reverses, looking every bit the rock star like Austin said. He fits into my life perfectly. I fit into his.

So why do I feel like I'm being ripped apart, one limb at a time, as we drive away?

Two weeks later . . .

CHAPTER THIRTY-FOUR

Love

I haven't been able to stop crying for the past two weeks. It's like my eyes sprang a leak and I don't have any putty.

Then finally, I woke up this morning knowing what I need to do next.

It's time to let Austin and his amazing friends and adorable family off the hook. I'm in D's bedroom, sitting on his black duvet cover in a room covered in steel accents, back where I belong. And I'm going live, so I can't change my mind.

"Girl, what's wrong with you?" D says, giving me a quick sideways glance, before refocusing on his game. He doesn't say it meanly, more like he'd love to know why I won't go back to being the way I was.

I don't think he'll understand I can't find that person anymore.

"I'm just emotional. All this up and down, people loving us and hating us." I sniffle. "I need to tell everyone we're back together and I feel bad for Austin, you know? I still feel like it was harsh of me to use him." That part at least is not a lie.

"Yeah, for sure," he says. "That's what I dig about you. You're a baddie with a big heart. It's hard for a kid like that, knowing he got beat out."

"Mm-hmm," I say, turning to face the ring-light tripod I have set up in front of me. I need to get this over with and then put Chicago and Highland Park, Ferris wheels and fireworks, behind me. Let Austin go on with his life so he can stop getting hounded online and find a nice, untwisted girl. And anyway, I'm uncanceled, and I got my sponsors and my single back. Mission accomplished. It would be gluttonous to want more.

I hit the Live button and watch as people instantly pop in. My heart skitters wildly in my chest when I see @austingreyhp in the lineup.

Do this, Love. Do this.

"So . . . ," I begin. "A lot of people have been asking me about my love life lately, and I want you to know it's all still really raw for me." Oh God, I'm not going to get through it. Tears are already leaking as I think about Austin in his room, dreaming of skyscrapers and hate-watching me.

"But I need to be real with you," I begin again, reciting the script Chris gave me. "First, I want you all to know the truth about the night of the video when I let you all down and fell on my face. I want you to know I was *not* drinking that night. It was all a misunderstanding. You might not believe that, but that's not spin, and if you know who I am, you know that's true.

"It's also true though that the bubbly person you see on my feeds isn't the real me. The real me has a hole inside. I didn't want to talk about it with y'all because you have your own stuff to deal with. But . . . it's gotten to the point where I have to. In trying to run away from that hole, I broke someone's heart. Someone I really love, all because I couldn't be honest with myself. But I realized, thanks to an amazing friend of mine, that you can't outrun your pain, and when I did, I was so terrified that he wouldn't take me back. Why would he? But then I thought, true love is unconditional. So I took a leap, and I'm so glad I did because . . ."

I force myself to turn the camera toward Damien. It'll be the death blow; that's for sure. Hundreds of thousands of people are watching, and the numbers keep growing. I can't see if Austin is still there in the blur of comments, and I force myself to get lost in the blur too.

Damien turns to the camera and throws a peace sign. "Wud up?"

I sniff back the snot and wipe away the tears. "I'm back with Lil' D, y'all!"

The clapping hands and hearts fly across the screen. There are a few angry emojis and downvotes too, and I agree with every one of them, but it's definitely not the majority. Chris was right. It worked better than even she imagined.

"We're dropping our first single together soon!" I say, trying to maintain my fake enthusiasm. "I'm not supposed to talk about it yet, but watch this space! It's going to be so exciting. More soon!"

"Dope video," D says when I end the live. "You did good. And of course I take you back. I forgive you. You're my girl."

"Thanks," I say.

But as soon as I say it, I don't know why I did.

"Aight, let's bounce," he says, dropping the controller and standing up before I can say any of the things I'm thinking. "Let's get to the party, boo!"

He heads for the door.

But I don't move.

"You know, I'm kind of tired. A movie in bed sounds better

than a party. Have you ever seen *Ferris Bueller's Day Off*?"

"Aw . . . c'mon. Jayden's place is gonna be sick. They just wrapped this music video, and all the girls are sticking around."

"Girls? Seriously?"

"I just mean it's going to be a good crowd. You know you're all the girl I need," he says. "It's chill if you don't want to come, but I'm going to swing by. For, like, a quick minute."

He pulls on his satin jacket, bends over, and kisses me, but I can tell his mind is already at Jayden's.

"Okay."

"Sure you don't want to come?"

"No . . . but I'll be here when you get back."

"All right. Sit tight. You get it, right? I have to stay in the loop. Gotta mingle."

"Yeah," I say. "Of course." But I can't help wondering why he would fight so hard to make sure I didn't leave him if he'd rather go out with them than stay here with me?

The door clicks behind D and I fall back on the bed. I know I shouldn't do what I'm about to, but I do it anyway. I open Instagram and click on Austin's feed. In the latest pic Austin gives Zoe a piggyback ride in the backyard and I can't help but laugh. It's good. They look happy. This is how it should be.

He's better off without me.

CHAPTER THIRTY-FIVE

Austin

Paige and Ty and Zoe and I are hanging out in a booth at the end of my shift. Vanilla shakes and fries aren't helping. I bet Emma's watching Love's live, probably with Chad. As soon as I have the thought though, I realize I don't even care anymore. That's one good thing, I guess. But Mom . . . I think she took the whole thing personally, like Love didn't think her son was good enough. Anytime anyone mentions Love, she shuts down and starts scrubbing something vigorously, which is what she's doing in the back right now.

"I'm not supposed to talk about it yet, but watch this space!" Love gives a big bullshit smile. "It's going to be so exciting. More soon!"

Her eyeliner is so deep, I can barely see her. She's got that Grad Girl mask painted on for her followers. There are many, many of them watching with us.

When she flips the camera toward Damien again, I realize I can't take this anymore and I shut it off.

"You all right, Big Brother?" Zoe asks. She's been helping Mom and me out this week, and I'm pretty sure it's so she can keep an eye on me. After Love left, I basically spent every second at the diner, and it took me days before I could tell her what happened. She and Mom both got that I didn't want to talk about it. So the house has gone back to normal. Mostly.

But I haven't gone a second without thinking about Love.

"Yeah, man," Ty says. "You okay?"

"I don't know," I say. "I think so."

"Want me to spam her Insta, telling her what an idiot she is?" Paige asks.

"I *want* to never talk about it again and for you guys to eat."

They look at me uneasily. "You'll tell us though, if you do need something?" Ty asks.

"Totally."

"It sucks," Paige says. "She seemed so legit."

"Whatever, she's stupid and she messed with my brother." Zoe shoves a Parmesan fry in her mouth. "I don't fuck with her anymore."

"Zoe!" Paige and I say in unison.

Ty laughs but Zoe's been different since she came back from her sleepover, ready to give us our phones back, sure she had executed the perfect plan for us to get together, but instead found a disaster. Her fists are back up, big time, and she barely even looks at her cell.

"I'm fine, Zoe," I lie, hoping if I say it enough, it'll be true, so she can be fine too.

"You're the better guy," Paige says.

"The best," Zoe agrees. "And Mom and me are lucky. Dad would be proud of you."

"Thank you," I say, our shakes and fries blurring.

But I'm not so sure about any of that. I don't know why I thought Love would pick me in the first place.

That's not how it goes.

At least not for me. It's like I traded one heartbreak for another.

CHAPTER THIRTY-SIX

Love

We're on set. My hair flies in the fake wind, water sprays, and my sequins gleam in the sun. I lip-sync, with Damien winding around me. The most insane fake ice-cream sundaes sit on tables, so huge, they're basically sugar bombs.

You thinkin' 'bout me every day, oh
I got that sweet taste, I know so
Head's buzzin', yeah, I'm that lush
That's me, your sugar rush

Damien licks my cheek seductively, then lip-syncs his part.

Lick you like a lollipop, so slow
Spin you round on the dance flo'
Head's buzzin', yeah, you lush
That's you, my sugar rush

Chris claps wildly as the director cuts. "That was awesome, guys! Once we get some footage, let's cross-post a little teaser, okay?" She squeals. "Power couple in the making. This is going to blow up on the socials. You did it! Together!"

"Dope," D says, smiling broadly. "That was so good, babe."

"Thanks," I say, searching for the enthusiasm I thought I would be feeling right now. I tell myself I can find the fire.

This is my *single*. It's not perfect, but I should be here for it!

Fiona runs over to me with a robe. "Here you go, Love."

"Can we go now?" I ask, teeth chattering from the cold, but also from all the excitement. Or is it dread? I can't even tell.

"We gotta do one more take, Love," the director says. "You doing okay?"

"I'm fine! So excited!"

"Reset! Back to one!" the AD calls.

I watch the crew as they roll the giant banana split I grind on halfway through back to its starting position, and think about Mom and my brothers. Are they going to be proud of me for this? I don't know. I can't even talk to Mom these days. The sperm donor is always lurking in the background and she won't stop trying to make me say hi to him. She wants peace between us and I want her to realize he's just a grifter. The boys have even gone to the dark side and are obsessed with "Dad." This is what happened last time, right before he left again.

At the thought of my dad and everything he's done to us, a new melody, plaintive and haunting, trickles through me the way so many songs have been lately. My heart aches with it. But here I am, trapped in a bowl of sugar, getting ready to hump a plastic banana, and the song in my head has no room to breathe.

"Hey, Chris," I say, as hair and makeup starts fussing with me.

She looks up. "Hmm?"

"I've been writing my own songs again. I . . . I started back up when I was in Chicago. I'd love to sing one for you when we're done."

She arches one eyebrow. "Love, let's not get ahead of ourselves, okay? Can we focus on this song for now?" She looks around as though to say, *Isn't this enough?* "Just do your job, get this done, and we'll see where we land after, okay? The release party is tonight—one more take of this, and then it's time to celebrate! Leave it all on the floor?"

"Yeah," I say. "I guess so."

I know how hard Chris worked to make this happen and that her plan is the reason I got it back, but sometimes I wish she'd stop telling me what to do and just *listen.* I think I might finally be finding my own voice. She might even like it. If she was willing to give it a chance, that is.

Every time we do another take on this video, I see Austin's face, him trying to be nice about the demo but not being able to hide the plain truth: It's not good. It's not brave. It's formulaic.

Still, formulas work for a reason. Commercial music is what gives clout. It's what makes money. It's how this world works. Austin doesn't understand that.

So maybe all our doubts about this single are wrong.

Maybe cheat codes work.

Or maybe Mom is right.

You don't get anything without bloody fucking toes.

We're on our way home from the single release party on Manhattan Beach. After the video shoot, I decided for once I was going to have a good time like everyone else and I drank a couple of hard seltzers. I grabbed three more on the way out, too, because fuck it. It's my party and I'll drink if I want to.

We're zooming down the coast and Damien keeps looking over at me. He knows I don't drink. He knows *why* I don't drink. Except now I do, because now I am.

And you know what? I feel fucking great.

Free.

I chug the rest of the can and then move on to the next one because #yum and also #whocares and also #iamsosickofworrying. So sick of my own brain and everything it has to say to me literally all the time.

Still, I watch the teaser reel of the video over and over. It's like I'm watching a stranger. Who even is that girl?

"That's, like, the fourth time in a row you've watched that," he says.

"Have you seen the comments?" I ask.

"No. I don't read that shit and neither should you."

"'This sounds like an Old Navy ad' . . . 'if clout could sing' . . . 'is there a volume lower than mute?'" I put the phone on my lap, losing that free feeling more by the second. The song and the reel have only been out a couple of hours and despite everyone gushing at the party, already it's a disaster. "Everyone hates it."

Damien snatches my phone away. "What did I tell you the first day we met? The people bringing you down are already below you."

I loll my head in his direction again. He pulls on his vape, tosses his arm back, spreads his legs wider, and gives me a half smile. He's sober this time but I don't want to look at his dumb face, still covered in pancake makeup. Even his voice is driving me insane. And not in the way it used to.

How did things change so much?

I don't know if it's the alcohol, or the other night when he left me for Jayden's, or everything hitting all at once, but suddenly I'm thinking maybe they didn't. Maybe I could have been any girl that day we met. I was so wrapped up in how perfect the story was, I didn't see that someone was writing it. Because now I'm thinking maybe Chris warned Damien that I was going to be there that day he was filming his video and told him to single me out. Maybe she even told him to show up at my hotel. She crafted the story of me and Austin. I should have seen it was easy because she'd done it before. I was so focused on changing my life, my dreams finally coming true, I didn't see what was happening right in front of me.

Damien doesn't care about me. He probably never did.

He cares about what I bring with me. The way I look. What I can do for him.

He's not the one who's changed. I am.

As we get closer to D's house, I'm suddenly desperate not to go there. And I can't be in here anymore either. I feel like I'm actually going to expire if I have to spend one more second in this car.

Through the window I spot a sea of bonfires burning on the beach. Bonfires. That's where people hang out and they hold hands and care about me. Maybe if I go to these fires, I will find someone good like Austin.

"Stop the car," I say, eyes trained on the beach. I have to get there.

"Huh?"

"Stop. The. Car."

"Okay . . ." D pulls over to the side of the road in front of a sign that says Dockweiler State Beach, looking worried. It's Thursday night, and the beach is packed. If I can just get there, to them, the people at the bonfires, everything will be okay.

I climb out of the car and start walking.

D follows after me, trying to get me to slow down as people start taking pictures of us. Some of them are filming. And you know what?

I don't care. I throw up a middle finger, stick out my tongue. Let them take pics.

"Do we have to do this right now?" D says, trailing behind. He lowers his voice. "We just got out of a mess. Do we need more trouble?"

I wheel around and almost lose my balance. "Just go home, okay? *GTA* is waiting for you." I trip on a pile of seaweed and it's a close one but I catch myself because I am literally *so* graceful. Dance training, bitch.

"Come on, babe . . . ," D tries again. "Let's get out of here."

"Go away!" I yell. It's not like he fixed any of my problems last time. Why do I need him now?

D looks to two guys with their phones on us, then back to me. "Fine, I'm out!" he says, tossing me my phone back. "You can call yourself an Uber or something."

A few minutes later I hear his precious ride peel out and he's gone. I'm glad. I don't want to go back to being the girl on the couch, the lip-syncing girl, the backup dancer. And I don't want a guy who is willing to send me into someone else's arms just to save his own ass.

I don't know what I'll be instead.

But not that.

The guys who were filming us turn out to be the nice people I'm looking for. They're named Nick and Riley and they take me over to a fading bonfire. They give me a beer that tastes like mouse pee, but I drink it anyway because it would be rude not to and I am *not* rude.

Fifteen minutes later, everything wobbles as I stare at the fire. The embers are pretty but it's *dying dying dying*, just like my heart. Because I was wrong. No one here is holding my hand or caring about me or asking what's wrong. Everyone is just watching me because I'm internet famous. But what am I even famous for? I mean . . . what have I really ever even done? Have I actually made an impact on anyone since Patty? Does that even count anymore now that Patty hates me? I wish they would stop looking.

The fire is still dying and all I can think is if Austin was here, it wouldn't die and neither would my heart. I snap a pic of it and tag it #myheart, then lie down on my back to watch the stars spinning spinning spinning overhead.

I wonder if they will ever stop.

CHAPTER THIRTY-SEVEN

Love

They do stop.

Everything stops.

Cold.

I'm cold all over.

Water is in my hair. I feel it rush over my face and I splutter awake. My eyes sting from saltwater and my hair, my hands, everything is covered in sand. My mouth tastes like briny dirt, my head is pounding, and all I can remember about last night is a bonfire, D leaving me, and those stars.

And now they're gone and the sun is rising.

As I stand, I see the remnants of the beach bonfire, abandoned. An older woman wearing a red-and-black sundress, an old tan jacket, and torn-up sneakers is walking by with a metal detector, but aside from her, the beach is now empty. I feel around for my phone and find it in my pocket, but it's long dead and considering I'm soaking wet, it's probably dead, dead.

"Hey! Can I borrow your phone?" I call to the woman.

She casts a slow, rheumy glance in my direction. Then her eyes widen and she scuttles away from me like a beetle.

"Rude," I mutter to myself. I'm sure I look rough, but all the more reason to help me out.

I stumble off the beach to the sidewalk, where a fit, tan couple are jogging in my direction. "Excuse me, can I borrow—"

"Sorry," the dude says, and he puts out a protective arm, shielding his girlfriend or wife or whatever . . . from me? What is going on?

They run past me and I feel my hair. It's crusty and gross, but I'm a very small person. I'm definitely not a threat to anyone. I spot a school nearby, a summer camp banner hanging over the outdoor basketball court. Perfect. Tweens always have their phones, and they are my audience.

No need to panic.

"Hey!" I yell through the fence, checking around for counselors. I don't see any. "Can one of you guys help me out?"

A girl with brown pigtails and an excellent ribbon in her hair runs over to me while the rest of her friends squint like I'm going to shove them into a white van. The girl gives me a judgmental once-over and grins. "Oh my God, are you *Grad Girl*?"

"Hi!" I say. "Yeah, I am! Listen, I'm a little lost and my phone is dead, so can I borrow yours for a sec?"

The girl takes hers out. But instead of handing it over, she starts taking pictures of me.

"Hey!" I put up my hands to cover my face, but when I peer out from between my fingers, she still has the phone pointed at me. "If you want a picture together, I'll totally do that, but can you wait until after I call? I had a thing on the beach and—"

"Guys! Love Thompson is here!" She beckons her little pack and they all run over.

They start snapping photos too and suddenly my head is throbbing worse. I feel like I'm about to break down. I mean, really break down. Like, I'm going to collapse and cry and maybe never stop. I don't know why they won't stop taking pictures, recording. Why they won't help me if they care that much?

"Guys! C'mon! I just need—" I snatch the phone from the first girl, when she's looking over her shoulder.

And that's when I see it. A photo of me, with Sharpie all over my face . . . Slut, it says. Whore, too. Penises are drawn at the edge of my mouth. Balls on my chin.

I can't breathe.

All those little twelve-year-old faces laughing at me. Judging me. Now multiply it by millions online who are surely about to see this too . . .

After all this time, I'm just right back where I was a month ago, only now it's so much worse. *I* brought this on. I remember last night, the drinking, wanting the whole thing to be over.

Well, it is now.

Everything is.

I was wrong again. Damien and I . . . we *are* meant to be.

We both pollute everything we touch.

When I get home, I plug in my phone to see if it might revive and scrub my face until it's red and raw. When the phone miraculously boots up, I call Mom.

"Love?" she says, a little breathless. Then, "Bus is going to be here in ten, Forest. River, get your lunch!"

"Mom," I say, and I hear her going somewhere, sliding a door closed.

"Pantry," she mutters. "It's the only place I can get any peace around here."

"Different house, same hustle?" I say, trying to cover up my misery.

It doesn't work.

"Love?" she says, fully present now. "What's wrong? What happened?"

"Nothing. Just. Some . . . bad pictures and reels are going to be all over the internet again."

"Oh my God, is it a—"

"I have my clothes on, if that's what you're worried about."

"What's going on?" she asks. "I've been trying to get a hold of you for days. I have to look at Instagram to know you're still alive. We haven't even talked about your trip to Chicago, and now suddenly you're back with Damien and you have a song out I know nothing about. I feel like I'm losing touch with you."

"I know, Mom. I—I need a little break from here, from this life. I tried to come back to LA after Chicago, but I can't. It's not working."

Mom takes a deep breath, lets it out into the phone speaker. I can picture her there, her head leaned against the doorjamb, dealing with the boys, probably wondering how she's going to take care of everything again. I feel like I'm letting her down. But instead she says, "You should come home. There's always a room for you here. You know that. I'd like it if you did . . . so much, baby."

I want to. I can imagine myself hanging out with the boys, lying around the pool outside, closing myself into the guest room, finally getting some peace. But.

"Is Dad still there?" I ask. "Will, I mean?"

"Yes, your father's here."

“Thing is, Mom, then I can’t be. I’m trying to get my shit together, not fall into a whole other doom spiral.” My heart breaks even further with how much I want to go to that house and how I hate that I can’t.

“Oh gosh,” Mom says, “honey bunny, I’ve been trying to tell you—it’s been better, really, it has. Your dad is not the same person he was.”

“I’m sorry, Mom. I just don’t believe you.”

“Well,” she says with another loud sigh. “I don’t know, Lovebug, but that is just really disappointing.”

Disappointing Mom has always been my biggest fear, but right now, after everything, it just feels like another blow. I can’t stay on with her another second.

“I have to go, Mom. Don’t worry about me,” I say, wiping at my cheeks with my palm.

“After asking for it from everyone in the world, you call me when you can find forgiveness in your heart for someone else, Love.”

I hang up without saying anything more.

What’s the point in saying anything when no one listens?

CHAPTER THIRTY-EIGHT

Austin

I'm in the process of looking up how to repair a boiler because Jo's out of town and Mom is already stressed, and maybe if I can figure it out on my own, we won't have to spend money we don't have to fix it. I'm contemplating whether or not this is a fake-it-till-you-make-it type situation or whether I might blow up the house by accident, when the doorbell rings.

I look through the peephole and then fall against the door, feeling the cool wood against my forehead.

Can guys have hot flashes?

Because that's what it feels like when I open it to Love standing there in big sunglasses and a hoodie once more, even though it's eight o'clock at night and the sun is setting. I can't believe she's here.

My mom and Zoe are going to lose their shit.

"Love . . . ," I say as I open the door wider. I should tell her to leave.

But as she pushes her shades up and I look into her eyes, I lose my resolve. They are red, tired, and free of makeup. She looks worn down to the bone.

"Can I come in?" she asks.

"Y-yeah. Of course." I don't know why I said that.

Not "of course."

She steps over the threshold.

"I'm sorry I didn't tell you I was coming. I threw away my phone."

"Seriously?"

"I couldn't look at those awful pictures anymore." She pauses. "You saw them, right?"

I try to keep my face neutral.

"I know you saw them. Everyone saw them."

She's not wrong. I quit following Love, Damien, and anyone with any remote connection to them, told Zoe not to even flame her in my presence, even told Paige and Ty not to send me updates. But this morning Paige said she thought I should see what was going viral. Screenshots of Love with writing all over her face and a reel of her swerving around a beach. A screenshot of her story—a fire, embers burning down—tagged #myheart. I hate how much that made me feel, how much I feel right now, looking at her in front of me, even after everything she did.

Once again I think I should ask her to leave before I feel anything else.

"What happened?" I ask instead as she slumps onto the couch. She looks right sitting there, like it's been waiting for her.

"I was passed out on a public beach. I got in a fight with D and . . . I had too much to drink."

"I thought you don't drink though."

"Yeah, tell that to Love at the single release party. She forgot."

"Everyone has at least one drunken night of misfortune," I say, trying to cheer her up.

"Yeah, well, mine was a little more than that. I was in bad shape. Someone should have called an ambulance or the police.

Instead they drew dicks on my face and took pictures."

"I'm sorry, Love . . ."

"It could have been so much worse though," she says, sniffling. "All they did was draw on me."

When I think of all the horrible things that could have happened to her in that state, it does make me feel relieved that she's here now, where she can't be hurt. I don't trust her not to hurt me though. "I'm really glad you're safe," I say, because it's the only thing I know I really mean.

"It's ironic, right? The thing I got canceled for the first time was totally wrong, but this time I deserve it."

"No one deserves that," I say quietly.

Her eyes fill and I just barely stop myself from pulling her into my chest and telling her it's okay. That's not my place anymore.

"I just need somewhere to disappear again for a little bit." She folds her arms across her chest. "A place where I have a . . . friend."

A virtual hurricane of questions kicks up in my head. Where is Damien? Where is her manager? Everything is punctuated by the word "friend" repeating on a loop.

For a moment I just stand there. Mom always says to beware of fair-weather friends, and I know better than almost anyone what happens when they turn on you.

But Love doesn't seem to have anyone at all. Not now.

"You've done more than I could have asked already, even letting me in. I know I don't deserve to ask for more, but can I lie low here for a few days? Just until I figure out what to do next? Then I'll be out of your way."

"You can stay as long as you want. You . . . have a friend here." *If my mother and sister don't run you out of the house.* I don't say that out loud.

I notice the word "friend" doesn't sting so much, looking at her now. I remember what I said to her that night about Emma. *Love is complicated.* That's probably even more true for her. I can put my feelings aside for a few days.

But Zoe is upstairs and Mom is doing something in the basement since we closed the diner early tonight due to lack of customers. I try not to think of the bills that are piling up at the diner as we speak. I need to get to Mom and Zoe before they get to Love.

I'm too late though. Zoe must have heard us because she's descending the stairs, watching Love the whole way before coming to stand in front of her, arms crossed. "No way," she says, looking Love up and down. "What do you think you're doing here?"

"I . . ." Love looks like she's been thrown off-balance. "I'm sorry, Zoe, for everything that happened. I made a mistake and I promise it won't happen again."

Zoe watches her for a minute, and Love seems genuinely nervous, everything in her tense. "It's up to Austin," Zoe says finally, "but if you hurt my brother again, we're going to have words."

My eyes get misty because I'm just that kind of sucker.

Love pins me with her gaze. "Never."

Just then, Mom comes up from the basement with a basket of laundry in hand. Alarm is all over her face as she looks from Love to me to Zoe to Love and back again. I try to get ahead of it.

"What are you—"

"Hey, Mom?" I say, hoping she'll read my expression before

going off. "Love is going to stay for a few days, okay?"

Mom's alarm dims to mild exasperation. She turns to Love and says, "Welcome back to Hotel Grey, I guess." I see Love exhale, as if she thought she'd get thrown out again.

"I'm so, so sorry to impose on you and your family again," Love stammers, painful emotions bubbling up. "After everything that happened, I know I don't deserve to be here, but I didn't know where else to go. God, I must sound so pathetic . . ."

"It's okay," my mom cuts in, her voice suddenly softening. I swear I see a flash of something like sympathy behind her eyes. Did she see all the hate against Love online? My mom can barely update a phone, but maybe she's been keeping tabs on Love too. "But unfortunately, our 'guest suite' is unavailable," Mom deadpans. "I started sorting through my husband's things and it's a mess right now." I look over at her in surprise. When did she decide to try again? "You'll have to stay with Zoe."

"I'm so sorry, Melanie. That must be really hard," Love says, and a silence blankets the room.

"It is," Mom manages finally. "But we'll get through it."

"You okay, Mom?" I ask.

"Oh yeah. Sure. Long day, that's all. Austin, why don't you get the blow-up mattress and I'll grab some fresh linens and we'll set Love up in Zoe's room. It's not the Ritz, but I think you'll be cozy enough in there for now."

"Thank you so much," Love says.

"Where are your things?" Mom asks, looking around.

"I'm sorry. I didn't bring anything except my purse."

"Huh," Mom says. "First trip you bring six suitcases, second trip none?"

“I needed to get out as quickly as possible,” Love admits.

“Eh, it will be a lot easier on the bellhop,” she cracks, trying to lighten the mood. “We’ll run to Target and get you some underwear, and I have some things from before I was pregnant that might fit you. I didn’t always have these hips, you know?” Mom beckons with her chin. “Come up. Let’s see what we can get together for you.”

“You’re screwed,” Zoe says to Love, confident in her analysis.

“Why?” Love raises an eyebrow.

“You’ll see.”

We all climb the stairs to Zoe’s room and Zoe immediately installs herself on two giant pillows and pulls out her nail polish kit. She pointedly doesn’t offer to do Love’s like I know she would have.

Mom leaves and comes back in a few minutes with a pile of sheets and blankets and the baggiest, ugliest pair of overalls I’ve ever seen. They’re blue and have patches all over them that must be from her Grateful Dead phase.

“Oh,” Love says, taking them tentatively out of Mom’s hands. “Thank you.”

She goes in the bathroom to try them on and when she emerges . . . wow. I’ve never seen her in anything but a dress or a crop top and shorts or pants, so this is . . . different. It looks like she’s wearing a potato sack. Even so, she is the cutest potato I’ve ever seen.

She’s only been in my house for ten minutes and I already feel back to where I was when she left two weeks ago, which is ridiculous.

Why am I like this?

I’m sure she’ll be gone again soon enough. All I can hope is that we'll get the chance to talk, really talk, before she disappears. I never got closure with Emma, and maybe that would have made the difference.

"Mother, Mother, please," Zoe says as she's blowing her pink nails dry. "She *can't* be seen in that." Her fashion sense is clearly overwhelming her commitment to icing Love out.

"It's okay, Zoe," Love says. "I'm off social media right now."

"You're on my eyes though." Zoe shoots up. "*I'll* find something for you."

I inflate the mattress while Zoe fusses around in her closet, looking for something that will fit Love.

"Try it out," I say when I'm done. "I can make it firmer or softer."

Zoe pops her head out of the closet and grins naughtily. "She wants you to make it firm."

"Zoe!" Mom and I say.

Love's face reddens, but she sits on the edge of the mattress. Gives it a little bounce. "It's great. Thanks."

Mom gives me a look. "You coming to take another look at the boiler?"

"Yeah," I say, "I . . . I'll be doing that, then."

"Of course," Love says, as Zoe hands her a giant T-shirt. "We're good here."

When we get down the hallway, Mom says, "Hey, you sure this is okay? I want her to be somewhere safe, but you're my son."

"Yes," I say, more confident than I feel. "I just know she needs someone right now. And I can be that."

Mom taps my cheek. "Oh, you make me so proud. You're a good man, Austin, and that's all I ever wanted. You've sacrificed so much for me and Zoe, for Love. Now all I want is for you to make sure you treat yourself right too. Go to school, get your life started . . . *your* life . . ."

"Thanks, Mom," I say, pulling away from her a little. Because school is feeling less and less like a possibility, but I can't say it out loud. Not yet. Not now.

For the moment, I need to go down the stairs, back to my pile of tools.

And even though it makes no sense and nothing has changed, for the first time since Love left, the anvil in my chest doesn't feel so heavy. At least for tonight.

CHAPTER THIRTY-NINE

Love

It's not that the air mattress isn't comfortable. I don't think I could sleep even if I was on my Tempur-Pedic at home. I'm sweaty, can't find a good position, and my head is still pounding. I can't even believe I'm here.

After I hung up with Mom, I Ubered right to LAX. I got a ticket for the next flight out and texted Chris to let her know where I was going.

Then I threw my phone into the trash.

And now I'm here.

With Austin.

He shouldn't even be talking to me right now. He should hate me. I think about what my mom said about forgiveness. I can't even forgive myself. I don't know how he can forgive me.

Damien is probably trying to reach me, but I'm glad he can't. I don't know why, but staring at this ceiling, in this unfamiliar room, I can see exactly how messed up we'd become. Damien being so reckless, driving me like that. Coming here and blackmailing me into getting back with him to save his career. Then leaving me on that beach, knowing what state I was in. He may have been my first love, but he's not my soulmate. And I'm not his. That'll always be his career. Or his car.

I can feel how well and truly over it is.

Because all I want to think about is Austin.

Finally, after an hour of trying to sleep, I realize it's hopeless. Too much has happened.

I roll out of bed, past the sleeping lump in the glittery eye mask that is Zoe, and creep downstairs, into the old office. The room that briefly was mine.

Austin's mom wasn't kidding. It is *chaos*. All the T-shirts, jeans, sweaters, and button-down shirts that were so neatly organized in the closet are now strewn over the bed. Several pairs of shoes, the sneakers well-worn, line the floor, and a whole side table is covered in baseball caps and beanies. Any other available space is littered with boxes that stand mostly empty.

I don't know how long I'm standing there, but I know it's a while.

Looking at all this stuff, it makes sense why Melanie wouldn't want to get rid of it. Every single item must hold a memory or an idea or an experience of Austin's dad. And when it's all gone, what will be left of him? How will he live on?

I think of Austin, trying so hard at the diner to maintain his legacy.

What will I leave behind when I'm gone? The photos of me plastered all over the internet? A dick drawn on my chin? A viral video that isn't what it seems? A song for people to make fun of in ten years?

None of that holds a candle to any of the stuff I'm looking at.

I don't know how I lost the person I used to be, the one with a plan, who knew what she wanted, who walked into Chris's office saying she wanted to be the next Lady Gaga. But I do know it doesn't make any sense to wait around for things to change anymore. When you know something is wrong, you have to make moves.

I need a new plan.

I want a real career, singing my own songs.

I want to be true to myself and share myself with someone else who sees the real me.

And when I'm gone, I want to have made an impact, and what I want left behind isn't just something viral, but something from my soul. Something real.

I get the feeling Austin's dad felt that way too, and for a second, it's like he's standing behind me, telling me to do the thing that scares me most, like he told Austin.

I grab my purse and pull out the only thing I brought with me: The journal Austin and Zoe gave me in the basket when I first got here.

Because I can finally, finally hear the whole song.

I turn on a little lamp in the living room and settle into the couch that has now become my favorite in the whole world.

And then I start trying to take the whole song in my head—the tune, the lyrics, the flow—and put it to paper.

A couple of hours later I'm in the breakfast nook with my third cup of coffee. I'm very, extremely awake. I think, maybe, I feel kind of . . . good? Which, yesterday, I would have said was impossible.

Austin trundles in and nods at me with surprise before getting some bread and dropping it in the toaster.

"You're up early," he says, voice scratchy sexy from sleep.

"You too." I yawn and look out the window into the backyard

where Austin and I spent the night not too long ago. The sun is still coming up and the dawn is soft and throws rosy color across the grass. "Why are you up?"

"I have to get to the diner. Food delivery day. What about you?"

"Just writing something."

He cocks his head and clocks the notebook. "Oh. Cool."

I suddenly feel totally shy. "It's a song actually."

He gives me a sleepy smile. "That's great. I'm glad you're putting yourself into it."

He remembers what we talked about that night too. He hasn't obliterated it from his thoughts. It gives me a hope I have no right to feel.

The toast pops out and Austin grabs it to go. "See ya later."

"You know, I'm not with Damien anymore," I blurt out before he can leave.

Ugh. That was so sloppy. But here's the thing: You know in books or movies when people don't tell each other things because they think they know what's best for the other person? I hate that, and yet, that's what I've been doing. Trying to protect Austin from me. But what if he doesn't need to be protected? I'm not lying to him or trying to be this thing I don't want to be anymore. And he opened the door to me when he didn't have to. So, what if . . . what if he would give me another chance?

"People get back together," he says, guarded.

I unfurl myself and stand up, then take a few steps toward him. "Not this time. Not after he left me on that beach alone."

"I'm sorry, Love."

I can't tell if he's saying sorry because he doesn't have feelings for me anymore, or sorry that happened to me. Either way, he shouldn't be apologizing. "I should be the one saying sorry. I bailed on you and all the potential we had between us for someone who wasn't ever really, totally there. Sometimes I wonder . . . what if I had stayed . . . here, I mean?"

He grabs his keys off the hook by the front door and I follow him. The toast hangs dry from his free hand. He looks at me like he has a novel's worth of things to say to me trapped inside him, but all he says is "At least you can put those feelings into your music." He opens the door and my heart is in my feet because he's leaving. But then he stops and turns back. "Are you thinking of doing a whole album?"

"Ha! Trying to write one full song is hard enough."

He lets this sit a minute, and the silence stretches out between us, but I can't be the one to break it this time. He still doesn't leave. "Well, if you ever want to bounce ideas off someone, I'm your dude," he says finally.

"You sure?" I say, surprised. "It's nothing like the last song—I promise."

He smiles and it's devastating. Delicious and sweet. He checks his watch. "I guess I have a little time now, before I leave."

I eye the piano. "We'll wake everyone up."

"Zoe slept through an earthquake at Disneyland and my mom is taking a shower." He smiles. "Fixed the boiler!"

"I can't . . ."

"Try," he says, leaning in the doorway. He looks so good when he leans.

I sit down on the bench, and fumble for a few chords, then hesitate.

"Keep going. It sounds great!" he says.

"I used to take lessons, but it's been a long time."

"C'mon. You're not a self-conscious person."

Oh, he has no idea, but I've pretended worse, so I try to fake that it's true. I'm scared for him to hear it, to lay it all bare for him. What if he thinks it's shit like the single? It would be the worst rejection.

But I remember what I decided last night. You don't change anything without making moves. I decide to take the leap.

"Okay," I say. "This song is called 'Lifeguard.'" I start again and this time my fingers move across the keys with a little more ease. I keep an eye on the paper with my lyrics, but pretty soon I don't need them. The words come from somewhere so deep, I already know them by heart. It feels like they've always been there, waiting for me to discover them. So I let myself go and sing:

I go to sleep
Drowning in the ocean
I drink its love
And swim in its emotion
But in the light of day
The tide of love has pulled away

I keep going to the end of what I have so far and when I'm done, Austin says, "Whoa."

"Bad?" I ask, cringing.

"No," he says. "Not bad."

"But not good?"

"No. Not good."

I nod. Of course. I didn't do justice to what I was imagining.

"It's great," he says. "Haunting. You."

"Oh." I close the top over the piano keys. I can't find the right place to put my hands. His compliment means so much more to me than all the comments and compliments I've ever gotten from strangers.

"So . . . ," he says. "Keep writing. I want to hear more when I get home."

That night, thanks to Austin, I'm back on the beach in much better circumstances.

I help Tyler, Paige, and Zoe build up a teepee of kindling for our bonfire while Austin goes to grab the lighter from the car. In a shallow pit on the sand, we lay small logs around the tinder in the center, like I'm back in summer camp playing with my friends.

Back when friends were just friends, and not followers.

Are Paige and Tyler my friends? In this moment, they don't seem to be. There's a tense quiet hanging over us that Paige finally breaks.

"So, do you plan to leave again? Go back to what's-his-face?" Paige says.

Tyler glances at us uncomfortably, then turns back to the logs. I can feel myself flush.

"Never. It's over. He's not the person I thought he was," I insist.

"You know, just because we're not stars doesn't mean we don't have value, that we don't feel things," Paige says. "We got all attached to you and then you were like a totally different person. You made our friend happy after a really shitty time and then you took it away."

"I'm sorry. A lot happened . . . ," I say.

"We saw," Tyler says, kicking up a little sand.

I feel stunned. I knew Paige and Ty would probably be upset for Austin. But I had no idea they'd be hurt themselves. I can't believe I took an actual friendship for granted again, especially after what happened with Patty. I shouldn't have come down here to play my song. I don't know why I let Austin talk me into it.

"Who's ready for a concert?" Austin bellows as he comes back on the beach. He hands the lighter to Tyler, who quickly gets to work at igniting our bonfire. I throw a nervous glance at the keyboard Austin pulled out of the basement for me.

"Not me," I admit.

"Come on." He pokes me gently with his elbow. "Play us your song."

Suddenly, the bonfire lights up. Brushing his hands off, Tyler stands back looking pleased with himself. Now I'm feeling the heat. Literally. "I don't know . . ." I try to back out. "I'm not sure I want to do any more ear violence on your friends after my single."

"Hey, that's what friends are for!" Paige ribs me and sits cross-legged by the fire. It's true, I'm not performing for the whole internet right now, just three of my friends. And there's part of me that desperately wants someone to hear it. So I take the keyboard off the sand and sit down with it.

I bang out the first chords. Then, I start to sing:

I see myself
And written on my body
All the words that say
Who can ever love me?
I wanna wash it off
Scrub until my skin is raw
I go to sleep

Drowning in the ocean

But when I dream, I see

You with me

The singing hurts my heart a little, but that's okay. Good, even. I look up at Austin, crouched down by the fire, skin lit up, orange, like he's sparking into flames himself. I can't take my eyes off him as I continue.

I hope he knows this song is for him.

All I want is to undo the stupid shit I did before.

All I want is a fresh start.

#gradgirl is dead. I want to know who is rising from the ashes. And I want Austin to be the one by her side.

When I finish, everyone is silent.

Oh God, they hated it.

"That—that's what I've got so far," I say, ready to actually bury myself in the sand and never come out again. I can't believe I thought this was ready to share with anyone. "It still needs work on the chorus, I know . . ."

"It's not fair," Paige says, finally. "How can one person be so good at everything? That song . . . it's really special."

"Really?" I say, surprised.

"Really," Ty says.

I want to hug them, but I feel like they're still deciding whether they want to murder me after what I did to Austin.

"Thanks . . . ," I say. "Austin helped me with some of the words."

"I'm sure he did," Zoe says, waggling her eyebrows.

"It's one hundred percent her," Austin says as he reaches for marshmallows. "I'm just a pair of ears."

"Your best feature. That and your giant . . . feet," Ty says.

• • •

Later, after they make me sing it a few more times, Zoe, Austin, and I head home. We rinse the sand off our feet with the frigid outdoor hose, and slip inside the house, trying to be as quiet as possible.

Austin looks like he's about to head up the stairs and disappear for the night, but I don't want him to go. "Hey," I say quickly, "I got a little chilly on the beach. Do you think we could make some tea or something?"

"Of course." He turns for the kitchen and I give Zoe a meaningful look.

"Okay, okay," she says with zero subtlety, "I get it. I'll leave you two alone."

"No, I mean, you don't have to," I say at the same time as Austin says, "Do you want some—"

"I said I get it! Sheesh." She disappears and it's just Austin and me. Melanie is already sleeping, I'm sure, and maybe tonight I actually will too, on that good old blow-up mattress. But not yet.

Austin brings me the tea and that didn't take long enough. Not nearly long enough. Minutes pass like seconds when I'm with him.

"Thanks." I sit on one of the gray suede barstools and it's comfortable, just like the rest of this house.

"There's honey, lemon, and ginger if you want." He slides a ramekin of each my way.

"Full-service," I say. "I'm gonna go for all three."

"Whoa. Adventurous."

I feel him study me as I pour in the honey and then squeeze some lemon over the top.

"Love?" he says.

My stomach flips as I throw in a couple of nail-sized slices of ginger. "Yeah?"

"Why did you come here instead of going back home?"

That definitely wasn't what I was expecting him to say. Remembering the conversation with Mom sends a wave of anxiety through me. "Sick of me already?"

"No. No! I'm happy you're here. But, I dunno . . . You're nineteen. Something terrible happened to you. Feels like prime parent time to me."

"They would have just made it worse."

"C'mon—they can't be that bad . . ."

"My mom's not," I admit. "I thought you wouldn't want me here and I did call her before I ditched my phone, but it's complicated."

"What do you mean?"

I stare at the green-tinted tea. "My mom got back together with my dad while I've been in LA, and I can't be around him."

"So her getting back together with your dad is a bad thing?"

I think about how to say this. "My dad's not like yours was. He didn't show up for recitals or homework or breakfast, even. And he has definitely never had any advice I gave a shit about." I take a sip of the hot, sweet tea. "He's an addict. When he's sober, he's okay. But he's usually not that way for long. And my mom's the type of person who wants to see the best in people. So no matter how many times she gets hurt, she'll always give him another chance. I can't be a part of that, especially not with all this happening. She says she loves him. But I don't know how and I definitely don't know why."

Now that I said that out loud, I start to see what Mom said

differently. Am I like my dad? Always screwing up and begging for second and third chances? I hope not. That's not who I want to be.

"Maybe that's why your mom named you 'Love,'" Austin says, dunking his own tea bag into his mug of hot water. "Because you're the best of what she saw in him."

"Maybe," I say, not sure how I feel about that.

Austin comes over and hugs me. "I think it's time for bed."

As we start upstairs with our tea, I don't know what he's thinking. I don't feel like he's totally over what happened before, but he takes my free hand and guides me in a way that gives me hope he could be, eventually.

So when he stops in front of Zoe's door, I feel a little crushed. I want to give myself completely to whatever this is. I can sing it to him, but I don't know how to *say* it. "I had a really amazing night," I say, trying to give him a little hint. "I wish it didn't have to end."

"Me too. It'll be hard to top a private beach concert from Love Thompson," he says.

I want to kiss him, to grab his hair, to feel his arms around me.

My blood pumps through my body as I wait. Wishing.

Kiss me. Kiss me. Kiss me.

"Anyway, good night," he says. But he doesn't move.

"Good night," I whisper. I also don't move.

He also doesn't kiss me.

I am going to combust if I stay here any longer. So I give him a kiss on the cheek, then step into Zoe's bedroom and close the door. I squeeze my eyes shut and sigh. "'I wish it didn't have to end.' I'm such an idiot . . ."

"No, you're not," Zoe says.

I jump and see she's sitting up in the dark on her bed. "You trying to jump-scare me? Because this is *Annabelle*-level creepy."

"So Austin dropped the ball, huh?" she says, ignoring me.

"Dropped what?"

"You know—"

"I think it's way past your bedtime," I say, cutting her off and slumping onto the air mattress. She has a night-light projecting the moon overhead, and stars light up my face. Outside, the wind blows and the trees rustle against the window.

"Austin used to be the most confident guy I knew. But now he's, like, beyond afraid of rejection. It's hard to blame him with everything he's been through," she says. "Because of Emma. Because of you . . . but he's not going to be the one to make a move, even if you slap him in the face with your boobs."

"Zoe! Aren't you, like, twelve?"

"I watch a lot of Netflix." She comes over to me, grabs me by the hand, and pulls me back up. She drags me into the hallway, then down to Austin's door, where she pauses under a portrait of her parents kissing. "Sometimes people need a little push," she says wisely. "G'night."

Zoe scampers off and I take a deep breath before I rap gently on the door. Austin opens it right away, almost like he was standing on the other side of it, waiting for me.

I don't wait this time. I wrap my arms around him and kiss him. When he kisses me back, it's not sweet like the first night. This time, it's urgent, like he can't get enough of me. He kicks the door shut with his foot, backs us into his room, still kissing me, savoring my lips. His arms are strong and he doesn't hesitate when

I pull his shirt over his head. He pulls off my shirt too, and we fall onto his bed, all limbs.

I'm straddling him and he flips me over. I can tell he's trying to catch his breath. "You sure?" he says, just above a whisper.

"*So* sure," I say.

He searches my eyes for another couple of seconds. "This feels like another do-or-die moment, like I shouldn't waste it."

He's so sweet, so thoughtful . . . but for right now, I'm going to make sure he is not worrying about anything, that he's just here with me, and that he can feel how much I care about him.

After the next kiss, neither of us is distracted again by worry, by life outside this room, by everything that could happen . . . not for a long, long time.

CHAPTER FORTY

Austin

Love is in my arms, in my bed, and I am perfectly comfortable. I think we slept for about forty-five minutes.

Worth it.

Love props herself up on an elbow and strokes my cheek. I feel it all the way down my body. "I don't want to drop in and out of your life anymore," she says.

"I don't want that either."

"So . . . Austin Grey, will you be my boyfriend?"

"Sounds so official," I say, grinning.

She smiles back, but I can see she feels vulnerable. I know Zoe would be telling me to *just say yes, stupid*, but I'm also scrolling through all the possibilities and questions I have. She's famous. No matter how she feels about it now or how many times she's canceled, she's from a totally different world, and that's where her dreams lie.

She sits up and scans me, blushing a little. "Don't leave a girl hanging."

I sit up too, letting the covers slip down to my waist. "It's just . . . Are you sure?"

"Austin, I'm in bed with you right now . . ."

"Okay, don't get me wrong, you're—incredible. But the thing is . . . I'm not."

"What do you mean?"

"Dating me isn't day after day of fireworks," I say. "It's more like a tingle every so often—"

"A tingle . . . ?"

"You know, like that feeling you get in your toes during a really nice massage."

"What's wrong with that?" she says.

"Or a first kiss," I say. "Don't you think you need fireworks?"

She leans in. "Actually, a foot massage sounds like the best thing in the world right now." Love kisses me, long and slow and deep. "But I don't think you're just a tingle, Austin. And I don't think you should make decisions based on what you think I'll think. We can figure it all out. I believe that. And anyway, this is the first time I've felt at home, maybe ever. So it's more than a tingle for me, you know?"

She looks down and away. I get how hard this is for her. It's hard for me, too.

But I'm not going to be so afraid anymore. If she thinks I'm worth it, why should I try to convince her I'm not? I pull her in close and kiss her again, tracing her spine.

Then I bounce out of bed.

"Where are you going?" she asks, confused. She looks good in my sheets.

"To give my girlfriend a massage," I say, and she beams at me at the word that finally answers her question. "But first I need to steal this amazing lotion from my mom."

I'm in my mom's bathroom, rooting around for the rosemary-mint massage cream she uses on her feet when she's had a long day, which is pretty much always, when my phone starts bouncing around where I've placed it on the counter.

When I see the words on the screen, my stomach plummets to the floor. This time the universe has been swift with its reminder of what happens when you open yourself up to someone.

It's Emma all over again. No, actually, it's just me again.

I am *such* a fucking fool.

When I finally gather the strength to go back into the bedroom, I see Love has picked up my copy of *The Two Towers* and is reading it. She looks up and smiles. "Yay! You're back!"

"Sorry," I say, still trying to make sense of how the world has shifted since I was last in here just five minutes ago. My lips and fingertips still burn from kissing her, holding her, and that makes this hurt all the more.

"Are you all right?" she says. "You seem really tense."

"I just got this." I hand her my phone. She reads the text sent from a number I don't know: yo bruh. i know u into love but she's lying to you. your whole time together before was a stunt to get uncanceled. thought u should know she's using u for clout. 🕶💀

Love looks up at me, storm clouds in her eyes. "He's such a rat bastard."

"Can you explain what this means?" I feel like I'm going to pass out.

"It's Damien messing with us. That's all. It's not true."

Okay, okay, okay. Maybe everything is okay. "So it's bullshit? The thing he said about the time we spent together?"

Love holds my gaze a beat too long, then studies the sheets. "It's . . . complicated."

"I'm such an idiot." And I am. Because it's all coming together now. Since the first time she came here, Love has been using me. Both times she showed up here after a scandal, when her reputation took a hit. All that filming and posting while she was here that first week, it wasn't just her job. It was a plan to fix her reputation. #myhero. She wanted to use how much people liked that video of me catching her in the mall to distract them from the *TMZ* video. And once her follower count was back up, suddenly who was in our driveway?

"You're still with Damien? Is that what this means? Have you even broken up?"

I half expect to see him out there again, right now. Damien. The thought of him holding this over me, rubbing my nose in it again . . . it's too much. I can barely breathe.

"No, I can explain," she starts miserably, but then stops. It sounds like she's got tears coming, but my sympathy has finally dried up. Who even knows what's real with this girl? I don't think *she* knows.

"Every time you've called me was after some PR nightmare," I say. "You needed, what? Someone clean and wholesome to scrub your image?"

She gets up on her knees and tries to reach for me, but I pull back out of her grasp. "Okay. Listen," she says. "That's how it all started. But that was before I got here and got to know you. This second time I came because I really missed you . . ."

"Why should I believe anything you say? Give me one reason. Please. Anything that tells me I have this wrong."

She picks up her T-shirt off the floor and slides it over her head. "It wasn't my idea, okay? That first time, I was desperate.

I panicked. And you were the first—*the only*—person I could think of who felt safe." She comes over and cinches me around the waist, holds on to me. She fits so well there, but that's probably just in my head too. "You don't know what it's like to have fifty million people suddenly think you're a drunk or a whore. To see everything you've sacrificed for going up in smoke. It's awful. It's like being burnt at the stake. You feel it under your skin."

I stiffen, feel myself turn to marble in her arms, and she lets me go. "Wow," I say.

"What?"

"You seriously made this about you. That's amazing."

"That's not what I'm trying to do. I know I should be the one saying sorry. I *am* sorry. I've been sorry since that first day I got here. I started falling for you even then, but I didn't know how to explain it in a way you'd believe me, and now I just want you to understand why I did it in the first place. So go on—call me a liar and selfish and a slut. Get angry. I deserve it. But then forgive me, okay?" She's crying now and I can't even look at her. "Because I love you."

"Don't say that."

"Say what?"

"Say *that*."

"But I mean it, Austin. I love you. I've never felt this way about—"

"Yes, you have. You say that to everyone. You say it to Damien. You say it to millions of your fans. Every day. Sometimes several times a day."

"I don't understand . . ."

"'Love' doesn't mean anything coming from you. And it

never will." I throw on a T-shirt myself and open the door. I don't even care if Zoe can hear us. What felt like the best morning of my life has turned into one of the worst. And I should be at the diner anyway, helping Mom. Enough with the distractions.

"Are we breaking up already?" she says, following me down the stairs. I just want to get away from her. "Let's talk about this . . . please," she says, but I already have my keys in hand. I'm done.

"None of this was ever real, Love, okay? I accept that. Let it go."

I don't turn around because if I see her face, I'll want to stay, and this has to be over. Once and for all. For good. I have finally learned my lesson.

I go outside, start my car, and I don't look back.

I never will again.

CHAPTER FORTY-ONE

Love

The wheels on the plane are barely making contact with the LAX runway when I go to track down Damien on Find My using the new phone I bought on my way to the airport. When we deboard and I feel that LA air, I push past the women with the facelifts and Louis Vuitton bags and Gucci slides and order myself an Uber right to his location.

I am about to end him the way he ended me and Austin.

When I arrive, Nobu is bumping, and I pass a string of Kardashians on my way out to the deck. The hostess gives me an alarmed glance as I walk right by her, but then I see her recognize me and she looks back down at her iPad.

This is where Damien brought me on our first dinner date. It's where he comes to be seen or bump into the people he wishes he knew. Sure enough, I spot him outside, sipping on some fruity cocktail, and sitting across from him in a sequined cocktail dress is Devyn, his supposed best friend Jayden's girl. She spots me and sits up straight, uncurling herself in her big loungy chair. The ocean shimmers and weaves, and the sun is a scoop of melon sherbet behind her.

As I stomp toward them, Devyn's expression becomes more alarmed, and she clutches her drink.

". . . and then she said, 'Lil' D?! More like BIG D!'—you know what I'm sayin'?" Damien laughs at his own joke.

I reach the table and he finally sees me. His vibe darkens slightly but his voice is chipper when he says, "Yo, Love! Didn't expect to see you."

"I got your little text message."

"What message are you—" he starts.

"Shut up," I say. I want to slap him, hurt him the way he's hurt me, the way he hurt Austin. Instead I grab a glass of water off the table and throw it in his face. "Stay the *hell* away from me! Don't ever contact me again. Or Austin. Don't let my name pass your lips. Ever. Again."

I turn on my heels, ignoring the stares I'm getting.

"Love!" he yells. "What message?!"

Yeah, right. I'm not falling for that. I'm done being a plaything and I'm done playing with other people.

This time, I'm the one canceling him.

Three months later . . .

September 16, 7:32 AM

Love

Hey Patty.
I miss you a lot. I'm sorry for everything.
I'm trying to fix it now and I hope when
I do you will find a way to forgive me.
I want to hear how you're doing.
I want to know all about your life.
Anyway, I'm sorry. You're the best friend
I ever had and I'm going to show you
the kind of person I really am.
You won't be able to reach me for a while,
but I hope you will want to, and I hope
we see each other soon. I love you.

CHAPTER FORTY-TWO

Austin

By September, she's everywhere.

Apple Music, Spotify, YouTube, TikTok, the radio. Love's gone viral again. But this time in a good way. At least for her. So I shouldn't be surprised when her voice pumps through the diner speakers.

It's just a little awkward, because I'm sitting here with Emma. We do our best to ignore it but the words come out clear and strong and we both sit quietly until it's over.

I go to sleep
Drowning in the ocean
But when I dream, I see
You with me
And you pull me out of the water
You stand in front of the slaughter
I'm tired of rock stars
Bring on the lifeguards
'Cause you pull me out of the water

"You know, this song is part of why I asked you to have a burger with me," she says. "It seems like it's about you."

"Yeah," I say, "well, it's in the past now." I wait a beat and say, "So was there something specific you wanted?"

"I guess . . ." She looks up from her Sprite Zero. "I wanted you to know that Chad and I broke up, kind of a while ago actually, before we left for school."

"Oh."

"Yeah and, I don't know . . . this song is everywhere on campus and every time I hear it, I think of what she said. Maybe I *was* stupid." She takes hold of my hand and squeezes. "She must be talking about you because you're that guy, Austin. Strong, stable, loyal . . . the kind of guy you want saving you, you know? I think I took that for granted. And I thought after, you were just punishing me for that. I should have realized everything that would get put on your shoulders."

All these months I have been waiting for closure. For Emma to apologize or at least acknowledge what happened, that it wasn't okay, that the way they handled their relationship was garbage, that the way they treated me all senior year was horrible, but now that she's here, I just . . . don't care.

"I appreciate that, I guess," I say, taking back my hand.

Emma sits back in the booth, looking disappointed. But I'm not the guy in that song.

"The thing is," I tell her, "I'm not the lifeguard. I'm the one who's drowning. I'm the one who needs saving, you know? And the second that was the case, you were looking for a way out. So I think I was the one who was wrong about you."

Zoe comes over to the booth, an order in hand, and I've never been so happy to see her. "Mom said to bring this out to you." She glances at Emma. "Oh, hi. Never thought I'd see you in here again."

"Hi, Zoe," Emma says. "You're so big now!"

"Yeah? And you're the same size you always were. Very, very small."

"Well," I say, scooting out of the booth, "I have to go back to work. Take care of yourself, Emma."

"Yeah," she says, frowning. "You too."

I head to the kitchen with Zoe a foot behind me.

I start the bechamel sauce for some mac 'n cheese and pull out the prepped pasta, while Zoe watches me from the doorway.

"Quit that," I say. "Go fill some ketchups, will you?"

"Austin, I just . . . ," she begins.

"Yeah?"

"I . . . I was wrong."

I don't think I've ever heard these words come out of her mouth. "About what?"

"About you needing to push the world around to get what you want. About being more of a man and needing to change who you are. Who you are is great and you make things better for the people in your life. What you're doing here to save Dad's dream; how you make sure I can go hang out with my friends and Mom doesn't just stay in her room crying. You take good care of us."

"Zoe," I start, but she puts up her hand. We're still not the kind of family who gushes at each other.

"Say nothing," she says, pushing the door open. "I'm going to go bus some tables."

I finish making the mac 'n cheese, and when I flip the next round of burgers, I do it just right.

CHAPTER FORTY-THREE

Love

I don't know how many times I've dreamed of singing my songs on the *Rowan Chase Show* in Los Angeles, but it's a lot. The part of me that wanted to write songs was smothered for so long, I thought a dream was all it would ever be, but here I am.

With both my parents, which is somehow even more surprising.

"I'm so proud of you," Mom says.

"Me too," Dad echoes. He looks ruddy, a little bleary from the trip, but he's six months sober today, so I decided to invite him.

Anyway, the Austin disaster taught me one big thing: Don't take love for granted. Don't throw it around and say it to everyone. Treat it like it's sacred. My mom *loves* me. I know now I shouldn't let my anger and spite take that for granted. And that means giving Dad another chance. If Mom says he's changed, and he's been sober, then I'm not going to poison their future. And I have to admit, he's been around longer this time than ever before.

"Good job, kiddo," he says.

"Thanks," I say.

"I'm going to go get a coffee," he says. "You girls want anything?"

"I'm fine. Thank you, honey," Mom says.

When he's gone I say, "I'm so happy you came, Mom."

She beams. "I'm so happy to be invited . . . with your father, no less. What made you change your mind?"

"I haven't changed my mind about him. Not fully anyway," I say, then pause. "But as someone who's had and lost a lot of second chances lately, I can't hold it against you for giving one to him. But he's going to have to prove himself worthy of it, like I'm trying to do, because, Mom . . . you deserve the best. I hope you know that."

"Oh, sweetheart," she says, into my hair. I hold her tight. It's always been me and her together, right from the beginning.

"You believe the best in people, Mom. You saw a girl, with no money, two crazy brothers, and gold dance shoes who hated the world because it seemed to hate her." I pull back and look my mom right in the eyes. "And you imagined all this. Then it was you who told me to remember I had my own songs to sing even when I stopped believing it. I wouldn't be here without you. Don't ever think I don't know that."

"I love you, Love."

A knock at the door interrupts us and Chris pops halfway in. "They're ready for you."

The studio is all glass and I'm sitting under a picture of Billie Eilish, singing here just like me. But I try not to think about her or the legendary stars who've been here before, or anything other than my song and what it means to me. It's a tunnel straight to Highland Park every single time, and like always, when I get to the chorus, I'm back on that beach with Austin, staring at the fireworks, staring at the sunset, staring at him, and I have to wrench strength from the deepest part of myself to get through it.

You pull me out of the water
You stand in front of the slaughter
I'm tired of rock stars
Bring on the lifeguards
'Cause you pull me out of the water

As I listen to the outro, trying to keep myself in one piece, I notice that Rowan Chase, famous kingmaker DJ, is swiping at his eyes.

I made *Rowan Chase* cry!

The song ends in a flurry of strings, and my guest cellist, Marina, lets the last note settle into the room, before giving me a thumbs-up.

"Wow," Rowan says, salt-and-pepper hair in a pompadour, leather jacket worn and buttery. Behind him, an intern named Brian is throwing hand signals and sipping aggressively on coffee. "For anyone joining us, that was Love Thompson performing 'Lifeguard' live here on the show. What a song!"

"Thanks," I say. It's still strange to get compliments for something that feels so personal.

"Now, you have spent five weeks at number one on *Billboard*'s Emerging Artists chart. How do you feel?"

"Uhh . . . cool, I guess."

"Cool? Cool?! Christ, I love your generation." He shakes his head.

But ever since I lost Austin, I can't fake anything, not even being cool. "No, the truth is I feel really grateful. It's just . . . this song brings up a lot of emotions, you know, so it's a weird thing to celebrate at the same time."

"So I'm guessing things never worked out with Mr. Lifeguard?"

It pains me, like actually physically pains me, that people saw so much of what happened between Austin and me. And Damien and me. Or at least they think they did.

And yet there's so much they have no idea about. They don't know what it was like to stare into Austin's eyes, to be touched by him, to have him ask questions about me and actually want to know the real answers. To want to know me, the person I *am*. And they don't know that I ruined all of it and the chance to know everything about him, just so they'd like me again.

"No, things didn't work out" is all I can manage.

Rowan is still looking at me from across that mic, waiting for me to say something else, but all I do is squeeze my seat like it's a stress ball. He squinches his eyebrows and clears his throat, pivoting. "Ah, playing it coy, I see, fair enough. Right, so . . . let's take some callers."

Brian says something into his phone from the other side of the soundproof glass and Rowan chuckles a bit. "Now, I'm told this caller got into a proper argument with my producer. She insisted that she knew you, and she must absolutely be given a question. I apologize in advance if she's just a mad stalker." He clicks a button and leans back in his chair, taking the mic with him. "All right, caller, you're on the air. What's your name and where are you from?"

"Hi! I'm Zoe from Chicago."

"Hello, Z—"

"Zoe! Oh my God!" I am literally screeching. I've never been so happy to hear from anyone ever in my life as I am to hear from that little heathen.

"So you *do* know each other?" Rowan sits up and leans on his elbows, interested. "But you're strangers enough that you communicate via radio show. Sounds complicated."

"I've been trying to reach you!" Zoe says, ignoring Rowan the way only she could. "Instagram, Facebook, everything . . ."

"I'm so sorry. I don't manage it myself anymore . . . I'll send you my new private number." Only Chris, Mom, the boys, and Patty have that number so far, and I like it that way. I'm so happy Patty decided to let me back into her life. I spent a week visiting her in Boston, and then she came out to LA and was in the studio while I recorded. I never forgot what Paige said, about remembering my friends' value. It's no wonder I made such a mess of things without Patty. She's a part of me I didn't realize was missing until I had her back. As far as socials go, ever since I got back from Highland Park, I've given the whole thing over to Chris. She insisted after I got into trouble the second time. I've wanted to reach out to Zoe so many times, but I felt sure the whole family must really hate me for good now. But now that she's the one calling me, I want to know everything about what's been happening with her, and okay, even more than that, I want to know what's going on with her brother.

There's a pause and then Zoe says, "That's so sweet, Love."

"That *is* sweet," Rowan interrupts, trying not to lose control of the interview. "But now that you do have Love on the line, Zoe, what's your question?"

"I wanted to say I'm so proud of you," Zoe says. "Ever since you first played this song on my piano, it's been stuck in my head. I hear it everywhere now, and it feels like you never left."

I feel the tears coming, but I don't want to let them slip over my lids. Rowan and the rest of Los Angeles don't deserve access to another public breakdown. "I miss you, too, Zoe," I say simply.

"Not a question, but a brilliant sentiment nonetheless." Rowan's finger hovers over the Disconnect button. "Thank you, Zoe. Next, we have—"

"Wait!" I say, desperate not to let her go, like if I do, I'll lose her permanently. "*I* have a question. Is she still there?"

"Yeah! Yeah! I'm still here." I can picture her in her house, in her pink room surrounded by all her pink things on her pink phone. In my mind, the blow-up mattress is still next to her bed, and Mrs. Grey's janky overalls are still flung across Zoe's desk.

"Oh good." I know his name shouldn't even, like, cross my lips, but I can't help it. It's like his name is an itch I have to scratch. "How's Austin? Is he liking school?"

"He's . . ." She hesitates. What is it? Does he have a girlfriend or something? "He didn't go."

"He didn't go to school?"

"Yeah. He's an idiot."

"Wait, what? But . . . what about his skyscraper?" For the last couple of months, all I've done is imagine him on campus learning how to build the buildings of his dreams with some beautiful young girl, who is wholesome and corn-fed and perfect for him. Not damaged and fucked-up like me. But he's exactly where I left him?

The diner.

It must not be doing well. If they couldn't hire a new chef, Austin would never leave his mom and Zoe alone to deal, or let it close.

"Yeah, it's pretty—" Zoe's line cuts off before I can hear more.

I shoot Rowan a look, but he shrugs. "And back to the radio

show, we are talking music with hit emerging artist Love Thompson. Caller, you're on the air."

The show goes on because shows always must, but my mind stays, as always, on Austin.

"The response has been incredible," Chris says over brunch the next morning. "Interscope wants you on tour ASAP, but I think it's better to stay small right now while we work on completing the rebrand of your image and you finish the rest of the record. So I'm thinking another pop-up tour with just the single would be the right move. A few cities? What do you think?"

"Yeah," I say. "Let's do it."

I'm opening Instagram, ready for my usual daily emotional-support scroll of Austin's profile. I may not post myself anymore, but I still check in on him. I can't help it.

Even though he almost never posts, his old photos and videos make me still feel connected to him somehow, and after talking to Zoe yesterday, I need that now more than ever.

"Great. That's what I thought too. Now, music video–wise, there are so many director options. We can go with Megan Price, she works a lot with Billie, but you might want to *differentiate* from Billie . . ."

"Right," I say, imagining the video on Austin's Instagram I'll go to first, one I've practically memorized. "Differentiate."

It's from right before his dad got sick, and he's carrying Zoe on his shoulders. The end, where he gives the camera a look and smiles before slapping his hand over the screen, is my favorite part. It's like for just a split second, you can see all the joy inside him finally let loose. But right now I can't find it.

I can't find his profile at all.

I try again, type in some different configurations of his name in case he's changed his handle.

"@austingrey"

"@greyaustin"

Oh no. Did he block me? I know everything Chris is saying should be important to me, but right now it's not. I'm panicking, feeling woozy, because what does that mean?

I type in "@zozogrey" and heave a sigh of relief when I see Zoe's picture pop up. I hungrily scan for signs of Austin, but it looks like he's not following her either, so he must have gotten off socials altogether.

I'm distracted from my spiral though by Zoe's latest post, a GoFundMe request with the hashtag #standbynathansdiner.

"I was thinking we could go with Chappell's director," Chris goes on, knocking back a shot of espresso. "So you're like Billie but less depressing."

"Yeah."

". . . or Big Bird could direct it and the other Muppets could be backup dancers," Chris finishes.

"Sure. Sounds great . . ."

Chris snatches my phone away. "Where's your head at, Love? What else could be so important?"

I take a sip of my crappy coffee and scan the room. I'm looking around now at the people in their trendy sunglasses and their black leggings and their tagged bags. The menu at this place is shit compared to the food at Nathan's, so why is it doing so much better? "I just don't get it."

"Get what?" Chris asks.

"How is this place so popular? The eggs are cold, the pastries are way too sweet, and the coffee is awful . . . but there's still a line out the door."

Chris folds her arms across her chest. "You really don't know?"

"No."

"It's because people like you eat here, silly."

I lean back in my booth and clock at least three other celebs from my seat. She's right.

And it gives me an idea. One I've been searching for since the show yesterday.

"Okay," Chris says, handing me back my phone and returning to hers. "Let's circle back on the video and talk about the mall tour. We drew up a list of cities that—"

"Actually, I *do* want to do the tour." I may have screwed up literally everything with Austin Grey, but I can fix one thing at least. "But we're not going to a mall. Come on, Chris. We have things to do."

"Yeah," she says, "I'm trying very hard to do them. I have a list a mile long—"

"No, not any of that." I stand up. "We're going to save a diner."

Chicago in November is the most beautiful thing there could possibly be, and when the wheels touch down at the airport, for the first time in so long, I feel like I'm at home.

That feeling gets even more intense as I near Nathan's. No one knows I'm coming—not Zoe, not Melanie, and definitely not Austin. I don't know if he'll throw something at me or if he'll make out with me or anything in between, and I don't really care. Well, I do vastly prefer one of those options, but either way, I have a proposal for him and his family that will allow me to finally give them something back after how much they gave to me. And how much I hurt him.

The window at Nathan's is plastered with signs letting the world know they're now serving acai bowls and breakfast burritos. Chris rolls her eyes and I stop her before we go inside.

"Look, I know that this isn't your favorite and you think I should be doing other things. But I was right about the song and I'm right about this, so I need you to support it, because doing this means more to me than all of it."

"I know," she says, and rubs me on the back in a way that I think is supposed to be soothing, but mostly feels condescending. "Let's just get it done so that you can get back to real life."

"That's the thing," I say. "I feel like *this* is real life."

Chris raises her eyebrows. "Well, it's not," she says. "Your real life is the opportunity in front of you. The video, all the success you're having now, is the thing you've been waiting for since you started dancing and singing in the first place. It's the thing we've wanted since we met. It almost didn't happen, Love, and I don't want to see you squander it all again for a guy."

That stings, but it doesn't feel like it should. Because in the end I didn't squander my career for a guy. I squandered the guy for my career. Now I need to use one to help save the other.

"He might throw a pie at me," I say, hesitating.

"Ooooh, that could make a great video," Chris says, and it's almost like she cheers up.

I walk into the empty diner as Melanie emerges from the kitchen. I'm searching behind her for signs of Austin, nerves jangling uncomfortably, but no one is out here except the two of us.

"Well, look what the cat dragged in," she says.

"Hey, Melanie!" I say, and it comes out overly chipper, because I know how pissed she must be after yet another screwup.

"You came all the way from Los Angeles for lunch? Or, wait . . . are you moving in again?"

"No." I can barely look at her. There's so much I want to explain to her, but I don't deserve to, not yet.

Chris slumps off to a booth, still typing. Melanie doesn't miss it. She stiffens and pulls out her order pad as I feel a flicker of irritation. "So what'll you have?"

"A veggie burger." I pause because Melanie is kind of scary right now, and I need to get to Austin. "But maybe I can tell the chef how I like it?"

"That's extra," Melanie says.

At first I think she's really not going to let me back. I get the feeling she's contemplating grabbing me and Chris by our shirts and tossing us into the street as she searches my face and I do everything in my power to project how much I love her son. Finally she says, "I'm going to open this door. I don't know why, but I'm doing it. Tread carefully though."

I take one last look around the diner, steel myself, and push through the double doors.

CHAPTER FORTY-FOUR

Austin

I'm in the walk-in, planning the special for the day based on what we have in there. It's looking like meat loaf with a sweet potato hash. I think I have enough for about twenty servings and just enough time to get it together. If it turns out we don't sell it, I'll take it to the unhoused shelter Dad used to take food to on the block. But I'm determined we will sell it, like a successful restaurant would. Some of the new menu offerings I've improvised have gotten us a little bump, but it's still not enough for me to be able to go to school. I think it's finally time to let that dream go.

Dad. If you're up there right now, can you show me a sign? Drop some broccoli on my head or something? Because I could really use your help.

"Hi."

That voice does not belong to my dead dad. It's the one that's everywhere.

I place the sweet potatoes carefully back onto the shelf before slowly turning around. It's been months since I've seen her, so I forgot a little how beautiful she is. Or tried to, but it all rushes back immediately when I see her. Her hair is swept back in a kerchief, her eyes glow, and her gold hoops dangle. She has no makeup on and is looking at me differently than last time. Like she's . . . scared. And maybe she should be—she can't just keep waltzing back into my life.

"Love?" I exit the walk-in and shut the door behind me. "What are you doing here?"

"I tried messaging you, but I think you changed your number. And you're off Insta . . ."

"Yeah," I say. "It's easier to move on without you popping up on my feed every five minutes or having to dodge a reporter calling me about the song."

"Right." She worries her hands and bites her bottom lip.

"So, uh—what do you want?" What *I* want is to get away from her, or since I can't go anywhere, for her to get away from me.

"Your sis told me about you not going to school," she says, when the silence stretches out between us. "And when I was looking for you, I found the GoFundMe."

"Dammit, Zoe," I mutter.

I didn't want Zoe to do that. It feels like begging, and I want to be able to take care of my family by myself. But in the end she won out.

"I want to help." She takes a step toward me. I take a step back.

"Yeah?" I say. "How do you feel about bussing tables?"

"Actually, I thought I could host a pop-up event at Nathan's . . ."

"Pop-up event?"

"Yeah, like, I invite fans here and they buy tickets to meet me. I bet there are a ton of people in Chicago who would come and then come back once they see how amazing it is . . ."

"No, thanks," I say immediately. People don't like the stink of death, the shroud of tragedy. We already have that with the fundraiser highlighting we're running on fumes, and my famous ex doing me a pity favor is only going to make that worse.

I trundle back into the walk-in to get my clipboard. Love follows right behind me, undeterred. She smells like a cookie.

Ugh.

"I don't want to be part of any more PR stunts," I say, walking back out and dropping the clipboard on the counter. I get the bucket from next to the sink and start filling it with scalding-hot water and soap. Like Dad always said, *If you don't know what to do, clean something.* Although that was definitely so he would have less things to clean himself.

"It's not a stunt for me," Love says, crossing her arms over her chest. "I swear."

"Sure." She's zero for two in the whole telling-the-truth realm, and I'm not risking a strikeout. Every time she shows up here, I break a little more. But I am not just taking care of myself. I have real issues that this doesn't solve. I grab the scrub brush and head back to the grill.

Love, absolutely not taking the hint, follows me again.

"Let me do something good with my fame. All it's done is cause problems and all I want is to fix something. I'd make sure the ticket proceeds would go straight to the diner—"

"Like people who follow you would come all the way to Highland Park, just to eat hot dogs. You don't get Chicago."

"Maybe not," she says undeterred, sliding up onto my counter again, just like on that first day. I wish she would sit anywhere else. "But I get tweens, and they will drag their parents across the state to have any lunch in the same room with me."

I give her a pointed look.

"It's not my ego. I didn't believe anyone would show up when I started, but that's really the way it is."

I scrub, scrub, scrub and the brush disappears in a foamy brown.

"And . . . I know what you're going to say about this—but hear me out. They would definitely show up if they thought we were back together . . ."

I stop and look at her. She cannot be serious. "So it *is* a stunt. Nooooo thank you."

"This isn't a trick, at least not on you. The one I did for the Arctic raised over a million dollars, and that was with no relationship intrigue."

A *million* dollars? For the first time, I pause. That would change everything. We're down to four thousand in the business account. "Why do you even care?" I say, stalling, sounding petulant, even to myself. "We don't deserve this more than polar bears."

"I owe you and your family. I took advantage of you guys and your kindness to save my rep, so this is the least I can do. I know how much this place means to you and I know about school. I want you to be able to keep your dad's dream alive without having to give up on yours. Please, please let me help." She seems to be actually, for once, telling the truth.

I know I can't say no to potentially a million dollars, but I also cannot let this girl back in.

"Look, it took me a long time to get over you—"

"I know—"

"No, you don't. You're not ever going to know, okay?" I shake my head and put the scrub brush down, trying to steady my thoughts. "Because this wasn't ever real for you. But it was real for me." She starts to protest, but I keep going. "So if we're gonna do this, I have one condition."

She audibly exhales. "Whatever you want."

"I want you to know that this time, it's all pretend for me, too. I don't ever want to get back together." She needs to know that, before we pull off one last bullshit show for Love and her fans.

"Okay," Love says in a small voice. "Whatever makes you happy."

We're a long way from happy here. Still, I nod, pretend I am. "Perfect."

But I've learned the hard way that nothing ever is.

CHAPTER FORTY-FIVE

Love

That Saturday we stand at the doors of Nathan's and it's like we're on *Good Morning America*. Chris and I have been staying downtown and I've spent all my energy posting to social media about this event. It seems to have paid off because hordes of tweens are holding up signs, banging on the windows and doors, and when they see me, they get hysterical. Faces redden. Bodies shake . . . it's approaching seizure territory.

"Fuck me," Zoe says, one hand on her hip.

"Zoe Jessica Grey!" Mrs. Grey says, but then takes a leap backward when a tiny girl with braces slams herself against the glass. Mrs. Grey's eyes dart my way, but only for a second. "Is it always like this for you?"

"Lately," I say. Austin is by my side and it feels like something missing has been returned. But then I have to remind myself: When I'm done with this, I'll lose him again.

"It's like a zombie apocalypse . . . ," Austin says.

". . . at an American Girl store," Zoe says.

"If I'm remembering correctly, these are your people," Austin says, arching an eyebrow at her.

"Austin," Zoe returns. "I'm *thirteen* now."

"All right! It's showtime." Chris pops up from the booth she's turned into a makeshift office. She has AirPods in her ears and Vans on her feet, and for once her phone is in a furry cross-body pouch that's more holster than purse.

I take a deep breath and look at Austin, trying to psych us both up. "You ready?"

He purses his lips, then sighs and says, "Let's get this over with."

Chris opens the doors, and the horde pushes in. She and Mrs. Grey collect tickets while Austin and I smile and wave from behind a velvet rope. They line up around us and a sea of cellphones flash in front of us. They chant, "We love Love! We love Love!" and "My hero!" and "Lifeguard!" I take Austin by the elbow, but it's obvious from the way he is standing that he would rather I didn't. Would rather be anywhere else.

I lean into him, trying to remind him why we're doing this. Eventually, I feel his tension release and he leans on me too.

Only then do I exhale.

It's a perfect PR stunt. All two thousand fans who preregistered line up for pics and vids with me while Chris live streams everything. The tickets were two hundred bucks each, and people are eating hot dogs or burgers and buying drinks on top of that. Paige and Ty are helping in the back so Austin and Melanie can be part of the meet and greet (I'm paying them. I insisted.), but the Greys keep running into the back to make sure everything's going the way it's supposed to. Which it is. Maybe even better.

There's even a new crowd forming outside, so we're prepping for another two hundred. If it's enough to help Austin and his family not to worry anymore, if it puts them back on the map, and Austin back on the road to college, it'll be worth it.

A super cute girlie with straight black hair steps up for her turn with me. "Hi, sweetie," I say, giving her a side-hug. "Thanks so much for coming to see me."

"I came here from Naperville."

"Oh my gosh!" I have no idea where Naperville is, but I make a big deal anyway.

"You're . . . so . . . nice . . . ," she says.

"Thanks," I say, blushing.

Austin is shifting around behind me. Maybe it's not the crowd. Maybe he's just uncomfortable being near me now.

Chris swoops in, phone in our faces as I talk to the girl, who I have discovered is named Cherry. "What do you love most about Love?" Chris asks her.

Awkward. I hate when Chris does this.

But the girl smiles huge and says, "She's, like, . . . like, compared to all the other stars, she's not as fake as them. She actually *wants* to talk to us!"

"Aw . . . that's so sweet." I hug her again as Austin snorts from behind me. We snap a pic both holding up peace signs and she is ushered away.

Suddenly, Chris swings the camera at Austin pointedly. "And what do you love about Love, Austin?"

Shit. Why would she do this?

"The authenticity," he drawls, crossing his arms over his chest. "Definitely."

Ignoring the sting of his sarcasm, I greet the next kids in line, a couple of thirteen-year-olds, a boy with his arm around his girl.

"It's so cool meeting you. Like, I've been following you since you were at fifty-k," the girl says.

"Wow. Thank you *so* much," I say, trying to ignore the weight that has just fallen over me.

"Hey, uh, do you mind if we take one with you *and* Austin?" the guy asks.

"Are you guys back together? You guys were, like, literally, #couplegoals for us."

I smile noncommittally, then pull on Austin's elbow. "No. We're just friends!"

"Yeah. Friends," he says, but his eyes are dead and his voice is dead and as the kids' parents slide up to frame the pic, I try to take his hand, but he pulls it away like I'm made of garbage.

Snap.

They take the photo, and Austin immediately gets as far away as he can and still look like he's with me.

"Check it out," Little Fanboy says, and he thrusts the pic in my face.

Austin looks gorgeous, but not like himself. He's muscular and tan, yet blank. No spark. His arms are tight by his side, mouth in a grimace-smile.

I've tried so hard to keep it together all day, but right now, looking at that, I can't. "Five-minute break!" I call out, and then I run out of there and into the bathroom before anyone can see me lose it.

When I burst into the white-tiled bathroom with the framed pics of all different people eating hot dogs with mustard though, I have to scoot past a bunch of fourteen-year-olds, who watch me beginning to cry in the mirrors like I've just stepped out of a TV.

Which, I guess to them, I did.

"Oh my God, is she okay?" I hear one whisper as I enter the farthest stall.

"Like, what's going on?" her friend says.

Tears spill over my cheeks and I try as hard as I can not to sniffle.

"I think it's her boyfriend," a third voice says.

"Maybe she cheated on him again. He's so hot though. I don't know why she would."

"Truth," the first voice says.

GO AWAY! I want to yell, but I crawl on top of the toilet seat instead.

The silent tears flow faster, and in that moment, I realize that actually, nothing's changed. I'm still that sad girl in high school at the mercy of everyone's opinions . . . and I'll be that girl forever. No matter how famous I am. There will always be another Bryce out there somewhere.

Suddenly, I hear someone burst in. Who now?

"Love? You in here?" Zoe asks.

"She's in there crying," one of the girls says.

"She cheated on her boyfriend."

"Like, with *a lot* of guys."

"Okay, uh . . . you bitches need to go right now," Zoe says, and I snort through my bawling.

"Like, what did you just say?" the first voice says.

"I said: You *bitches* need to go right now!"

That's my girl.

I peer under the door and see three pairs of UGGs beginning to surround Zoe's Converse. She might be in trouble.

"Or what?" Girl One says.

Her UGGs lurch toward the Converse, but then Zoe says, "Or I'll break that expensive little nose of yours . . ."

The girls seem to believe her because they scatter out of the bathroom, and when I'm sure they're not coming back, I join Zoe at the sink. "I wish I knew how to do that."

"It's a lot easier to confront other people's bullies than your own," she says, like the wise little sage she is.

"Right."

I get a paper towel and try to blot the runny makeup off my face.

"What's wrong?" Zoe says.

I throw the paper towel in the trash and grab some lip gloss, but hesitate. I should reapply, but I just can't make myself care about any of it. Not without Austin. "It's just, I realized I can make millions of people love me, except for the one who matters most."

"Who? My brother?"

"Yeah . . ."

"Sometimes he's an idiot," Zoe says. "But it's not totally his fault. Emma, the sea hag, messed him up, and he thinks you're going to be the same as her because your thing followed the same pattern. He let himself fall for her and she trashed him, and it kinda seemed like that's what you were doing too . . . you know, with all the social media stuff at the start."

I groan. Just thinking about that first week, about Damien, leaves me flushed and embarrassed.

"But you're not going to *end* up like that," Zoe says, patting me on the back maternally.

"How do you know?"

"Because one, you are not a sea hag. And two, look how you met. You literally smacked right into each other."

"He smacked into me," I say. That day in the mall. I was so nervous for the dance, wishing Damien was sober, so hungry and tired, wishing for a single that would make it all worth it, but now all I'm wishing is that I could take it all back, start over. I would do everything differently. Except one thing: I would still fall into his arms. It's just . . . I would stay there.

"Whatever. It's fate-y," Zoe says. "So I wouldn't worry about it. Because fate is fate."

But Austin doesn't seem interested in fate taking the wheel, and I've gotten myself in trouble thinking that way before. "Why did he ever want me in the first place?"

"What? Are you serious?" Zoe puts her hands on her hips. "You made mistakes, but that's not who you are. You're an amazing person. You're pretty and brave and talented and fun to hang out with. Of course he wanted you."

"Thanks, Zoe," I say, but it only makes me feel worse. Because Austin did make me feel like I was all those things, but "wanted" is past tense. I already blew my chance.

Chance*s*.

Zoe is watching me carefully. Finally, she says, "Ever since our dad died, Austin lost his mojo. He changed from my badass older brother into a guy who was scared of the world. But when you fell off that escalator, it's like everything changed. You gave him confidence. Now he just needs to find it again . . . for himself."

It gives me an idea. One last chance to take.

"Are you okay?" Zoe says as I march out of the bathroom to the waiting crowd.

"HEY, EVERYBODY!" I yell.

The crowd quiets.

"Who wants to learn some dances?"

An excited squeal rises from the crowd. I briefly meet Austin's questioning eyes from where he's standing at the back of the crowd, but then I look away.

"Meet me in the parking lot!" I yell.

"What the hell?" Chris whispers in my ear, teeth clenched, her hand tight on my arm. "What are you doing?"

"What needs to be done," I tell her. "Now let me go."

I smile big and wide to the crowd, then say, "I've got a surprise for you, and it's going to be *lit*!"

I run outside into the freezing, bright day, bubbling with determination once more.

After this, I won't have any more questions or what-ifs.

After this, I'll know.

CHAPTER FORTY-SIX

Austin

Everyone is outside and I have no idea what's going on with Love. More antics and shenanigans for the 'gram, I bet. We have a temporary PA system set up on the patio and glitter is everywhere. The kids pressed against the window look like they're seconds away from busting through the glass.

I'm not here for it.

"Any idea where she is?" Mom asks.

"No."

Zoe has her phone out and is filming the horrifying crowd of rabid tweens, but she looks back sharply at my reply. "Of course you don't," she snaps.

"What's that supposed to mean?"

"You've been so cold to her this whole time."

"No, I haven't!" I lean against the brick diner wall and meet Zoe's withering stare. Okay, maybe I have been trying to keep my distance, but how can she blame me?

"I get that she hurt you. I hate that. But she's literally saving the restaurant to try to make it up to you. At last count, Mom said we've brought in almost half a million already; plus the GoFundMe has been blowing up ever since she shared it."

That's . . . more than I ever could have dreamed of this whole last year of struggling. "Yeah, it means a lot, but it also doesn't change what happened," I say with a shrug.

"Why not?" Mom surprises me by interjecting. "Austin, I know you think you're scared that she's going to lie or hurt you again. But . . . I think you're actually more scared about what if she doesn't? Just like I think you're scared of leaving the diner for school. But what is your life going to be if you stay here and don't follow your own heart? You're going to have to stop using Zoe and me as an excuse, especially now. We're going to be fine. But if you let her go, let school go, and don't see what could be, you're only going to be half alive. We have to take risks in life, big, messy, gross ones, you know?" She takes my hands in hers. "The last year has taught me that, because staying stuck doesn't make things better. And I want you to really hear this, Austin: Love does not come often, not a love like this, where a person would do something like this for you. And when it does, sometimes it doesn't last as long as you want it to." She sets her jaw and eyes me severely. "But you don't squander that. You can either go for it or let not doing so eat you up. Trust me, by the time you're my age, you see the consequences of wasting even a minute. Don't do it. Follow love and be brave enough to see where it takes you." She releases me. "Like me and your dad."

Finally, I let myself see why I haven't been able to shake Love in all these months. I have always known love exists because of my parents. I thought I understood it, witnessing it from the outside. But it's so different from how I felt about Emma. So much deeper. It's how I feel about Love.

But I don't know how she really feels. I don't know how to trust it, even if she tells me. "Did she say something to you?" I ask.

Zoe scowls at me. "Why don't you go ask her yourself?"

"Fine, I'll go look for her."

"You're not going to have to look far," Mom says, pointing up.

I scoot around so I can see. "Oh shit."

Love is on the roof. There's something sweaty and unhinged about her expression, like she's gone feral. I'm glad it hasn't snowed in the last week.

"Hey, guys!" she screams. "Who's ready to dance?!"

Zoe hits Pause on her phone and glares at me. "This is your fault, and if she hurts herself, that will also be your fault."

"Jesus, Zoe."

"Don't 'Jesus, Zoe' me. She wouldn't be up there if you had been half a human today. She loves you, idiot."

She *loves* me? Present tense? She said it that day we broke it off. I didn't think she could mean it, but what would she have to gain from lying about that now, if she's doing better than ever? She hasn't asked me for anything; she's trying to help me. I remember what I thought that day, listening to her song on the radio, how no one was ever there to save me. But now she has saved the diner. And my skyscraper dreams. She's my lifeguard.

My lifeguard, who is now up on a roof with no water to break her fall, surrounded by fans, all filming.

I feel dizzy and out of sorts and like I might throw up. I will *definitely* throw up if she hurts herself doing something stupid on this roof.

"Who's ready to daaaance?" Love yells.

The crowd around us starts to undulate. "ME ME ME ME," they chant.

"I think you know what we're gonna start with. Hit it, Chris!"

"Replay" starts up, and all the kids start to dance on the spot.

"Actually, wait, hold up, hold up, hold up!" The music cuts out and Chris sighs impatiently. "I have something to say before we do this dance."

The crowd goes silent again immediately. She's the maestro, the magician, and everyone is riveted.

"I wanted to start with this song because it's how I met the love of my life," she says.

For a second, I think she's going to say something about Damien again.

And that's what makes me admit to myself how badly I want her to say it's me.

"And he's the reason why we're all here right now, to save this amazing place," Love says.

She *does* mean me. Literally everyone is now staring at me, except her. She keeps her eyes on the crowd, like she doesn't want to see my reaction. I wave, weakly.

"This is a Miley-level meltdown," Zoe says.

"We gotta get her off the roof," I say.

"I'll go get her," Mom says, fanning herself like she's in the throes of a hot flash. "We don't want a panic. Or a lawsuit."

She runs inside.

"Okay, everybody ready to learn this dance?"

"YES!!!" the tweens scream, a single horde of hormones and adoration.

"This one's easy," Love says. "First you go, boom boom—" She sticks out her arms. "Then boom boom—" She raises them up. "Then boom boom—" She throws her hands on her hips. "And boom boom boom boom boom!" She breaks into the swiveling moves she did on the principal in the first Grad Girl video, except she doesn't have anyone to lean on. Then her reckless eyes land on me. "Let's all try that first part. You too, Austin!"

Just to keep her from trying anything else until my mom gets to her, I try to do the dance. It's not great. My phone buzzes in my pocket.

It's my mom. THE DOOR IS LOCKED. I CAN'T GET TO HER! it says.

Shit shit fucker shit.

I try to keep a smile pasted on my face as I move through the crowd to the front with Zoe, while Love leads her fans through the final piece of choreography.

"Then it's boom boom, and finally . . . the fall!" Suddenly, she slips—then pulls back. "Just kidding!" she says, laughing.

Everyone around me starts laughing too. But this is not funny though. She's right at the edge of the building, and this is the original Grad Girl, willing to do anything for someone she loves. And there are only two ways off the roof: down the stairs that lead back inside, or jumping off.

If I know Love the way I thought I once did, I know what she has planned.

It would be just like my life to have the girl of my dreams say I'm the love of her life and then immediately die.

"Okay!" she says. "Who's ready to try with music?"

"You better get ready," Zoe says, and I position myself as best I can directly beneath her in case I'm right, but I'm *not* ready. Everyone around us is dancing, oblivious. It's chaos, that madness Love inspires in her fans. But then, just like last time, I lock eyes with her, and everything clears.

She is going to jump.

I am going to catch her.

I know I can.

I know I am the man she loves.

I know I am strong enough to hold her.

I am not afraid.

Just like Mom said, I am not going to let myself get eaten up, be a person living a half-life.

I am going to go for Love.

My arms stretch out and . . .

She jumps.

Once again, she lands soundly in my arms.

The crowd roars as she opens her eyes. She looks like she's about to say something, but the crowd roars as the tweens scream, "KISS KISS KISS!"

That's all I want to do. She is so incredibly beautiful, but this cheering crowd telling us what to do reminds me that even if I believe her, these people are still running a major part of her life and her dreams. I wish all this didn't have to be in the public eye, but everything with Love always is, always will be.

What will she have to do the next time something goes wrong? What will she do if her fans suddenly turn on me? She's not going to give up her career being bigger than ever right now to, what, hang out with me while I sketch skyscrapers?

Love closes her eyes and I know she expects what the crowd expects, but I put her down. "I'm sorry. All this . . . everything you've done today has been amazing. *You're* amazing. But me and you . . . I can't."

I start to head inside. I'm sorry to disappoint Mom and I'm

even sorrier to disappoint Love, but this . . . us . . . it doesn't make sense.

"Austin, wait!"

"What?" I have my hand on the door, but I stop.

"You really feel nothing?" she asks.

"What I feel isn't real," I say. "You said it yourself. None of this is."

"*I'm* real." She's begging me to hear her, to believe her, but then she looks at the crowd that's gathered around us. Everyone is recording us on their cellphones, and I see her wince.

"I think we should take a break," she says.

"What? We're not—"

"I mean we—" She turns to her devoted followers and raises her voice over the crowd, though she doesn't need to. It is so very quiet right now. "We should take a break."

A gasp rips through the crowd.

"For most of my life, I thought the world hated me. I wanted so badly to be loved by everyone. But living to be loved isn't living at all. It's pretend. Performance. And I'm so tired of performing my life rather than living it." She looks right at me. "To love is to live and I love you, Austin."

"I—" I start, not even sure what I'm going to say, but whatever it is gets drowned out.

A girl screams, "NO!"

A boy yells, "YOU CAN'T!"

Shouts of "I love you" and "I hate you" and "no way" get louder and louder, and that's when I realize a wave of frenzied tweens is crashing toward us. Chris springs into action and grabs Love by the hand.

"We need to go. Now!" She pulls Love to the alley, where her town car is waiting.

Love looks back at me as she and Chris flee the fans and dive through the back doors of the car. Love's is barely closed before they speed off to make their getaway, the die-hard tweens running after the car.

And just like every time before, as suddenly as she dropped back into my life, she's gone again. And I'm too late.

"What do I do now?" I say to Zoe and Mom.

"You need to say goodbye," Mom says.

"It's too late to do that. She's gone."

Mom turns my shoulders square with hers. "I mean, you need to say goodbye to us."

"What?

"You need to say goodbye to the diner . . . and to your father."

"Mom—"

"Let me finish," she says. "I can't speak for Nathan. But I can tell you what every parent wants: for their child to achieve their dream. To truly honor your father, you have to go out and get yours . . . do you understand?"

I let the tears streak my cheeks as I think about Dad and life and everything that has happened this year plus. The three of us hug for a long while.

When we separate, Mom says, "Now, part of that dream just took off down Main Street and is being chased by her fans." She squeezes my arm. "But rumor has it, you're good in the clutch."

"I am," I say, the confidence from catching her lingering.

Zoe hands me the keys to my car. "Well, then . . . quit your dawdling, God!"

CHAPTER FORTY-SEVEN

Love

The tween horde is chasing the town car.

Chris is typing on her phone like nothing else is happening. I want to throw it out the window. "Okay, we can spin this," she says. "The pressure of all this success was getting to you. You were drunk, or on pills . . . Wait, *are* you drunk right now?"

"No! Holy shit, I am *not* drunk and I don't pop pills. I only drank the one time and what makes you think I would do something like that after everything I've been through? I'm just a person who made a choice about what's best for me."

She looks up, surveys me with her usual absolute certainty about whatever words of wisdom she's going to deliver. "I know you're a person, Love. But this is why you have *people*. To tell you what choices are *actually* best for you. Don't worry about any of this. I'll call your publicist—we'll damage-control."

The thing is, I know who I am. I know what I want. It's not "people" who think they know what's best for me. Chris has done so much for me. Hell, she's here right now. But that doesn't mean she knows me better than myself. I have to make her understand that.

She starts typing on the phone again and I lay my hand over

the screen. “I meant every word I said, Chris. I’m taking a break from all this.”

“You can’t do that!”

“Sure I can.”

I open TikTok and enter the settings. But before I can hit Delete Account, Chris snatches the phone out of my hand. “No, you can’t. We have a contract. And in that contract it says that you will ‘apply yourself to your career to the best of your abilities.’”

“And I will. I want to keep singing and songwriting, performing, even. But that doesn’t have to include documenting my every move on social media. Not anymore.”

“You need to trust me,” she says, pleading now. “You wanted to be a singer, and I made you a star, just like you asked me to.”

It’s my turn to look at her incredulously. After all the times she ignored and dismissed me, wouldn’t even listen to my music, and had me running ragged, she has the balls to claim she’s the only reason I’m successful? No. “You didn’t make me anything,” I tell her. “I did that. I made the Grad Girl dance. I wrote ‘Lifeguard.’”

“And you were going to throw it all away until I stopped you,” she snaps. As soon as it’s out of her mouth, she looks like she wishes she could take it back.

But she can’t. My skin prickles dangerously.

“What are you talking about?” I ask.

“Take us to the airport,” she says to the driver, ignoring my question.

I’m not letting her off the hook. “I’m serious, Chris—what are you talking about?”

She glances over at me, but she can’t meet my eyes. “You blew up the image we had *just* managed to fix and went completely off the grid to be with that bland boy again! I knew this time you wouldn't leave, so I had to pretend to be Damien and tell him the truth!" Chris shrugs when she sees the look on my face. "What? It was the only way to get you to come back to LA and keep you from destroying yourself completely."

A chill rolls down my spine. "*You* wrote the message? The one that ruined one of the only times I can remember truly being happy in my life?" All this time I thought maybe Chris was obnoxious or overly driven or didn't listen to me as much as I wished she would, but I trusted her. I never thought she would do something like that.

I tap the driver on the shoulder. "Stop the car, please!"

The guy pulls over immediately. I don't know where we are, but I'm not sitting here for another second with Chris. There is only one person on this planet I trust outside my family and only one place I want to be, even if it's surrounded by an angry mob.

"Where are you going?" Chris mewls, but I'm done listening to her. I grab my phone and jump out of the car.

"Love! Love!" she calls sweetly. "Get back in the car! Let's discuss!"

I slam the door shut and run as fast as I can.

The town car follows alongside me, window rolling down.

I'm never going to be able to outrun Christine.

"LOVE! YOU SPOILED LITTLE B—"

But before she can finish, a familiar Jeep slides up out of nowhere and pulls over across the street. Austin throws open the door and yells, "Get in!"

I rush across and jump in as I hear Chris yelling after me about how I'm going to regret this. Blah blah blah.

There are a lot of things I regret. This isn't one of them.

Inside Austin's Jeep, it's finally quiet. He's driving calmly toward the beach, toward the water, like he didn't just rescue me yet again.

"I think I just fired Chris," I say, after a minute.

"Wow. Lots of breakups today," he says.

"And maybe one makeup?"

Austin takes my hand and smiles at me. "And one makeup." We drive a little while, away from the crowd, and then he says, "I've decided I'm going to school, you know, thanks to you."

"Really?"

"I hope Dad's diner is around forever. But I want to be an architect, build something of my own. Mom and Zoe think he'd want that for me."

I smile. "I *know* he would."

"But I'll look for schools in LA. I'll apply for next year. The reason I couldn't say yes before was I didn't know how we'd make it work, and I don't want you to have to give anything else up after what you've already done."

"No . . . I like it here. There are amazing musicians everywhere. If Interscope wants to keep me badly enough after 'Lifeguard,' they'll figure it out."

"Yeah?" he says.

"Yeah. I just want to be with you. Anywhere. For real."

As we get to the lake, the sun is setting, and Austin guides me out of the car and down to the water's edge. It is so quiet here, like the whole universe knows we need a minute. Everything is blanketed in flat winter light as snow begins to drop from the sky. It's magical.

"Man, this would be the perfect Instagram. All we're missing is the fireworks," Austin says.

"I got some right here for you . . ." I take his face in my hands, and we kiss. As I lean into him and he wraps me up in his arms, I can feel how well we fit. This is the beginning I've been waiting for. When he pulls me in even closer, I know . . . I was right.

Total fireworks.

ACKNOWLEDGMENTS

This story began as a screenplay. When you write a screenplay, your greatest hope is that this story will become a movie, because a screenplay isn't something that will ever be read or seen by an audience. It's more of a blueprint: all the dialogue, the action, and the settings are there, but the heart, body, and soul is missing. It takes dozens, sometimes hundreds, of people (and millions of dollars) to turn a screenplay into a movie. So most never draw breath.

Ours did. In this book. And we are eternally grateful to the people who helped us bring this story to life. First among them is our cowriter, Estelle Laure. When we first started this process with her, we joked that she's like an actor who plays every role in the movie. But she's also the production designer . . . and the cinematographer, too. Every line of dialogue in the screenplay had to be motivated and internalized by Estelle. She *played* Love, she *played* Austin, and she even managed to play Lil' D. Her prose created the world of *Love Goes Viral.* And her heart brought these characters to life.

If Estelle is our incredible actor, then Alexa Pastor, our editor, is the director of this book. It was her vision that made this novel possible. She saw the potential of our story as a novel and knew the path to get there. And it was a twisty one. Her feedback and insight inspired us to revisit the screenplay and craft a story so much richer than the one we started with. We still can't believe how seamlessly she moved between our film language and the language of novels. Alexa, Justin Chanda, and the rest of the Simon & Schuster team have been a dream to work with. This story, and its authors, are forever in their debt.

Our producer on the film, Mark Ross, was the first person to see our screenplay as a book. He connected us with Alexa and is an incredible champion of this story. Mark is also, quite literally, the nicest person we know. His relentless optimism has kept us going. We struggle to put it into words, and even if we did, its bright cheeriness would probably blind you (and then how would you read the rest of this)?

We also want to thank our manager, Sidney Sherman. He has believed in our stories from the very beginning. His feedback has helped this story soar from the initial screenplay pitch (what if *Notting Hill*, but kids . . . ?) to the rich character-driven novel that you just finished.

Finally, thank you to Richard Curtis. You showed us what romantic comedies could and should be.

—C. S and A. B.

First off, huge gratitude to Camille Stochitch and Alexander Berman for choosing me as your collaborator and for conceiving of these characters. Working on this project was a joy on every level, and I do believe we made a little magic.

Confession: I have long coveted Alexa Pastor as an editor and was beyond thrilled to have the opportunity to work with her. And guess what? Her rep is not hype! Thank you, Alexa, for all your insightful notes and comprehensive letters, and for being so instrumental in bringing these characters to life. Beyond that, thank you for getting as excited about the little things as I do and for really backing the art of the writing process. I am a big fan of you.

Everyone on the production side at Simon Teen: I love the team over there, and I thank each of you for your exceptional work. Veronica Meleksetian, it is a true pleasure to be your colleague. Of course, always, my agent, boss, and most excellent friend, Emily van Beek, who has been the human portal to all my dreams . . . I am forever grateful for the moment you came into my life and for every day since.

My family: five siblings and all partners concerned, all three parents, many lovely cousins, aunts, uncles, and my nieces, Violet and Ellie—because of all of you, my life is an embarrassment of riches. Let's keep on singing and dancing every chance we get, yeah?

And finally, my immense affection, loyalty, and forever love to my brilliant, passionate children, Lilu and Bodhi; to Killian for being a kick-ass extra kid; and to my ridiculously just-about-perfect husband, Chris. If I wasn't so scared of heights I would leap from a rooftop for any of you, and I know you would catch me . . . every time.

—E. L.

Scan here to listen to Love's song "Lifeguard"!